The Ears of a Dog is the very promising debut novel of the young Canadian writer E. I. Vernon. It traces the lives of a set of characters making their own ways, in different parts of the world, through the Suez crisis in 1956. Historical novels are notoriously difficult to control but Vernon does so with an adept and gentle hand, assuredly tracing out the relationships of his characters, whose personal lives take twists and turns around the developing crisis. The book challenges us to look at how people's lives weave a fabric of history as it might appear in a canonical sense. It questions how and when we get involved in events around us, what our motivations are, and how, ultimately, we can justify it. A thoroughly enjoyable first novel. I am already looking forward to Vernon's next book.
K. P. Clarke, University College, Oxford

E. I. Vernon's characters in *The Ears of a Dog* have finely crafted voices; their emotional and psychological complexity gives them a richness and depth that captivates the reader. The sidelines are crammed full of equally subtle, complex and utterly believable characters. The inner turmoil of the main characters is highlighted and exacerbated by the international turmoil of the Suez Canal crisis of 1956. The geo-political circumstances of a couple of weeks in the autumn of 1956 function as far more than backdrop. Vernon uses a fictional form to make a powerful historical point: that international geo-politics touch, often in devastating, violent and wasteful ways, the lives of real people. Vernon's skills as a historian and novelist are truly impressive.
Francine McKenzie, author of *Parties Long Estranged*

E I Vernon

THE EARS OF A DOG

Matador
9 De Montfort Mews
Leicester LE1 7FW, UK
Tel: (+44) 116 255 9311 / 9312
Email: books@troubador.co.uk
Web: www.troubador.co.uk/matador

In this work of fiction, the characters, places
and events depicted are either the product
of the author's imagination or they are
used entirely fictionally.

Cover graphic: detail of an original lithographic plate from
*Mittheilungen aus Justus Perthes' Geographischer Anstalt
über Wichtige neue Erforschungen auf dem Gesammtgebiete der
Geographie von Dr. A. Petermann*, Justus Perthes, Gotha, 1861.

ISBN 1 905237 85 5

Typeset in 11pt Stempel Garamond by Troubador Publishing Ltd, Leicester, UK
Printed by The Cromwell Press, Trowbridge, Wilts, UK

Matador is an imprint of Troubador Publishing Ltd

In memory of my grandfather, Roy Vernon

I am greatly indebted to David Graham for reading my manuscript in bits and pieces as it was being formed, and for providing some most valuable suggestions and truly heartening encouragement while this story was taking shape. Special thanks are also due to Jordan Ellison, Eldar Kleiner and Julia Moses, whose early readings of the first draft, and helpful comments, are much appreciated; to Chen Tamir, for challenging me to justify certain aspects of my historical and character depictions; to Holger Nehring, for his time and interest; and not least to Craig Beeston, for his good company along the way. Thanks too to Saul Lemer, for confirming a theoretical point of English law.

I owe much to Keith Kyle for his masterful and inspirational scholarly presentation of the 1956 Suez crisis, Suez: Britain's End of Empire in the Middle East, *from which much of my understanding of the crisis is drawn. Also very helpful were Sir Percival Griffiths's* History of the Indian Tea Industry, *Mohamed Heikal's* Cutting the Lion's Tail *and Moshe Dayan's* Diary of the Sinai Campaign. *I am especially fortunate that so fluent a statesman as Abba Eban was at the United Nations to represent his country as movingly as he did during the crisis, in a speech which I have chopped up and adulterated shamefully on pages 74 to 95, and I am grateful to Israel's Ministry of Foreign Affairs for making the text of that speech publicly available. The part about the manipulation of combination locks in Richard Feynman's* Surely You're Joking Mr. Feynman *was inspiration for a section of the chapter in Part IV titled 'Concentration of Moments'.*

These citations, of course, must not give rise to the impression that the fictional tale which follows is altogether historically accurate. There are bound to be errors within, and not only historical, and they are entirely my own. Certainly all characters, other than the mostly unnamed political and military figures who seem to pull the strings in the background, are wholly made up and not meant to depict any real person. It should be added that nothing in this book, but with particular reference to the chapter in Part IV titled

'The Client's Business', should necessarily be considered a valid expression of English (or any other) legal doctrine nor be relied upon as an accurate statement of English (or any other) law.

As for the historical backdrop, the story relies broadly on the unfolding of certain world affairs in 1956, but I have taken my own inadequate understanding of those events, brutally pared away most of the richness of historical detail to leave just a dusty skeleton of developments, then painted on layers of new and imaginary cosmetic nuance. Chronology is mildly askew in parts, accuracy sacrificed to drama. Was it really raining in the City of London on the morning of 25 October 1956? I've not bothered to look it up. I bid the reader indulge such audacities.

Thanks most of all to my mother, father, sister, brothers and to Grace.

I

Bearings

THE SUN burned a deep orange against the shimmering east horizon, floating heavily on the patient waters of the Bay of Bengal. They were partners there in a way, the sun and the sea. Willingly or not, it doesn't matter, though one likes to think willingly. Together they cast a troupe of little dancing flecks of warm light, choreographed in tight formation, twirling and leaping and bowing momentarily, en masse, a long glittering stripe across the sea. A dance show on the black dawn waters for Naveen's pleasure.

There was no discernable roll to the ship just then, and the calm would have eased him back into sleep, were he in a position to sleep. But it was just the beginning of his shift.

He was standing on the main deck of the *Majesty*, a Calcutta Maritime Company ship, supposedly on his way to the hold for a final inspection of the braces securing the tea chests before they hit deeper waters and gathered speed. He knew there was no rush, despite the Second Officer's command to hurry. The chests had been secured and checked thrice over in port. It would take dynamite to dislodge them. The order really meant not that the chests had to be inspected, but that *he* had to inspect them. The Second Officer had decreed it, as he had decreed many useless things for Naveen to do over the last few days.

It was quite apparent the Second Officer had it in for him. Indeed, the Second Officer would readily have admitted to any trusted acquaintance that he had reviled the keen new cadet from the moment they met and for no express cause, and was perpetually inventing what they both knew were pretexts to send him off the bridge and out of his sight. It was just a grating feeling the cadet gave him with his irritating conscientiousness and exceedingly correct behaviour.

A bit of penetrating introspection might have yielded some more sophisticated reasons for his distaste. The cadet reminded him of his own embarrassingly overeager self at that age. He would

3

rather have forgotten the slow, servile climb he had made up the rungs of marine management, the enthusiasm he initially showed quickly snuffed out by condescending superiors. It annoyed him that the cadet was not losing his cheer as rapidly as he had.

The boy did not know the subtleties of character interaction in the hierarchy of career seamen. *He* had striven years to attain a perfect personality balance among the officers on this ship. He was content with his position and with the delicate but reassuring web of mutual support and friendship among these officers who had spent a lifetime on the high seas with only each other's steadfastness, humour, skill and comradeship to get by on. It maddened him that the Company troubled to accommodate this youngster who should have been training on the Company's Australia line and would have been but for his inability to obtain the appropriate travel documents on time. No such charity would have been shown him in his day as a cadet.

And it maddened him that he appeared to be the only one maddened by the cadet. The Captain, the Chief Officer and the others displayed no annoyance of him at all.

Above all, it maddened him simply that he allowed the cadet to madden him.

But straightforwardly identifiable as these currents of animus would have been to a psychoanalyst, the Second Officer was unaware of them as reasons for his snappishness towards Naveen. They subsisted beneath the thick membrane of his consciousness.

And Naveen? Snappishness, hatred, even revulsion he accepted, for they were to be expected between certain people, even though he considered it remarkably early for the Second Officer to have developed so intense a dislike towards him. But mockery he could not abide at any stage, and his situation was approaching mockery.

Yesterday the Second Officer caused him particular insult.

'Cadet!'

'Sir!'

'What you are doing in the wheel room?' The wheel's *l* flipped into the room's *r* as the Second Officer's Rajasthani tongue rolled forward along his palate. Wheerllroom. Most of the officers were from the northwest, and yet on duty all spoke English on board.

4

'Checking engine indicator readings for accuracy as Third Officer ordered, sir.'

'That is *un*necessary. The engineers can do measurements themselves from engine room.'

Naveen stood away from the panel, unsure what to do. He remained motionless for perhaps two minutes, taking care not to glance in the direction of the indicators, while the Second Officer stared out to sea.

The floor hummed and creaked and a meter was ticking somewhere.

'Cadet!'

'Sir!'

'*Now* what are you doing?'

'Awaiting orders, sir.'

'Awaiting. Orders.' Sarcastic tone. 'Have you no mind of your own? Must we supervise your every action?'

Naveen felt it wisest not to reply.

'Go and stand guard on the main deck. Keep an eye off the stern for pirates.'

The command was uttered with studied nonchalance and the Second Officer again turned his attention to the sea, while Naveen felt heat rush to his face. He inhaled sharply and his chest filled with suppressed anger. Everyone knew there had been no piracy reported in this expanse for years. The Second Officer would have given no such order had another senior officer been with them on the bridge.

'Aye, sir.'

Naveen feared his frequent absence from the wheel room on such errands of stupidity would marginalise him in the Captain's awareness, or worse, wrongly show him up as slack in his duties. Nonetheless, there was no obvious way out of his bind. He dared not complain to the Captain, for the Second Officer was the Captain's nephew's brother-in-law and trusted friend, and he was Mr Nobody on board. Even were there no special bond between the two it would be inappropriate for someone of his station to circumvent the chain of authority.

But if he was nobody on board he was still somebody to his family and friends in Jaipur and his classmates in Calcutta. He had a fair helping of self-respect and he would not accept his humiliation in utter servitude. While scanning the horizon yesterday for pirates, he resolved to carry out the Second Officer's ridiculous orders with the utmost laxity. After brief consideration, he concluded it was acceptable to dishonour the chain of command in the face of such abuse of power. He felt it morally and operationally permissible under these circumstances to be arbiter of which of the Second Officer's commands were legitimate and not blindly to acquiesce to each of them. Besides, no matter what they wanted you to believe at the academy, the merchant navy was not the military. Of course to preserve his own future career at sea any disobedience flowing from this conclusion must be surreptitious.

And so it was, as the sun chose to grace his view at daybreak with a brilliant performance of glistening movement, that he chose surreptitiously to linger at the rail, to inhale slowly the warm salted vapours of the bay and forget his loneliness and degradation among the officers.

He gazed at the rippling wake, and reminded himself that he was where he had always dreamed of being. He had just graduated from the merchant marine academy and it was his first voyage. They were headed for England and he was an officer-in-training.

The boat was gliding southeastward as they cleared the shallows. A lone seagull circled and swirled and flitted on invisible breezes overhead, unnoticed by any person, majestically overseeing the ship's departure from the unmarked boundaries of his shrilly proclaimed dominion near the Mahanadi Delta. The bird watched purposefully and intently as the vessel slipped away and into the brightening distance, beyond the one hundred fathom point due east of Puri.

*

'Pour us another, will you?'

'Jim, over here! Haven't seen you since... God, it must have been when we all went for dinner after Twickenham last December. Here, have a, have a... oh, whatever this is. Got it for you. Still a naughty bachelor, are we? Noticed you made your entrance alone. That's my Jim.'

'Nice to see you too, Percy. How's work? How's Helen?'

'The family's just splendid, thank you.'

'Family? Forgive me, Percy, but Helen and yourself are not a family. You're a pair of overgrown undergraduates who love the fast life and who incidentally, by the way, as an inconsequential aside, happen to be grown up and married and *both* working full tilt at a newspaper.'

'No, Jim,' a smile playing at the corners of his eyes, his dimples deepening, 'you've got us all wrong. We're a pair of very respectable journalists, I'll grant you that, but...'

'Respectable! And I'm...'

'Yes, respectable, I'll grant you that, Jim, but we're also the parents of a very adorable baby boy who looks just like his father Percy.'

'My word, Percy, I never would have thought you had it in you. Well, congratulations!'

'Had it in me? What's that supposed to mean?'

'Percy, I only meant to congratulate you. It's wonderful news and I'm very happy for both of you.'

'Why thank you, Jim.'

'Looks just like you, does he?' A heartbeat's delay. 'I always thought you did have a babyish face and a sort of pudge about you.'

'Jim, Percy, I want you to meet Siren. She works at the London office of the central bank of some distant and exotic country whose name I've forgotten.'

'Hullo, Roger. Pleased to meet you, Siren.' Siren as in fatally alluring temptress or siren as in air raid? He glanced at Percy and they both had to stifle giggles. Siren as in this is my chance to escape from Percy. In fact I'm tired and I'd rather be in bed. No, not with Siren. Alone, asleep, so I'll have my head about me tomorrow.

'Jim, join us for a drink on the balcony, will you?'

'Delighted to, Miller. Excuse me, Roger, Siren. Good to see you again, Percy.'

A glass shattered somewhere in another room and after the briefest of pauses (you wouldn't have noticed had you not listened for it; people were so damned polite) the buzz of conversation resumed at exactly the same pitch.

Jim Roper stepped out onto the narrow balcony overlooking a Mayfair street and took a breath of air with a hint of moist chestnut wood (imagine picking that out, he thought), a touch of automobile exhaust and various undertones of damp stone and pavement.

He used to enjoy these parties, which tended to attract what once seemed to him a nice mix of young professionals from different walks of London life. It had been exciting at first when he joined these circles of the up-and-coming. The company was stimulating, and the talk was often intelligent, occasionally scandalous. So long as it had been new it had been enlivening.

Lately he'd begun to feel differently, to find the conversation contrived and pretentious. He came only reluctantly now, feeling almost trapped by his social position into attending. It had all become just a dizzying array of names he somehow managed to associate with the faces bobbing about him, the babble of voices penetrating his mind, superficial differences like hair colour and spectacles often the only markers helping him distinguish people.

He would rather be somewhere else.

A taxi hurtled by beneath just as Amy stepped out onto the balcony, with Miller somehow wrapped around her like a pesky vine.

'So, Jimmy, how treats you the law?'

'John, you know he doesn't like Jimmy. It's Jim; or *James* when he's feeling posh.' She winked. 'And he's probably sick to death of talking about the law, what with the endless hours he spends at the firm, aren't you Jim? John Miller, you are a drunken disgrace. Take your hand off my face. That's right, now off my waist. Good lad.'

Roper was beginning to feel ill, despite the fresh air.

'Actually, I don't mind, Amy.' He was unfailingly polite. 'The law is treating my soul poorly and my pocket very well, Johnny. There's little more to say. Forgive me, Amy, but I'm feeling a tad unwell. I think I'll take my leave of the hosts.'

He shook John's hand solidly. John liked that manly sort of thing, especially on those evenings when drunkenness had sapped away half his masculinity.

He stepped back inside.

'Jim, legal question over where those people are standing. The stunning blonde and the donnish looking chap in brown. We despise solicitors, of course, and wish to take every advantage of them. That's why we've cornered you for free advice at a party. Heavens, that's probably why you were invited.'

'Shut up, Bradley.'

His temples were starting to throb.

'My point exactly, Roper. Now defy your profession and be a good sport. It was a question about murder.'

He was being propelled by the elbow towards the donnish chap.

'Murder,' said the blonde.

Chairs scraped and someone turned up the gramophone and the chattering of idle people all around him was taking over an ever greater portion of his consciousness.

'Actually, the question was somewhat broader,' said the donnish chap.

'Jimmy, I thought you were leaving!' Miller was shouting drunkenly at him across the room. 'You were only trying to get away from us.'

The blonde had bright red lipstick that reflected the overhead light almost as a glare at Roper's eyes.

'As I was saying,' the man in brown sputtered on, 'the question goes beyond murder. In fact, it could apply to any number of crimes.'

'I know very little about the criminal law.'

'Surely you're being too modest. Bradley tells me you were on scholarship at St John's in Oxford.'

'Ask him the question,' the blonde insisted in a domineering tone Roper found distasteful. 'I want to know the answer.' It became evident she was American, if her accent was any indication.

'The broader question is this.'

Roper leaned against the wall and readied himself to think. He was just too bloody tired for this.

'Criminal law is concerned to a large degree with moral culpability, is it not?'

'I should hope so.'

'To be morally culpable for an act...'

'Or omission,' said Roper.

'To be morally culpable for an act or omission a person must as a precondition be a morally responsible actor. That is to say, if he...'

'Or she,' said the blonde.

'If he or she committed a crime and was apprehended and tried and given a penal sentence, the penal sentence would be unjust unless he or she intended for the act to be committed or for the omission to be made.'

'Sounds right to me, although if you're nitpicking you'd swap intent for mental element, but I have a feeling that won't be relevant to your question, when it eventually arrives.'

The American smiled knowingly at Roper, her brilliant white teeth assaulting his now bloodshot eyes with further glare. She seemed pleased to have identified Roper's light facetiousness, and turned to the donnish chap: 'Get to the point, honey.'

'Implicit in the general precondition of autonomy to the imposition of punishment is, and this is taken for granted, that the criminal and the punished must be one and the same person. In other words, the requirement of autonomy presupposes the requirement that the perpetrator be the one punished.'

'I suppose, although I'm not sure I follow entirely.' Roper's head was spinning and he was beginning to sweat, but he forced a reply. 'Correspondence between the criminal and the punishment doesn't require autonomy. We could punish unintentional killers by jailing them notwithstanding their lack of intent.'

'Ah yes, but we don't. You see, I was demonstrating *a fortiori* that...'

Bradley and the blonde had somehow both disappeared.

'...since we go to lengths to find an actor's autonomy before punishing him...'

Roper turned to the far corner of the room where there happened to be a ten second lull in conversation. Sudden silence, even an isolated corner of silence in a room full of chatter, always drew notice at these social occasions. Somehow he drowned out the lecturer as his eyes locked in mutual gaze with a woman, a member of the paused conversation, sitting on a deep red sofa with shoulder-length black hair and Mediterranean skin and the most absorbing, transporting gaze he believed he had ever encountered. His breath shortened and his heart waited an extra long time between beats before taking off rapidly. Neither one smiled nor blinked. It was just a stare. He stopped trying to catalogue the minutiae of her appearance and soaked in something more engrossing. He was sure in those brief moments that her soul had boldly stepped towards his and grasped it in a fierce embrace. Their spirits grappled, locked in invisible and irresistible combat through their connected eyes, his soul defending the pure pale blue territory of his irises, blockading her entry into the chasm of his being. But hers, issuing steadily forth through the black coals, her eyes, conduits of fiery energy, was gaining the upper hand. At once his heart raced, his loins stirred, and he felt as though he may be dying. And someone next to her spoke to her and she turned her head.

His ears accepted snippets again from the don.

'...and halt me if you disagree, but such a theory, if validated, would have shattering consequences...'

She turned her head back to him briefly. They were both hungry for more of the visual combat, but she was again distracted.

This was utterly ridiculous. This whole evening was utterly ridiculous.

'I'm terribly sorry, but the whiskey has got to my head. I'm really not following. I really hate to disappoint and it sounds terribly interesting. Perhaps we could take it up at another time.'

'The essential point is this: if we are never, from one moment to the next, the same person, and are instead an infinite number of different people at every different moment in time, time being infinitely divisible into smaller and smaller moments, how could the act of a person at one moment give rise to his culpability at a later moment? At the later moment he is one person, and it would be wrong to punish him for the crime of the earlier incarnation of himself, another person.'

Roper escaped. 'Another person' echoed in his head as he stumbled down the stairs and out onto the street.

*

'Bearing two-eight-five.'
'Two-eight-five.'
Three minutes passed.

'Two-nine-five.'

'Two-nine-five.'

The monsoons were well over and the sea was still calm as they rounded the southern tip of Ceylon. Naveen was pleased to learn they would not be stopping at Colombo, which the ship sometimes did to collect a few chests of Ceylon tea. He had been stationary long enough waiting to embark and was keen to maintain full speed. He stood several feet behind the Captain, watching the latter oversee the manual steering as they pointed the ship in the direction of the Gulf of Aden. They were just over five degrees north of the equator, seventy-nine degrees east of Greenwich.

The Captain turned and leaned towards him.

'Cadet.'

'Sir!'

'Have you heard of Marco Polo?'

'Yes, sir.'

'Did you know he was a sailor?'

'No, sir.'

'I see.'

As often was the case on board, Naveen was unsure how to react, so he did nothing. The Captain turned his attention back to the steering.

'Two-nine-seven.' The course was old hat for the navigator.

As it was for the helmsman. 'Two-nine-seven.'

'Cadet.'

'Sir!'

'On his way back from China to Europe, Marco Polo sailed part of the way. He was bringing commodities to the Occident, just as we are. Trade between the East and the West fuels the world economy, Cadet. It began with him, and it continues with us.'

'Yes, sir.'

'History has a funny way about her, cadet, a way of coming back to remind us of our place and the significance of our destiny. What would you say if I told you that right now, we were sailing around the island of Ceylon *just* as Marco Polo did in his day, on the very same course, crossing the very same set of coordinates?'

Naveen did not know what he would say. He began to wish they had docked at Colombo and avoided Marco Polo's wake.

The Bus

THE BUS shuddered and Nan's head vibrated against the window. She looked up for about three seconds, Clare reckoned, and turned her head about before dozing off again, evidently satisfied they were distant enough from their stop to allow her ancient brain some more time to communicate with other worlds. Clare was sure this was what Nan did when she slept. Nan was old enough and wise enough and mysterious enough to have friends in other worlds. Perhaps enemies too. Nan had suggested as much last winter. They were making wreaths together and Nan dozed off and Clare had watched, fascinated, as Nan's eyes darted back and forth under the wrinkled skins of her eyelids.

'Why do your eyes move when you sleep, Nan?'

'Because I'm in another world, my dear, looking wildly about to see if there's anyone I know to keep me company. Mind you, at the same time I'm being extremely cautious.' She drew out 'extremely' for a long time, and peered around the room as though making sure no one was lurking, listening. 'I look everywhere to make sure the bad spirits are nowhere near me.'

Clare assumed these were secret enemies Nan had accumulated over a lifetime spent disciplining rascal children. Nan must meet them in her dreams, which was where Clare met all sorts of her own monsters. Thank goodness *she* was well behaved, for she loved Nan and would not want to be her enemy.

Nan was not her grandmother, like Emily's Nan. She was a different sort of Nan, who looked after her while father attended to important business and mother carried out a lady's duties. Without Nan to see to her, said mother, Clare would be little more than a filthy sewer creature.

The family driver had taken ill earlier in the week and was in hospital with cancer. Nan came alone to fetch Clare from St Agnes Girls' School and they walked together to the bus stop on Hammersmith Road and caught a fast, tall, turny bus home. Every time it rounded a corner the upper deck swayed slightly.

13

Nan hated it upstairs but Clare begged to go up every time and Nan eventually agreed every time. Her old legs were not made for climbing any more stairs than were strictly necessary, and Clare was hastening her invalidity. One of these days her knees might buckle and she would topple down the stairs and Clare would have to gather up her dry scattered bones into a large paper bag and take them home and explain to mother and father just why Nan was no longer in one piece. Clare considered this a feeble excuse and refused to believe it. She often wondered why old people were so lazy.

The bus shuddered again as it came to a stop, and this time Nan did not stir, which signalled deep sleep. They were seated five rows back from the front window, and a man with a brown cap was sitting three rows in front of them. He had smelled gently of mildew when he walked by earlier, and now he was deeply engrossed in a broadsheet newspaper. Both observations indicated to Clare that he was not a man to worry about. She peeked up and down the aisle, confirming that they were the only three people on the upper deck. The time was ripe for exploration.

She slid herself very slowly off the seat and tiptoed backwards down the aisle, softly as a mouse, holding on to the top of each seat as she went. She paused at the back, one foot on the first step down, the other still on the upper deck, and looked out the window to their left. They were moving slowly along a busy road. A brown stone bank building passed them by, then a leather merchant. They slowed to a near stop, just inching along with traffic, and her eyes locked upon two dark figures talking in an archway in front of a boarded up door. One was tall and the other short and the tall one leaned to conspire with the other in his ear.

The bus came to a full stop and everything seemed to stand still. The man in the cap up front was staring at his newspaper, holding the pages open rigidly. Not even a paper crinkle from him. The window had a film of dirt on the outside so the exterior scene presented itself as an imprecise painting. A sense of decorum told Clare to remain motionless amid this stillness and she wondered if this was how people felt who lived in picture books.

A few long, dreamy seconds passed.

Then all at once the scene was again in motion. God had

turned the page. The bus axles squeaked forward and the newspaper rustled and the short figure ran out from the archway towards the bottom of the picture until he was out of Clare's view, and she heard two feet clomp on the floor below.

Coins clattered.

Nan was still dead asleep and she felt her mission must take her to the lower deck. Upstairs they were in the sitting room of a great nobleman's mansion and the servants in their quarters below were exploited like African slaves in America, even though they were freeborn Englishmen and Englishwomen. It was unjust and they were bored and worn out and wanted cheering up by the young lady of the house and she must help but Nan forbade her from mixing with them. Although the governess believed Clare was nine she was in fact twelve and knew better than to obey her every command.

Lithely twirling to face herself forwards down the stairs, one hand on the railing, she rushed to the bottom and saw an opening on the seat between two old ladies. One was fat and the other was very small and was knitting.

She determined temporarily to suspend her adventure with the servants. She had more pressingly to deal with the real world need to remain inconspicuous. The last thing she wanted was for someone to speak up at her arrival and for Nan to discover her absence. So she walked gently across to the old ladies, eyes to the ground, and nestled in between them. Her legs dangled and swayed from left to right to left as the bus accelerated and slowed. She remained still so as to settle her nervous excitement, and then looked around studiously, orienting herself among the strangers who peopled the lower deck. She felt exhilaration and foreboding at once, and completely forgot the pretence of her presence there as spontaneously as she had conceived it. It was terribly adult and important of her to be on a bus on her own, even though she felt very much nine years old again. And something did seem wrong and guilty about sneaking away from Nan.

Never mind. Nan needn't ever learn of it. If she did, Clare could think up an excuse. Anne had explained to her about white lies, and Anne's mother had confirmed that a white lie was better than the truth at times. When the truth was upsetting, it should be suppressed if it was of no real consequence. And Nan would certainly be upset if she learned the truth about Clare and her adventure.

When her father once said with a laugh that she was an adventuresome little thing, Nan had clucked like a hen in disapproval, shaking her head ominously and staring gravely at Clare.

'Not on my watch,' she had said.

The bus lurched to a stop and the conductor held out his arm to the old lady on Clare's right, the fat one, helping her alight.

They rolled forward again and out of nowhere a grubby little boy appeared at her side, where the fat old lady had been. She peeked at him discreetly. He sniffled as he breathed. She was careful not to stare. But she stole a second glance and discovered he was one of the two figures she had seen conspiring in the archway.

'Don't stare at me, miss. I'm no funnier looking than you.'

She turned away quickly, embarrassed, wanting to appear like any other passenger and not draw attention.

A sudden pang as she thought about Nan. She had better go back upstairs. What should she say to the people seated here to explain? Surely they would think it odd that she came downstairs, only to go right back up again.

In unwitting confirmation of her nervousness, the boy leaned to her ear and whispered into it.

'I bet you're a scaredy-cat.'

'What on earth do you mean? Leave me alone. I was just on my way upstairs.'

This dirty boy made her uneasy and she contemplated complaining to the conductor, but then thought again. She would just go quietly back to Nan. Better not to raise a fuss or Nan might wake and be furious. Better to abide the nuisance. Perhaps the boy had no Nan, and was becoming a filthy sewer creature as a result. It wasn't his fault. She resolved to ignore the rude comment. But he wouldn't let up.

'You're a real chicken, aren't you missy?'

'I am not.'

'Bet you are.'

'Don't be silly.'

She stared at him continually this time and he turned to her and flashed an impish smile. His grubby cheeks became little red balls and three gaps were displayed in his front teeth and there was dirt caked under his nose.

'Bet you're such a scaredy-cat you wouldn't stand up and sing.'

Of course she wouldn't stand up and sing.

'My Nan is sleeping upstairs and I wouldn't want to wake her.'

'Your Nan's upstairs?' He pondered for a moment. 'Tell you what. Prove you're not frightened. Go over to the conductor and pull his sleeve.'

'That would be silly. I have nothing to ask him.'

'I knew it! You're a scaredy-cat. The biggest one I ever met.' Some spittle landed on her cheek with 'biggest'.. How sickening.

'I *am* not! You spat on me!'

They were seated next to the rear door where the conductor stood. He noticed the whispered exclamation and turned towards them. The boy cleared his throat, looked out the window and started whistling. She looked down at her lap, and felt very uneasy. After a few seconds the conductor turned back to counting coins.

'Go do it now! Go pull his sleeve.'

This was becoming absurd. She was not scared and she resolved once and for all to prove it. It would shut the boy up. Besides, all she had to do was think up a question to ask the conductor to make it all look genuine.

The conductor was still hunched over his stacks of coins. She knew if she waited she would never do it. She hopped up and tugged on his left sleeve. 'Sir?' He swivelled abruptly, annoyed, but his stern features softened when he saw her.

'Yes, my sweet.'

'May I ask you a question?'

'Course you can, love.'

The boy got up and slid behind the conductor, but her full attention was in the exchange with this adult stranger and she took no real notice. She had thought up a question.

'Why do some buses have two floors and others have just one? When I was a little girl my Nan took me on flat buses.'

A man sitting opposite called over to her, 'double deckers are only for grown-ups, and now you're on one you must be grown up.'

The old lady knitting scolded him. 'Don't fool with the girl. Shame on you!'

Quick as a wink, concealed from everyone's view behind the conductor, the boy pocketed three tall stacks of silver coins as all attention was turned to Clare.

'Actually, love, these buses are called Routemasters. They were just introduced a few months ago. You never rode them when you were little because there weren't any. But just you wait. London will soon be full of them. Marvellous contraption, isn't it?'

She nodded.

'Right, then. That answer your question?'

The boy pulled three stacks of copper coins from beneath the conductor's stand and placed them where the silver ones had been.

Only Clare noticed.

She didn't know what to do. She wanted to cry out to the kindly conductor to tell him what she had seen, but she also felt a reluctant partnership with the boy, the thief. He had made her an important part of his plan and she had helped him.

'What's the matter, dear? Did I get your question wrong?'

Clare shook her head.

'No sir, you answered it. Thank you very much.'

The conductor paused for a second, then smiled and winked at her.

A man hopped on board as they were moving, out of breath. He had been running alongside the bus. The conductor turned to him. 'Fare, please.'

When she returned to her seat, the boy was already there. She was about to berate him but he pre-empted her.

'Run back up to your Nan before she wakes.'

He stood up, one hand on the rail by the door, and she felt oddly compliant. As she passed him to climb the stairs, he grabbed hold of her hand and pressed a fistful of coins into it.

'Swear you won't tell.'

She hesitated.

'Swear!'

She nodded.

He gave her a serious look, his lips scrunched into an almost scowl, and hopped out the door. She watched as he dashed with much agility through the traffic and then she went upstairs and sat down next to Nan, who was snoring.

Clare tucked the coins one by one into the waistband of her skirt, separated to avoid clinking together. In her mind the boy was still dashing between cars, looking very much like a naughty rabbit in Mr MacGregor's garden.

The mildewy man with the newspaper turned back towards them and she stopped adjusting the coins, dead still. His eyebrows were scrunched and his forehead furrowed and he looked stern and she was sure he knew. She began to worry about the law.

Rain, Fruit and Women

A MEDLEY of raindrops splattering onto slate roofs and runoff jangling through drains and into the sewers accompanied Roper as he emerged from Moorgate Station and dashed across Ropemaker Street, ducked into Finsbury Lane and finally met shelter under the awning of an out of place fruit and vegetable seller. Better to wait it out. He seldom bothered with an umbrella, a nuisance to carry about with him everywhere, and there was no particular hurry this morning in any case. The shop was empty of customers, and a bearded man in a faded black frock stained with the sludge of years of produce stood silently behind him, watching the little chutes of water tumble off his awning.

The rain was mesmerising. Roper stared at the gushing gutter and watched the drops assault its surface then be swept away without any hope of keeping up their individuality. And they *were* individual.

A foreigner once remarked to him on the peculiarity of English rain. 'Like its people, England's rain refuses to conform to a sensible standard. You insist on farthings and tuppence and threepence and sixpence and shillings and all manner of unexplainable shapes and sizes and antique measurements from out of time. So your raindrops all at once fall in many sizes and at unreliable distances apart.' Indeed, raindrops large, small and medium were falling all at once, unequal distances apart, into the puddles all around him. He had always thought the irregularity normal.

What was abnormal was the presence of a fruiterer in this part of the City. From the look of the sign and the furnishings, the shop was a relic of a different era in Finsbury. It touched him to see such small institutions persevere out of place, 'out of time', as the raindrop foreigner would say.

The rain didn't appear to be abating and he would just have to run for it. But first he turned to the silent proprietor, determined to lend a token of support to this lonely fruit enterprise. Or was it that he felt responsible to the man for occupying his shelter uninvited? The proprietor's silence was a powerful incentive for Roper to buy. He would have felt no obligation towards a talkative man, but this bearded fellow who shared the rainfall with him unobtrusively and in silence awakened a melancholy sympathy in him. Almost a need for his approval. A desire to commiserate, at the very least.

'What would you say is in season?'

'Pears are at their peak.'

'I'll have one please. No... wait. I'll have three.'

'That'll be two shillings please.'

'Do you deliver?'

'If the order's large enough.'

'A crate of pears?'

'Depends how far.'

'Just round the corner. Offices of Crossley & Broke.'

'Yes, I can do that, but you'll have to pay in advance.'

The man named a sum and Roper reached into his pockets and pulled out the appropriate notes and coins.

The rain dwindled to drizzle, on its own idiosyncratic schedule as is the fashion with London weather, and Roper walked the balance of the way to work, unmindful of the wet, wondering why on earth he had just purchased a case of pears. And three in a paper bag besides.

Up the steps and through the shiny painted black door with a gleaming brass knob and into the cosy but well appointed reception area.

'Oh, you're all wet, Jim.'

Roper insisted the receptionist call him Jim. She was always a distracting start to his workday. He had subtly encouraged their flirtation for months (or had she?), coaxing more and more intimacy out of her. Never anything that crossed the unspoken bounds. Just innocent gestures of interest whenever they passed one another, just a little more ripe with invitation to linger and smile and glance than was formal. Very subtle. It woke them both up. Nowadays she did more of it than he.

'Shall I take your raincoat?'

'Yes please, Penny.'

He walked ahead of her to the cloakroom and might as well

have hung it up himself, her heels clicking behind him on the marble, then on the wood of the cloakroom floor. She held out a hanger and he handed her the coat with prolonged eye contact and a smile, which she reciprocated, and helped her with one of the shoulders. Their hands met only through the fabric of the coat.

'Thank you, Penny. After you.'

No one could see him and he quite shamelessly watched her behind move up and down with each step. Once he would have felt some guilt, but that had left him lately.

Back in the reception room, she safely seated, Roper walking towards the corridor for the offices, she called after him.

'I'm so disappointed, Jim.' Playful. 'I rather thought you had something for me in that paper bag.'

He turned around.

'Fancy a pear?'

'A what?'

'A pear.'

'As in the fruit?'

'Here, enjoy. And think of me while you do.'

She bit into it as he strode away, her eyes level with his adorable firm bottom, fitted in so nicely beneath his straight back and square shoulders. Did he know that whenever he spoke to her with his confident, earnest and gentle voice her spine tingled and her legs felt all warm?

He pushed through a door and was gone.

'Good morning, Jim.'

His secretary was also to call him by first name. She was plainer than Penny but buxom and more forward. No, not forward. Direct. More direct and prodding. And a shorter skirt. Christ, why could he think of nothing else? It was time he got a male secretary and started avoiding the firm's front entrance. Or married. But he had a feeling marriage wouldn't solve his distraction.

'Morning, Sarah.' Work. Getting down to work would do it. 'Messages?'

'Mr Selling would like to see you.'

'That all?'

'Erm...' She flipped through to the right page. 'October...

twenty-fifth. Nothing in the diary.'

Roper was two years qualified and had joined a medium-sized and very reputable boutique practice. Its specialties were commercial contracts, charterparties, dry shipping, and, thanks to the presence of a shadowy junior partner called Pinsky, anything to do with the international transportation of diamonds.

Selling was one of four senior partners, the sort of man whose reputation and exploits clattered about him like a junk heap as he paraded down the firm's corridors. Distinction in the navy, experience at his father's shipping firm, then articles in law, 'out of seasickness.' You could almost see the medals on his chest, his father walking behind him with a hand on his shoulder, the giant moustache that was once his pride but which he now got by without because of a foolish bet.

Roper secretly disbelieved the moustache story. It was not fashionable for lawyers, especially in the City, to sport whiskers, and Roper suspected Selling of having shaved his off the moment he realised he was to begin a career in law. He thought Selling's style fraudulent, though he couldn't put a finger on why precisely. Perhaps it was because he felt Selling should have had a large belly and little red capillaries showing on his face and a slight wheeze as he walked but had none of these things and in fact appeared quite fit for a man of sixty.

He knocked on Selling's door.

'Good morning, Mr Selling.'

'Ah, Roper...'

Inexplicably, right there and then, for the first time since the party the other night, an image of the woman flashed in his mind's eye. The one who had wrestled him out onto the street with just her eyes.

He forced his attention back to Selling.

'...Stockton Lavery are to begin importing some of their soap ingredients from Brazil and will be here for a meeting about drawing up new contracts. They like a serious young man to work with and I'll leave them in your hands from now on.'

This meant Selling considered the switch to Brazil foolhardy, believed it would result in the client's ultimate demise, and would rather someone else's name be associated with them at the firm.

'Our favourite beer exporter is being sued over breach of a

warranty in the c.i.f. which *we* drafted and I've looked at it over and over and we do not have a case. I advised them to settle for thirty-nine thousand and they refuse. This is going to be messy and I'd rather someone able like you do the honours than leave it to, say, well, I won't say to who. Prepare the instructions and I'll leave the choice of barrister to you.'

'Mr Selling, you know I've got rather a lot on my desk at the moment. Not that I'm not up to the extra work, but don't you think it would be a better allocation of our...' he searched for a word, '...manpower, if Bigby or Rounthwaite took one of these matters? I know for certain Bigby is having a light week, and we both know Rounthwaite needs a kick in the backside for laziness, if you'll pardon me for saying so.'

'No, Roper, I would like you on these jobs. Oh, and there's one more thing. Just a trifle. Simon and the others agree with me that we need the corridors carpeted in the client areas. The wood is getting worn out but it would ruin us to replace it. We've decided on a nice dark yellow. Navy trimming. Sort of modernise us, we think, and give us a bit of the maritime touch we like to portray. Simon will give you the details and you just have to find a good carpeter to do the job. Should be a breeze.'

Yellow! Disastrous! This would become a matter of hilarity in the City, he just knew. And it would *not* ruin them to replace the wood. These old bastards were all going to retire soon, and were imposing their hopeless tastes on the rest of the lawyers as a parting gift. Avoiding reflooring would protect their own profit margin the year or two before they quit for Brighton or the south of France, and would leave everybody else with a great embarrassment of a building.

'Will that be all, Mr Selling?'

But Selling was already on the telephone and waved him out of the office. Bloody old man.

Sarah was calling to him from her desk.

'Jim, you...'

He walked into his office but left the door open.

'Sarah, cancel my dinner with Rogers. And see if one of the students can take over the Raleigh file for the next couple of days.'

'Yes, Jim.' Pause. 'Jim?'

He picked up the stack of papers on his desk.

'And see if the librarian can rustle up something for me on Anglo-Brazilian commercial precedents.'

'Of course, Jim.'

'And what do you think of yellow carpets, Sarah?'

'Jim!'

'What!'

'There's someone waiting for you at reception.'

'You're joking. You said I didn't have anything in the calendar today!'

'Better hurry. Penny called about it a few minutes ago but I didn't want to disturb your meeting with Mr Selling.'

He was already out the door of his office and he slammed the papers he was holding down onto Sarah's desk. Back down the corridor and out into the reception lounge. Penny was on the telephone, but looked up and nodded in the direction of the couches. Standing next to them was a somewhat dishevelled, bearded man in a smudged black frock. Beside him, on the polished chestnut table, next to the morning newspapers, there rested a large wooden crate of Williams pears.

Rude Awakenings

ABOUT THREE months before Naveen and Clare and Roper took their places in this story, there was an echoed crack!, and a bullet whirred past Azim's face and landed with a swish and muffled thud in the sand twenty feet to his right. For several moments he was too stunned to move, and stared in the direction of the bullet's resting place.

'Drop, Azim!' In Arabic.

He fell to his chest and crawled over to his rifle, his scalp and torso prickling with heat and his arms trembling slightly. There was shouting all around him.

'The enemy is attacking!'

Frantic activity behind him in the supply tent.

His ears rang with the shock of three rifle shots discharged right behind him. Someone from his section was already returning fire. His instinct was to crawl behind the tent to try and get a more secure vantage point, but he knew the tent was useless as a shield and would probably be a target, so he stayed put, cocked his rifle and lay on his belly.

The sergeant was yelling.

'Command did not tell us of this! This is a surprise attack! Walid, radio with command and find out what is going on!'

Azim began to take aim in the direction of the bullet's origin, at a group of men in the distance. They appeared to be running and were advancing toward them quickly. His stomach tightened into a knot.

'We are outnumbered, sergeant.'

He heard shouting from the direction of the attackers.

'Bring me the field glasses,' the sergeant shouted.

Nobody moved.

'Bring me the field glasses!' He shrieked the order so ferociously his voice gave out partway through.

Walid dropped the radio receiver, grabbed the field glasses, dropped onto his belly, and elbowed his way over to the sergeant.

The shouting from the direction of the attackers was growing louder. Azim put his finger on the trigger and took aim. Better to fight, even though they were outnumbered. If they were Israelis it was the only honourable course. The attackers were waving their arms like madmen. His finger tightened on the trigger, feeling its tension, his right eye level with the barrel.

'Don't shoot! Don't shoot! Don't shoot!'

Azim had already fired.

It appeared he hit one of the attackers in the leg. They were about a hundred feet away but when the man fell, grabbing onto his shin in pain, the others dispersed and started running away in various directions.

'Don't shoot!' The sergeant hurled the field glasses at Azim's head. '*Masryeen hom!*' They're Egyptian.

*

On reflection they realised it was absurd to have assumed an attack. They were on Egyptian territory, surrounded by Egyptian infantry, all doing exercises in the vast sandy wastes of the northern Sinai. No planes had flown to drop foreign paratroopers, they were miles from the coast, and intelligence would have been aware of movements near the Israeli frontier. The commanders would have cancelled the exercises, put them on standby, and Hafez would have rallied his *fedayeen* to deal with any nuisance. The French, who were suspected of growing friendship with the Zionists, had trouble up to their necks in Algeria. Even a British threat was not possible; although they had exchanged shots with some British in recent months, there had been confirmation that the last British troops withdrew from the Canal more than three weeks ago. And the radio reports told of a very good management arrangement they had just made with the British over the Canal.

It was just that none of them had experienced friendly fire before. They couldn't be blamed for their reaction. Besides, the Israeli aggression in Gaza in April had set them all on edge. If Israelis could kill Egyptian civilians in cold blood, what horrors they might inflict on soldiers were the stuff of extreme nightmares.

And the politics in Cairo were very alive. Too alive. There was the air of big things happening. Not good news for a soldier of Azim's placid temperament, who preferred evenings smoking his pipe and playing *sheshbesh* with his section to the prospect of being killed by some Zionist crusaders. Arafat was leading student demonstrations, agitating for action against Israel, and Colonel Nasser had just been elected president after hovering around for months as prime minister following Neguib's resignation. Azim had much preferred Neguib's style. He sensed that the Colonel was a man whose ambition burned too strongly for Egyptians to be left in peace. The Colonel viewed Egypt as the hero of the Arab world, and was determined for Egypt to champion the Arab cause on behalf of all the others. Why not leave such efforts to Syria?

It worried Azim that he had recently been issued a shiny new Soviet rifle. Perhaps he should quit the army, return to his flat for good and look for work as a civil engineer. He ought to put his training to good use rather than play these silly and increasingly dangerous games in the sand. Then again, he had voted for the Colonel. Not that there was anyone else to vote for.

He could not deny it made his heart proud that for the first time in over two thousand years there was a native Egyptian leading his country, bearing promises of great things for Egypt. But when he thought awhile about his life he realised he would happily sacrifice pride for ease of mind.

For heaven's sake, he had just come within two inches of losing his face thanks to the common nervousness around him. But praise to God that nobody had been hit. The fallen man had sprained his ankle while running towards Azim's group, although in the heat of the moment everyone involved thought he was shot.

Azim's sergeant and the commander of the other section agreed that the incident would not be reported, and that they would carry on as normal. Walid was ordered to run around the encampment five hundred times for his hesitation with the binoculars. Azim was given the same five hundred laps and had his guard duty extended by two hours a night for the duration of the exercises.

He didn't know about Walid, but he would just as soon give up his wife as run five hundred laps in the desert sun. He made elaborate arrangements with several soldiers who would be in key positions during his punishment run, and succeeded in reducing his ordeal to a manageable one hundred laps, carefully spaced out over the time it would have taken to endure the full five hundred, his sergeant none the wiser. This cost him seven Egyptian pounds, all his American magazines and nearly his entire supply of strawberry flavoured tobacco.

He did not consider it necessary nor worth the expense to avoid the extra guard duty. With three small children in his Giza flat, dogs barking outside his window and vagrants fighting in the streets all night, he was accustomed to surviving on inadequate sleep. When on leave at home he normally lay in a state of semi-consciousness all night and drifted off properly just before dawn, only to be awakened minutes later by the muezzin, reminding him cheerfully that prayer is better than sleep. He would wake his wife, sometimes make love to her briefly, and send her downstairs to make sure their eldest was walking in the direction of school. She would return with bread and cheese and olives and Canada Dry from the street vendor, which he lived on.

He would spend the daytime idling contentedly in his flat, snoozing in his chair by a stack of backdated newspapers, his ashtray full with dozens of crushed cigarette butts.

He particularly liked the lazy feel of drifting off with the paper folded in his lap, a cigarette smouldering in the ashtray, the electric fan humming by the window and his wife puttering reassuringly in the kitchen. In the background, the radio would, more often than not, be playing the deep and sultry and lilting voice of Umm Koulthoum singing her latest song. His mind would begin floating, and her music would gradually come to dominate his head. She would transport him out of his flat and onto the streets of Cairo, carry him like a child on her back as she walked down the path by the river, her melody entering his head and filling his chest and possessing his limbs until his whole body was in a gentle buzzing vibration. People would stand on the bridges and smile at the sound. They smiled at him, upon him, and he knew he was lucky to have been chosen by Umm Koulthoum. She became his mother and he slept in her arms, his head rested against one of her breasts, and he watched dreamily as a great many feluccas drifted in a long line down the Nile.

'Azim, wake up you lazy fool!'

He opened his eyes to find himself slumped on the ground, his head leaning on a cold, hard tent pole, sand in his pants, and Khalid's boot heel digging into his shin. Time to hand over the weighty responsibility of vigilance to the next man on night duty.

He crawled into a tent, plopped himself down heavily on the ground, his head still thick with sleep, and rolled over onto his side. But he immediately changed position because of a jarring pain when his head came into contact with the ground. This was due to a very large and very raw welt a couple of inches above his left ear, which had developed, hitherto unnoticed, on account of the intimate connection Azim had recently sustained, in the heat of false battle, with a pair of manually propelled field glasses.

*

Not long thereafter, the Indian Pandit sat in a plush seat on board the new Egyptian president's airplane. They were returning together from an exciting conference at Tito's Adriatic resort. A few others had been there, leaders interested in forming an alignment of nations that could stand apart from the Cold War power struggle and through cooperation avoid being swept into the global game of intimidation as American or Russian playthings. He had been so heartened watching the Colonel at the discussions, a man of strong moral voice to justify a movement of non-aligned nations.

Since Stalin had gone, the Yugoslavs were perceived, rightly or wrongly, as too geopolitically associated with the Russian bloc and isolated from the rest of Europe for them truly to succeed as leaders of such a movement. Key European members they could be, but not leaders. India, with its firm democratic process, its huge economic potential, its teeming mass of popular support, would naturally form the substance and bedrock of the association; but his observation of the Colonel at the meeting had confirmed to the Pandit that Egypt would be their true source of promise and initiative.

The Colonel had a brazen and fiery energy, exuded tremendous charisma, had much potential for sway over the vast Arab world, could mobilise Egypt in an instant to support the movement. He wielded the Suez. He was the joint linking east and west. He held the rapt diplomatic attention of the Americans and the strategic fascination of the Soviets and the respect of the Africans and possessed some real estate that was very dear to the hearts of old colonial Europe. And he had the independence of spirit to pursue a vision.

The Pandit's daughter sat next to him, and contentedly he followed her gaze out the window as they banked slightly to the right. The Mediterranean shone up at them, a great unblemished surface of deep blue emotion, stretched taut across the divide of continents.

At the other end of the cabin the Colonel was being briefed in hushed tones by his aide. He had just been informed of a radio transmission. He looked over at the Pandit.

'The Americans have betrayed us.' His tone was matter of fact.

He had tested the sincerity of the American State Department and they had shown themselves up as the double-crossing brigands he instinctively knew them to be. It was all calculated on his part. They promised him money to relieve some of the financing burden of the Aswan Dam project, out of fear the Soviets would do it first. The British had convinced the Americans it was a good idea, and the Colonel had found this development quite convenient. He knew he could play everyone off against each other at least for a short while, and he took an old Egyptian bargaining stance he knew would cause the Americans frustration. He delayed and delayed, and encouraged prolonged wrangling over minor and inconsequential terms of the loan.

America was too self-important to put up with such tomfoolery, and when it was frustrated it either lashed out or lost interest. Here it was not worth lashing out. Here he knew they would lose interest in the offer they had made, lose interest in him as a partner, and only once that occurred did he accept their offer. Of course by that point their answer had to be no. They would try to brush him off like a fly. And he would teach them all a lesson. Maybe not the Americans, who didn't understand or didn't care enough to understand his politics, but certainly the British, who were exceedingly uptight about their rules and regulations and their shipping interests.

It was so very amusing to watch the British pretend not to get worked up over his activities, to watch them acting so self-righteously and feigning disinterest. They always had one eye on their balance books and the other on their history books. Their accounts had to add up at all costs, while their scribes had to vindicate the actions they took to make ends meet in reassuring terms of duty and responsibility. The British were in the comic business of trying to keep up a failing empire on a shoestring budget and in good conscience.

In due course he would show them all that Egypt was not a pawn to be sacrificed so casually. He had planned the American refusal from the beginning, and they arrogantly thought *they* were teaching *him* who was boss. The West would pay for this American treachery.

But while toying with the world's great behemoths it was also essential to maintain solidarity with the world's losers if he were to have real power. The Pandit was a convenient audience for a show of victimhood.

'The State Department have indicated that their offer to meet our interest burden for the Aswan project has been withdrawn. They have made fools of all Egyptians. They made a fool of *me*!'

He began to pace up and down the aisle, feigning great aggravation.

The Pandit had a reply at the ready for such occasions.

'What arrogance they have! This is very unfortunate news, my dear Colonel. I am most distressed to hear it. But I daresay it does not surprise me. Western colonialists cannot see beyond the gold rims of their own spectacles, and this quality makes them very fickle partners indeed.'

He got up and walked over to the Colonel, put his hand on his shoulder and spoke to him in soothing tones, dropping light hints at irregular intervals that it would bear fruit for Egypt to cultivate non-alignment as its primary political tool.

*

As soon as Clare arrived home the day she assisted the thief in the bus, she went up to her room and hid her loot in a secret place. Although she was considerably vexed over what had happened, a good night's sleep and the renewal the next morning of her strict daily routine made her forget the episode for a couple of days.

Warriors in High Places

IT WOULD be unavoidable. The Prime Minister would have to be notified before the end of his dinner with the Iraqi dignitaries. It was most regrettable and he had held off as long as he thought appropriate, but it was not his place as Private Secretary to withhold delivery of a sensitive message.

He glanced up to see Admiral Sir Charles Thompson cast him a glare of disapproval, in oil colour. King George II sneered down at him, decidedly unimpressed.

The brilliant, luminous chandelier, giving the impression of deriving its angelic glow from the orbs of heaven, looked ready to crash down onto the long table. But he had always sustained an irrational fear of chandeliers falling and did his utmost to avoid being stationed directly beneath one.

The man he knew to be the Prime Minister's most favoured guest, formerly an associate of Lawrence of Arabia (in more virile times) and about as English-looking as one would like an Iraqi to be without risking confusion, was slicing gingerly through the last of his string beans. The Iraqi King was in rapt dialogue with the Leader of the Opposition, and various top Cabinet Ministers were pecking at their plates while animatedly holding up several threads of discussion simultaneously. Conversation was lively and the meal might drag on and he might be sacked for failing to convey the information before too late. A private secretary must possess and exercise the ability to recognise those rare occasions when exceptions to official etiquette were required.

He approached the Prime Minister and leaned, bent at the waist, towards his ear. An inch closer and his master's moustache would have brushed his cheek. He conveyed the news.

The Prime Minister wasted no time in sharing it. 'Gentlemen, our dear Colonel has just purported to nationalise the Suez, and with a show of force.' The Leader of the Opposition cautiously pressed for further information and garnered a hint or two of possible direction from the Foreign Secretary.

The Prime Minister stood up, not a crinkle in his suit, his hair in its perpetually just-combed look. But he waited before speaking for the last fork to be set to rest against its plate.

'You'll please forgive me, and accept my sincere apologies for excusing myself so abruptly. Whilst you enjoy the pudding, I expect to spend the rest of the night on bitter coffee and distressing policy alternatives. My Ministers, I'm afraid, shall have to join me in that fate.'

Brief, liquid, monosyllabic murmurs of sympathy all the way down the table, but mainly silence.

He began walking for the door and the Ministers readied to follow him.

To the Iraqis, 'please do carry on,' and before any of them had a chance to stand up, 'don't stand up. I shall have to make this up to you. Good night.'

The Iraqis left shortly after.

*

In the Cabinet Room the Prime Minister displayed lividity.

'The Colonel must not be allowed to have his hand on our windpipe.'

The First Sea Lord and the Chief of the Imperial General Staff had been summoned. Did that mean there would be military action? Prompt military action? And someone had thought to call in the French Ambassador and the American Chargé d'Affaires. A military coalition?

A brilliant coincidence occurred to the First Sea Lord and he barely managed to refrain from a visible demonstration of excitement. But he calmed himself before speaking up.

'As it happens, Prime Minister, the Mediterranean Fleet is awaiting my inspection at Malta. They should be ready to sail at four to eight hours' notice. If we were to send a signal now they would sail for Egypt no later than dawn. Two days at full steam will bring them to Port Said, including a diversion to collect twelve hundred Royal Marine Commandos from Cyprus.' The First Sea Lord was also the Earl of Burma.

Several minutes of general conferring before a firm reply.

'I fear such a course of action will be too dangerous for us

34

without the prospect of immediate reinforcements to follow them in should matters deteriorate at Port Said. Besides, how will an occupation of Port Said secure the Canal for us?'

The First Sea Lord took solace in the sequence of the reasons. The Prime Minister's instincts had not rejected a sea-borne invasion out of hand.

The French Ambassador spoke up. He had been getting up throughout the meeting to send and receive cables and this had been agitating the Prime Minister.

'Prime Minister, I have been informed that France has no more then eight days' supply of oil in reserve. That is, eight days for all of France. I don't presume to know the situation here.'

Calls were made and notes pushed back and forth and it emerged that Britain had only twenty days of oil to fall back on.

By midnight the First Sea Lord was looking edgy, as if he wanted to get up and pace. Smoking had been forbidden in the Cabinet Room for some years. The French Ambassador had sucked in his cheeks so tightly that his expression was unreadable, and the Prime Minister was clearly mortified. His face had been alternating between shades of bluish-grey and bright pink. The Chief of the Imperial General Staff looked busy, poring over sheaves of notes. He was not an Earl of anywhere yet. The American had contributed little to the proceedings and had not seen fit to supply the present company with his country's oil reserve estimates. He continued to appear earnest but unconcerned, and the warm July night wore on and on.

*

As it happened, the Colonel stopped no boats. The oil continued to pass through to Europe, and the situation at Suez was even more ordinary than ordinary. Shipowners continued paying dues to the Canal Company. The captain of an Israeli merchant ship was shocked to find himself sailing through the Canal entirely unopposed. Six Suez crewmen had come on board to pilot him through as though it were the most normal thing in the world (it wasn't). But never mind the show of normalcy. The French public, abuzz with righteous outrage (did the vision of De Lesseps mean nothing?), stood unanimously in favour of crushing the

Colonel. The British Prime Minister felt in his bones that there was no natural or honourable course for his island but to teach the Colonel his place.

*

There is a quiet, lush Paris suburb which displays its wealth and dignity by way of many large trees. Its grand and genteel homes are so sure of themselves they don't mind being obscured by foliage. There is no sense of protest in its rich and fragrant air. The energy of the nearly empty streets is of tacit consent. The odd person on a stroll one October evening might have felt as though the semblage of dwellings and pavement and trees and railings all agreed with one another about the proper way of the world.

Inside one of the homes in that suburb that evening stood the Commander-in-Chief of Israel's defence forces, his confident silhouette framed in the open front doorway. He had an unconscious, relaxed control over his posture that one paradoxically might have described as flowing from a spirit of rugged resignation, a spirit borne of having waged many battles with deep purpose, human failure simply not an option. He watched with a combined sense of irony and moment and wonder as the backs of the two British statesmen moved rapidly away down the pavement. It seemed to him that these British would sooner have been caught in a park with cheap French prostitutes than be known to have colluded with Israeli leaders. But they had inscribed their names on a secret protocol of war and there was no turning back. They certainly didn't look back. They looked rather as though they were suppressing an instinct to flee. As they hastily took their leave a minute earlier they had mumbled words of politeness, tinged with astringent and defeatist humour not altogether clear to him.

The Old Man he had accompanied to this place, a couple of other Israeli officials, and their welcoming French hosts, had gone back inside. He shut the door softly and returned to join them. The Old Man had fever and was sunk into a soft chair. The others were all quite pleased with themselves. Imagine finally drawing in the British. Imagine! *Un vrai coup de maître.*

Friday's Child

'LAST DAY of the wee-eek!'

Anne's singsong voice tickled Clare's eardrums and woke a sense of song in her. With all the brown leaves falling around them in the schoolyard it might have been a melancholy melody which stirred, but instead it was a spontaneous mood of goodness. In autumn the plants began to die but people began to return to life after the lazy days of summer. Clare felt a warmth of common purpose once school began. Things began to happen. New subjects and teachers, and new stories from school friends whom she had nearly forgotten.

Seven summer weeks at her aunt's Cotswold estate had kept her rosy-cheeked and energetic and were the occasion of some splendid secret adventures, but autumn meant the resumption of dining with her mother and father every evening, which was a reassuring daily highlight, and doing the usual proper things with Nan, which simply felt right. Grey skies and the patter of rain on window panes while teachers offered her new formulas and formalities of knowledge out of thick books gave her a renewed and businesslike feel. And so the melody that animated her mind in the schoolyard was purposeful and happy.

She sat on a carved log and watched half absently as girls ran about and made lots of noise and bobbed up and up and up over skipping ropes, her imagination taking a part of her away on other magic journeys. The elaborate redbrick schoolhouse was a wizard's castle, the playing girls spellbound little assistants who were captive to his powerful dark forces, she a spy from the land of wise old women, sent to find a weakness in the wizard's scheme without being detected, to save the girls and send them back home so they could get on with their lives. She would have to carry on as though she were one of them in order to avoid discovery.

Her eyes, set into the distance, came back into focus to meet a girl running towards her. Buckled blue shoes clapped the pavement in rapid steps and gravel crunched and Anne came to a breathless halt before her.

'Last day of the week, Clare. Aren't you pleased? What will you do at the weekend? I shall go to department stores with mother and shop for winter wear.'

Ellen and Maxine joined them.

'You ought to buy ribbons, Anne, just for the four of us. It would be our special group ribbon that no one else has.'

All the girls liked that idea and agreed on yellow.

'I can't. I haven't any of my own money to buy things. Mother buys what she likes for me and I don't reckon she would buy something like that.'

Until then Clare had been content not to remember the incident on the bus, but at that moment it occurred to her, with a shock of danger that she brushed aside in her mind, that her coins could be employed. Wouldn't it be alright to use them for friendship's sake?

'I've got money.'

'You *have?*' Ellen was incredulous, as she knew just how strict Clare's Nan was and could not imagine her permitting Clare to keep money.

'Anne could use it to buy us ribbons,' said Clare. 'We should then be a secret group. The Yellow Spies.'

'Why spies?' asked Maxine. 'What are we going to spy on? Let's be the Yellow Princesses. Only girls who we choose to join us might become Yellow Princesses.'

'Where did you get money, Clare?'

'I shan't tell you why I have it but I do. It's not important where it came from if we use it well.' As she spoke she already felt pangs of guilt and foreboding.

'So shall we be Yellow Princesses?' Maxine was pushful at times.

'We don't have to decide right now. Let's buy the ribbons first and decide later.' Ellen was always more reasonable.

A girl Clare didn't recognise from past years had been standing alone, watching them from a distance. Clare had seen her in the classroom but not taken a particular interest, being too busy reacquainting herself with her old friends and the familiar surroundings. Now in the schoolyard she registered that the girl had dark braided hair and a freckled face and the awkward look of someone who was too shy to introduce herself but at the same time did not want to appear as though she were hovering about alone because of friendlessness.

'Will you give Anne the money, Clare?' Maxine was fully taken by the idea of the ribbons.

As the prospect of buying them became more and more likely, Anne began to look uneasy.

'Even if I have money it won't be a simple matter to buy ribbons. I shall have to explain to mother why I want them and where I got the money.'

'You mustn't say I gave it to you.' Clare began to regret having spoken up about her coins.

'Then what shall I say?'

Maxine interrupted bossily. 'You *will* give Anne the money, won't you Clare?'

The braided girl had just taken a small step of strength, having summoned some hidden boldness and determined to join the group of chatty girls by the fence at the edge of the schoolyard. She felt so foolish standing on her own at this new school, and knew that to overcome her exclusion she would have to take matters into her own hands and become outgoing. She had next to no experience in such matters but was determined to turn her position around quickly.

She stepped up to Clare's group.

'Let me introduce myself...'

'Why should we?'

Clare was aghast. 'Maxine!'

Surprised frustration showed in the new girl's face; she had imagined all sorts of possible responses but never that one exactly.

She tried again.

'My name is Prudence and...'

Ellen, who was always the kindest of the group, audibly suppressed a giggle when she heard the name Prudence pronounced with such earnestness and sincerity. She hadn't meant to react meanly but the presence of the other girls impinged on her pattern of behaviour, prompting unexpected results. And the girl was enunciating her words so seriously and had given a funny little nod at the start of her introduction. She tried very hard to hide her reaction.

'... and I wondered if I might stay with you at the next break. Only I'm new here and would like to get to know you.'

All four girls stared at her without a response, until Ellen began to say 'yes' and Clare sighed with relief. But before Ellen could carry on Anne whispered something in Maxine's ear and Maxine spoke up to interrupt.

'You can't join us. We don't know you and we've just built a special group that others aren't to join.'

'No we haven't.'

It was the most Clare could bring herself to say without feeling she was being disloyal, and she stopped herself from carrying on when Maxine shot her a very angry look.

Irreparable damage had in any event already been done. To the new girl, as she registered the words exchanged, the world seemed to sway, and her eyes lost focus on the group of four girls she had attempted to join. Her body felt light and hot, and as she quickly regained her inner grounding and sense of place she felt a hard lump grow in her throat which at once made her want to swallow and prevented her from doing so. She blinked rapidly to frustrate the tears that threatened to pour as these girls stared at her wordlessly, and with a surge of will she managed something remarkable. A smile. And a friendly nod as she turned her back on them. The sobbing she was able to postpone for the three minutes it took her to gain permission from the teacher to go inside the school and then find a deserted lavatory in which to crumble.

'Who does she think she is?' asked Maxine.

'She's an odd one,' said Anne, in a tone Clare could imagine Anne's mother taking. 'Prudence. What a silly name!'

Clare and Ellen were silent and for a while none of the four had anything to say at all. Then Clare, who was feeling very sorry for not having spoken up to make the girl welcome and at the same time admiring Ellen for attempting to do so, said, 'maybe we should let her be part of our group.'

'We don't want strange ones in our group,' said Maxine. 'Anne, you *will* buy those ribbons, won't you?'

Clare's mind was spinning in a guilty whirl. Taking the money from the boy on the bus had been naughty, and she hadn't felt able to stop it occurring. It had just happened and she hadn't the slightest inclination to protest until it was far too late. The boy was now perpetually hopping through traffic in her thoughts and there was no catching him to bring him back, no returning to the scene to set it right. And her group of friends turning away this girl made her feel similarly powerless to stop bad things happening. Why could she not act to prevent what Nan would call evil when it was going on right before her? Even when it involved her directly? She mustn't let it continue. She would place herself on the path of good and she would shun evil, and Nan (though she was constrained from confiding in Nan on these matters for it would surely mean punishment) would be proud. She resolved just then that she would not provide the improperly acquired money for her friends' ribbons. That would be a step in the right direction. And she would eat everything her mother told her to eat without whining like a piglet.

'Clare, how will I get the money from you?'

Denying the money was going to be harder than she anticipated five seconds ago. But she had pledged herself to withholding the stolen coins and would not now turn back from her commitment. Their teacher began ringing the bell in her severe way, her wrist limp as she flopped it back and forth, but the sound somehow issuing from it in perfectly regular intervals, as though she commanded it by witchcraft. A ringing metronome drawing them back to the classroom with hypnotic magnetic propulsion.

'Clare! How will Anne get the money?'

'I've not got it with me. It's at home.'

'Then how will she get it before the week end? How will we buy the ribbons?'

'I shall have to bring it to school next Friday. I will give it to her then.'

'I won't be out shopping then, I don't think.'

'You can keep it with you until next time you go out to shop with your mother.'

Why had she said that? Why not use the impracticability as an excuse to let herself out of the promise to provide the money? She suffered a paralysis of resolve. The urge and intent to do right were in her, but the attendant actions failed to follow. Was the pressure Maxine exerted on her so strong?

More likely the root of Clare's incorrigibly complicit manner was to be found somewhere in her own character. Maybe it was her compulsion to make tangible contributions to the bond between her friends. Providing the practical, activity-oriented nourishment in their group sustained her involvement in their regular interaction even though she lacked the assertive nature of Maxine or the easy talkativeness of Ellen or the adult condescension of Anne to hold up her end of the canopy of friendship. She felt intuitively, for she certainly did not reason these matters out in her mind, that it was her strongest personal point of interest to the group that she encouraged things rather than just words to happen, and that this was primarily what made her company continue to be desired.

And who, at what age, anywhere, does not, at least secretly, at least fleetingly, wish their company to be desired by those they respect and from time to time revere, those whose company they themselves desire?

II

AROUND the Kafr the ridges and dips and paths are dusted with beige pebble. Dark green thorny shrubs, ankle high, jealously guard the roadsides. The wind rises from the Great Sea to the west, on a course for the holy hills of Judea, where it collides with divine easterlies and disperses and enters secret rock crevices to shroud and caress the hidden bones of beloved ancestors. How precious a task, to minister to the earthly remnants of ancient parents of singular faith, devoted forebears of the moral tenets of our civilisation, who dwelled in those parts.

Those sprouts of the west breeze without the force to reach maturity over Judea whisper along the coastal plain and satisfy themselves among the orange trees and graze the olive groves of the foothills, where humble farming families share their lives with the stubborn soil and with its thistles with little yellow flowers and the scorpions and their goats and donkeys and intimately and warmly with each other.

A woman carries her husband's name in her womb, and he plants an olive tree to stand as a blessing for his father's grandson.

Most of those who lived in this particular frontier village cared little for politics and less for war. Since *al-Naqba* they were resigned to their new Jewish masters, who up to that day, if all was told, were by no means monstrous towards them. The village inhabitants tilled modest tracts of earth and tended small herds and a number of olive trees in the fields surrounding the village, and good potable water filled their wells. Far better, far less insulting, to have Arab masters, none would disagree, but nobody wanted to summon a storm. They were simple people. Politics in their memory had always been attended by violence and various upheaval, and they would rather carry on pressing olives and marrying their children off (and occasionally conceal a blood feud) than engage in protest and incur the interest of Israeli guns, to be herded around like sheep by young Israeli boys who ate an excess of beef and lacked any veneration for tradition.

They could not smile at Israel, for it had stolen their honour, but protest was for young men in the towns, for the educated. It was eminently practicable and emotionally tolerable for them and

45

the Israelis to carry on their business in tandem and without much friction. They would husband the land as they were meant to do, and if he willed it God would one day restore the dignity of Arab dominion over their village and the villages of their cousins. But one Monday the soldiers came, and they were in unusually sombre form. As the sun pounded on them from dead above, at midday, they received orders to enforce a curfew. To publish it and enforce it. No exceptions. They were at war. 'Violators to be halted with much prejudice.' Somewhere along the line of command it had become 'violators to be shot on sight'.

Nobody wanted to do any shooting but nobody wanted to die either. If the orders were to shoot the situation must be really serious. Orders were orders. The integrity of the freshly minted State, the ancient homeland, depended on the intense cooperation of every last man and woman and tight concert between the men of strategy, those watching and directing the battles from the crow's nest. The eagle's nest. But in this country the eagles fought on their feet, on the hills and down the valleys and gritting the sands with everyone else.

Something went wrong and the curfew order did not reach the village mayor until after four o'clock. The lockdown was to start at five and not a minute later.

Scrawny black and white cats with burning eyes and the typical local petulance would not leave the soldiers alone all afternoon, shamelessly soliciting some imagined scraps that the soldiers did not actually possess. Perhaps they looked more robust to the cats than the villagers, and they sensed these young men were associated with nourishment. Perhaps they scented blood.

'Please, you must permit the people to return after five o'clock. It will be impossible to notify every man, woman and child working in the fields that they must be in their homes in under twenty minutes. It will be impossible! Your commanders will surely make an exception. It is beyond our control. You have asked the unreasonable. Please, be reasonable. We are reasonable people.'

The young man wavered momentarily, but regained resolve. Orders were orders. This was war. The soldiers in his presence must be taught firmness. He did not reply to the mayor, who was nearing tears. A woman ran with all her energy and then some, her skirt catching between her legs and then releasing, her head disappearing over the hilltop. She had heard of the curfew and was screaming the names of her husband and two sons, desperate to bring them back on time. She had thirty-five minutes to live. Her sons had twenty-two. Her husband, who came from a different direction and three minutes later than the others, heard gunshots and screams and lay low and survived, a ravaged man all his remaining years.

As the evening arrived and their stomachs and the creeping chill in the late October air urged them home from the fields and groves, forty-three people, old men with staffs, women and girls with pails and baskets, boys with donkeys, men with bicycles, teenagers with goats, trickled back to the village road and made their way along it toward the small cluster of soldiers blockading the point of entry. As the returning villagers approached, the soldiers took aim and shot every last one. They made sure to add a fatal round to anyone who was only wounded on the first go. The sky rent with the echoes of their cries and the beige pebbles soaked red, then hardened to brown. The cats, for once, steered clear.

The same curfew orders had been issued for all other villages, and the same poor calculation meant hundreds of Arabs would be unable to honour it, no fault of their own. But only one young man and his subordinates at the one village, the one Kafr, cut themselves off from the fabric of humanity to impose a leaden regime of strict liability upon *their* Arabs.

History, if it could be given personality, would offer up the whole range of fact, all of it precise and neutral (it cannot but we pretend). We the people would sit, as we do, in living rooms and television studios and libraries and post judgment on the moral goodness and badness and mediocrity of its offerings. We take the bad along with the mediocre, the heinous along with the saintly. We have no choice. The young men had.

And so to war.

And So To War

AT FIVE o'clock, four hundred Israeli paratroopers hit the Sinai sands at nine hours' fast marching distance from the outskirts of the town of Suez, where Azim's section was stationed. The paratroopers were to be reinforced several hours later by an army travelling overland from Israel. But they had a specific pact with the Europeans to achieve precise objectives in Egypt, so they avoided combat and simply took up the appropriate tactical positions.

The word ran through the Egyptian army like a flame on oiled twine. The Sinai had been invaded.

Azim quickly learned that the Israelis had gone mad and were attacking not the Egyptians but the sands. Truly unwelcome news. If there were two things he held by as a soldier, one was his conviction that the Israelis were cold and calculating and certainly not mad, and the other was his terror of fighting their war machines. If they appeared weak it was a ruse. If they seemed to have lost their senses it was a trick. He had fought them in 1948 and never wanted to fight them again. Israel was a ruthless cancer in the Middle East and he wished it would go away so that his nerves might be soothed. God protect him now.

'Azim, you are trained as an engineer, no?'

Azim stared at a crack in the plaster on the wall, following it with his eyes from the ceiling and down a sometimes jagged, sometimes squiggling path to the floor.

'Are you not, Azim?'

He looked up.

'Yes, sergeant, I am an engineer.'

'Azim, I have volunteered you for a special mission.'

Of course.

'Our section will cross the Canal in two hours to meet the aggressors, but you will stay behind. You will wait for instructions from Lieutenant Hamid.'

Who?

'He will identify himself to you as soon as he arrives tonight.'
Lieutenant sounded ominous. Tonight. Trust the Israelis to attack at night.

He stayed put in his seat until the last of his section had left the compound, shifting in it only to relieve the tingling and numbness that kept building up in his legs. He missed lunch that day because he had wanted to stroll in the streets, and by dinnertime he was too anxious about the invasion to eat, and now his pangs of hunger were stifled by a complete disinterest in food.

At such times of anxiety he settled into an outwardly deceiving listlessness. He appeared utterly bored, a look of monotonous calm about him, and in a way he *was* calm, but not in a healthy way. In a knotted and self-destructive way. Nobody was there to observe his disposition tonight in any case. He shared his inner feeling of rot with some flies and the crack in the plaster and a weak lightbulb overhead.

At nine he finally got up to relieve himself, and discovered while urinating that what he really wanted was a cigarette. He trudged outside the building and stared at the stars, and thought briefly of his wife and children. A dog barked and a diesel motor ground itself into the night air. He looked to see the guard opening the gate for an old, dark red Mercedes. Perhaps the arrival had cigarettes.

The car was waved through and it rolled up to the building in a civilised coast as the driver cut the engine and the lights. Its sole occupant, a slight man in civilian clothes, stepped out and walked over to face him, without expression. Not with interest, not with disinterest.

'You are Azim Husseini?'

'Do you have cigarettes?'

'You are Azim Husseini? I am Lieutenant Hamid.'

Azim gave a barely discernable nod, feeling no compulsion to respond with 'sir' to this man who wore no uniform and drove an old Mercedes. But he would have felt disrespectful towards anyone that evening.

The man did not reach down to offer from the pack of cigarettes Azim could see in his shirt pocket. He looked at Azim with a subtle tinge of meanness in his unexcited gaze, a mixture of coldness and directness and inscrutability.

'You know explosives?'

'More or less.'

'You love Egypt?'

'From deep within my breast.'

'You will join our camp further down the Canal. You may help us to destroy a beautiful piece of Egypt. It has been commanded. The President himself...' He trailed off, and the dog barked again, further away this time.

'Perhaps it will not be necessary,' he resumed. 'We shall wait at the camp and see. Now we drive there in my car. In ten minutes.'

*

Meanwhile Walid and Khalid and the rest of Azim's section were plunging down the desert road to meet the battle of their lives. They expected to fight, but had no premonition of the intensity of the encounter which hung over their future. Nor did they expect to wait as long as a day before engaging the first enemy foot soldiers.

That night they were tormented from the black skies as they forged their way off the road, some to the right, some to the left, up rocky hills to stake their footholds among the hard caves and stone emplacements of Mitla.

Metal birds of war rained down fire upon their approach to the ambush site, but they pushed through, interlocking their fates with ridges of mineral and sand, stepping over little dry shrubs. Will I get a better shot from behind this outcropping? Am I more likely to survive by waiting inside this cave where I'm invisible? Or will it become my trap? They dispersed in small groups along the two main ridges overlooking the desert road from both sides, and became carnivorous creatures, waiting patiently to pounce. Hawks' eyes, sharpened with anticipation; claws like tigers, waiting patiently to tear into the flesh of another species; hearts of predators. Jewish fighters the prey.

*

Earlier that day, Clare sat in the classroom and stared at Prudence's braids. Thoughts of the coins had again slipped out of her mind over the weekend, and only now, at school, was she reminded of the dilemma she had wrought for herself the previous Friday by speaking up about her money (*her* money!).

As the teacher nattered on about the meaning of the word 'tradition'; as the Prime Minister paced distraughtly to and fro in his rooms and Israeli radio conveyed the curfew message to those whose receivers were tuned, and as Azim was strolling the avenues of the town of Suez on his lunch hour; as these things took place, Clare decided once and for all that the coins would have to be returned to a Hammersmith bus. Using them for friendship's sake was well and good, but not when they rightly belonged to someone else, such as the owner of her tall, turny, Routemaster double-decker.

The family's driver had been discharged from hospital but was recuperating at his home and still most unfit for work. Clare overheard her father saying that actually, they had sent him home to die, but when she asked Nan about it, she was told she needed her ears washed out with a soapy sponge.

Nan took up collecting Clare from school in a taxi when father, who previously thought that bus rides might be informative for Clare, had lately changed his mind about his little girl being dragged about on 'the crowded wagons of the great unwashed.' Father had the same mood then as he had the time he told Clare with a tight smile that he was 'a very rich man indeed.'

Unwashed.

Why had he used that word? How could he possibly have known about the dirty boy?

After passing many hours fraught with anxious deliberation, Clare finally reasoned that her father's choice of word must have been coincidental. But it had not been easy for that rational conclusion to overcome her guilty suspicion that he knew everything and was just waiting for her to confess to whoring after evil.

Oh, it was all just becoming too much. Tonight she would sneak out of the house and take the coins with her up to the high street and hand them over to a policeman. If she couldn't find a policeman, she would get on a bus and leave the coins with a conductor and hop off before he could ask any questions. She had never gone out alone before, but she knew it would not be a hard thing to pull off.

When she arrived home that afternoon, she retrieved the coins from their secret place and tucked them once again into the waistband of her skirt, spaced apart from each other just as she had placed them before, ready this time to be smuggled out into the streets.

*

'Suppose we encounter hostility. It is not worth the risk. Think of the alternatives. On the one hand, Captain, we enter Canal to keep up to schedule, and find ourselves caught in crossfire, maybe boarded, maybe looted. Maybe we are killed, Captain. Maybe we are hit from the air by a stray bomb. On the other hand, we divert and take one week longer to arrive. The economic loss is significant, but nothing considering the great risk we would run otherwise. Management will not hold it against you.'

'Management will hold it against me.'

'Captain, you could make convincing argument about acting in Company's interests. Steering clear of danger will show investors that we are aware of safety.'

He had meant to say 'shippers', not 'investors', but it was too late.

'The Company is a family enterprise and not interested in attracting outside investors! You know this! I think you are afraid, Chief Officer. And even if it were a traded company, speed, efficiency and willingness to take minor risks to gain time are more attractive in a shipping line. Our cargo must find its way into English teapots by teatime. That is what matters above all. You do not matter. I do not matter. The last transmission from the Canal authorities has been to assure us that all traffic is proceeding as normal, so please, tell me, what good excuse will we have for avoiding Suez?'

'The excuse is that they have never felt it necessary to make us any assurances in the past.'

'We will carry on into the Gulf of Suez. If you wish me to record your objections in the log I will do so.'

'That will not be necessary, sir.'

The Captain looked at the Chief Officer, trying to read his face for signs of serious disaffection. The two knew each other very well, but still the Captain could not make out whether he ought to be concerned about possible insubordination as they neared the war zone, or whether his first mate was simply carrying out his duty to voice reasonable concerns. Nor did he have any more desire to sail into an air assault than the Chief Officer. The difference was that he knew beyond any doubt what the Company would insist on, what danger they would want their ship to be put through and when to forbear from proceeding, whereas the Chief Officer had always projected a little too much of his own humanity onto the fat directors at the shipping line's headquarters. To the Captain they were money men who pulled strings. To the Chief Officer, who happened to be a devout Catholic, they were better.

Naveen overheard their conversation.

They must have assumed the rushing water at the sink where he stood, washing the day's stack of tea and coffee cups used by the various bridge officers, drowned out what they were saying. But what they said had not bothered him. It tickled of adventure. Adventure was welcome to come and corrupt what had now become to Naveen a very routine existence at sea. He dreamed of catastrophe, caring nothing for the welfare of the ship itself, though in his imaginings no harm ever came to the officers or crew. The notion of disaster was pregnant with chances of special new (typically heroic) roles for him far outside the everyday constraints of his station on the ship. He did not yet have a wife or children depending on him, nor a cemented reputation that could not be repaired later on should things go foul, nor had he sealed off as many avenues of life as had the senior officers who were fully committed to their careers. Not that he hoped to lose anything, only that he was yet of the age and temperament where risk and adventure, and all the great rewards that pair of ideas offers to the intrepid, stirred far more excitement in him than fear.

The Second Officer arrived in the wheel room ten minutes before he was due. He knew the Chief Officer liked to end his shift early so that he had a chance to wash before catching the tail end of dinner, and he was pleased to facilitate that. He and the

Chief Officer showed each other many secret favours, making both their sea lives all the more endurable. But they had an understanding that when the Captain happened to be on the bridge, for he came and went as he pleased, the Chief Officer would not leave early. Instead, all three senior officers would person the command centre.

Naveen watched now as the three stood, side by side, to face the waters. They saw a dull grey-blue horizon at eye level, and quietly shared the mesmerising feel of forward motion over the waves, the effect of low-grade petroleum propulsion seen but not felt, the ship's underbelly faithfully treading the soft surface of the sea.

The Second Officer stood stooped with collapsed shoulders, a man of stability and security who was easily shaken by the disruption of any part of his routine, his comfort. His years of service allowed him his own command, yet he chose to remain on board this ship, near but not at the top.

Next to him the Chief Officer, steady and tall and not a bit expanded at the midriff. A kind man. On the outside of the door to his cabin hung a large brass crucifix. It was against regulations but he was too well liked for anyone to take notice. Inside, he kept one cupboard stuffed with yellowed, creased paperbacks, another laden with sickly sweet spirits, and on the small shelf above his desk he had a leather-bound copy of the King James Bible. Naveen felt sure he read it often. Once they had shared the bridge at dawn and the Chief Officer spoke to him.

'Behold, Cadet. The night is far spent, the day is at hand; let us therefore cast off the works of darkness, and let us put on the armour of light. It is from the Bible.' Naveen was a Brahmin.

Now to the Chief Officer's right stood the aging Captain, who wore a face of experience. The creases by his eyes were not cynical, only weary. And trustworthy. His frank way of speaking inspired confidence. He looked as though he had witnessed much, and knew the hearts of all his sailors. One tended to feel confiding towards him, expecting he had at various points in his long past already endured and successfully weathered all the same personal crises any one of his sailors might be experiencing. It was the way Naveen felt a captain should be, and he no longer even minded when the Captain occasionally indulged in patronising lectures on the grand scheme of history and politics and trade. Though at first Naveen had been uncomfortable and not known how to react to such excurses, he now knew he was expected simply to express a word or two of acknowledgment and appreciation at the Captain's insights. '*Most* fascinating, sir.' Or, 'I was verily unaware of that, sir. How interesting.'

Presently, the Captain and Chief Officer left the bridge together. Only Naveen and the Second Officer remained, and Naveen's heart sank as usual. But the Second Officer let him be for a good hour while Naveen studied the charts, plotting the course for his first navigation through the Suez waterway.

Then out of the blue the Second Officer asked him, 'what do *you* think?'

'Sir?'

'Do you think we should enter Suez, or do you think it is too dangerous?'

He had been trapped. He knew that any answer would be unacceptable. If he chanced to choose the view favoured by the Second Officer, he would be told he was unqualified to utter such opinions and should have declined to reply with any firm view. If he expressed an opinion that happened to differ from that of the Second Officer, he would be told in a smug tone that he was wrong, and subjected to a point-by-point explanation of why. If he hedged, he would be accused of ignorance or indecision.

'I do not think my uneducated opinion could be of much value to a man such as yourself, sir, as you have far greater experience in these matters.'

And so he disarmed the Second Officer. And so the Second Officer continued to hate him.

*

They were joined on board that night by the Canal Company pilot and crew who were to take them into the Suez.

Melbury Road

ON THE outside it was a large and dignified reddish house with careful brickwork patterns and limestone slabs framing tall windows. The chimney was broad and gave vent to several clay pipes. Little outcroppings of rooms and windows protruded smartly from various odd parts of the roof. Standing guard on the ground was a simple wrought iron fence, protecting a modest rose garden and barring entry without obscuring the property's general display of calmly beneficent grandeur.

Tonight the house was blanketed in mist and its bricks moist with drizzle.

On the inside servants were bustling and candles burning and it was time for dinner. Clare was called downstairs to the dining room, where mother was already at the table, looking beautiful and distant. Mother preferred to wear white and light colours in the house, even in the evenings, and usually a pearl necklace for dinner. She looked to Clare like an angel.

Clare walked over to her for their customary exchange of kisses.

Father had not yet arrived, but he had telephoned to say they could expect him by half past seven. It was now nearly eight and they were just readying to begin without him when they heard the garage gate slam shut and the front door open and the thick leather soles of his black shoes resounding along the front hall carpet.

'So sorry you had to wait, my dear ladies.'

He patted Clare on the head before taking his seat, and she smelled sandalwood musk and automobile leather.

Mother said nothing, and the servants began to serve.

'Have you had a nice day, darling?' he asked Clare's mother.

'The weather was hideous, so Madame Bourdeille cancelled her garden party. I was so hoping to meet the new Bulgarian ambassador's wife. We could have talked politics. I think ladies ought to talk politics more, don't you, dear? Talking literature used to be alright, but Madame Bourdeille's guests are always such a mix of foreigners and none of them appreciates our classics.'

Her favourite activity in the society of ladies was gossip, but she preferred her husband to consider her intellectually interesting. She had not recognised his repeated hints that he objected to intellectual women.

'I imagine so, dear.'

'We could have discussed the situation in Hungary. Bulgaria is near Hungary, isn't it?'

Clare knew where Bulgaria was on the map, but also knew that her mother preferred her to remain silent until spoken to.

'You don't think it would have been insensitive to raise the issue of Hungary with her, do you? I mean, one can't be sure of her views.'

'No doubt they match her husband's views to the letter. The potatoes are just right this evening, aren't they, darling?'

'Mm. Do you think the Russians will let Hungary get away with what they've done? They *do* seem so courageous and one would just die to see them trampled on. Do you think there might be a war?'

'I shouldn't think so.'

'I wonder how Eisenhower will react. Or do you think Dulles is the man we ought to be watching?'

'Don't know. I think we ought to take a note of these potatoes.' He called the butler. 'Dewey, do make sure the cook keeps using this type of potato. It's quite superior.'

'So I sat at home and read the newspapers instead, darling. Was your meeting with the new warehouse manager a success?'

'Quite. He's a bloody fool. He rejected my suggestion of a western extension to his building out of hand.'

'Oh, darling...'

'One large storeroom is quite enough, he said. He positively trembled at the prospect of taking on a debt to extend the building. He's a short-sighted bloody fool. He can't see that the terminal at Felixstowe will soon be the end of all the London warehouses if they don't start looking to the future. And I told him as much. They'll need to begin distinguishing themselves somehow. A separate storeroom just for whole leaf grade, for instance. If I wanted Golden Flowery Orange Pekoe I should just waltz in and inspect it in the Whole Leaf Room. If I could do that it would keep me going to the riverside. As things stand I might begin making other arrangements. Maybe even send my own shipments elsewhere.'

'He sounds so dreadfully unimaginative. Not a man of vision like you, darling.'

Father was slicing into his steak, and didn't reply. Clare wouldn't eat steak. It was so thick and meaty and it smelled of blood. They had tried to force her but she had simply left it untouched on her plate every time it was served for dinner for three weeks, and mother finally capitulated and had her fed chicken instead. Even fowl Clare would only eat if the gravy contained treacle and lime juice. And she would never eat fish. Nor cabbage unless it had butter and salt, nor carrots unless they were ungarnished. But she happily ate every variety of pudding.

She had, without thinking, seated herself with one leg folded beneath her on the chair. Mother would have a fit if she noticed this, so Clare had been extremely still and tried not to make it evident that she was sitting slightly taller than normal and lopsided. But it was beginning to hurt, and she would have to shift ever so gently.

She tried to move her leg by grabbing hold of her ankle and pulling it with one hand, but the weight of her body was too heavy and the leg wouldn't budge. She yanked it harder, and suddenly it gained a life of its own and extracted itself in a great jerky motion. As this occurred, some of the coins from her waistband dislodged and clattered onto the hardwood floor. Mother and father looked coldly at her as one coin rolled on its edge in a seemingly endless circular journey beneath the table. It stopped finally when it collided with her father's shoe. She was mortified and found herself unable to look up to meet either of her parents' stares.

Her father bent down and picked up the sixpence which rested at his feet. He held the coin up in front of his eye and rolled it between his fingers and examined it, tilting it back and forth by the light of the candle, then changing position to view it in the light of the electric bulbs overhead.

'Well, I don't know what to make of this, Clare,' he said. 'I confess to being slightly surprised to see you carrying money. I can't imagine where you got it. I thought everything you needed was provided for you at home and at school.'

'Go on, Clare, don't sit there like a lump of rotting flesh. Pick up what you dropped.' Mother was cross.

'And once you've done that, I should like to learn about the source of your income.' Father pocketed the coin as Clare gathered up the others that fell. Some had remained in her waistband.

It was an ominous sign that they were not yelling at her. Being told off loudly and soundly was perfectly bearable. But when father exhibited calculated thoughtfulness, and mother's rude words were spoken with quiet control, Clare's predicament was grave.

And it was far worse for her than they could know, because she bore the burden of a secret which took her to a crossroads of unacceptable choices. Setting off down the way of complete truth would lead to her punishment, to untold repercussions for Nan for dozing with Clare in her care (she had great loyalty to Nan), and to an eschewal of what she considered to be her oath of secrecy to the boy thief. Selecting the path of falsehood opened up an infinity of new possible roads, each with its own special pitfalls, but all sharing as well a common hazard: the evil of deceiving her parents. Moreover she had the bus owner to consider. She mustn't take a course that would bar her from returning the coins which remained in her possession, for then she would continue to be the holder of thieved property. At least she already resolved not to use them for her group's ribbons. One less weight to upset the balance of moral clarity.

Her thoughts were nonetheless askew as the pressure of the moment bore upon her, her crackling sparks of reason prevented from coalescing into a quick bolt of rational decision. Possessing a strong sense of morality on account of Nan's puritanical guidance (reinforced with lessons in virtuous behaviour from her teachers) made the moment all the more trying. It set the stakes high. A decision based solely on material self-protection or physical self-preservation (avoiding a spanking) would have been straightforward. But the sanity of Clare's soul was at stake as well. The morality served by any one option promised to compromise the normative principles contained in the other options, threatened to chip away irreparably from her granite slab of metaphysical integrity. The granite of Clare.

The words issued from her mouth on their own. 'I found them on the doorstep.'

One lie uttered, the rest tumbled out.

'Today when Nan brought me home I saw them gleaming there, on the ground, and as Nan was pulling the bell I got down and picked them up. I don't think Nan noticed. She was busy with the doorbell. I thought they might belong to the gardener and I was going to ask Nan but I had to come in and wash my hands before anything else and then she went to sleep. I forgot about them and set them down on the chair. When I shifted position they just fell. I'm sorry for the rude interruption to our dinner.'

Clare's mother laboured hard to conceal a wave of tenderness and pity. But her father was shrewd with liars. He knew them better. Sometimes it suited him to let them lie, and lie and lie until one day he could turn around at just the most devastating moment and with a carefully placed remark cause their card houses to come tumbling down on their heads. He forgot no lies. They were simply too valuable. Toward his small daughter of course he harboured no such malevolent or vindictive designs, but his manipulative streak ran deep. Stringing along a liar came naturally.

'Oh, yes, Clare, those were mine. I knew I had some coins in my pocket this morning. When I arrived at work they were gone. They must have fallen out whilst I was hurrying out the gate.'

The trap would only work if she replied impulsively, and she did.

'No, they weren't yours, father.'

'I beg your pardon?'

She hesitated and unconsciously rubbed her finger along her lower lip. Liar identification result: positive. It would take her a few moments to follow up with an explanation as to how she could be so sure they were not his. *If* she possessed full calm. Otherwise her reaction might be one of several. She could buy time by pretending not to have heard (of which the sub-possibilities were to change the topic abruptly, carry on in silence, or ask him to repeat his last phrase). She could pretend not to understand, and ask him what he meant. She could laugh or smile, instinctive methods of disarmament. She could play the victim, sending feminine body language of helplessness and need, tools available even to many young girls, in an attempt to melt him down and distract his course of pursuit. Or look over to her mother for assistance (a desperate measure). She could seek physical escape, and excuse herself to the toilet.

Or, if she were fully self-possessed, she would have a clever and effortless explanation, a quick way, without sounding contrived or grasping, to qualify her negation of his assertion of ownership over the coins. But rubbing the lip as a first reaction signalled that this would be unlikely.

'I didn't think you carried coins. I thought you were rich enough not to need small change.' Something in between.

'Sometimes I might carry coins. Being rich doesn't mean you don't occasionally need to buy the little things bought by everyone else. What if I wanted to buy a different newspaper on the way to work, Clare?'

She shrugged, wrigglingly uncomfortable under the directness of her father's address.

'But this morning I had no coins, as you were right to suppose. I only wanted to show you how possible it is to catch someone out. And also challenge your little explanation, which went on long enough to become suspect in my ears. You sound quite sure of yourself but I don't think you've shared the whole truth with us about how you... about how you came by your little fortune. Until I hear the truth I think you ought to be punished in some way.'

'She shall not have pudding until she confesses. And dinner will be served to her without gravy or dressing.'

Mother got up and removed Clare's plate of food from before her eyes.

'Bring Clare a serving of dry chicken without gravy. And she'll have no pudding tonight.'

The butler acknowledged these instructions solemnly as Clare stifled tears.

The rest of dinner was consumed in silence, except for when father returned to Clare the coin he had pocketed, saying one punishment ought to be sufficient, and that he knew *he* had no good claim to the coin. Then off to bed.

*

She lay staring at the ceiling, tears rolling off her face, her cheeks drying, her mind calming, then more tears.

She heard a distant muffled bell strike midnight, which meant she had rested awake for three hours.

Finally her agitation settled and her ears filled with a babble of voices and unstructured sound, perhaps a droning melody in the background of her skull, and she descended into the first level of sleep, falling and drifting and falling all light and floating and birds walking, their beaks large and people skating on a frozen pond and ringing, repeated ringing, bring bring... brring brring... She was dragged to the surface by the net of wakefulness. She was awake again.

Her little desk clock read five past midnight.

She heard her father's voice. No distinct words, just the blurred outline of the sound vibrations stamped with his trademark, the familiar pitch of his voicebox. Unusual. Normally he slept at ten.

She rolled back the heavy covers and stepped onto the blue oval carpet by her bed. And tiptoed out the door, swinging it forcefully and stopping it abruptly, a trick she had learned to avoid squeaking the hinges.

She followed his spurts of voice down the corridor, down a flight of stairs, round a corner into another corridor, creeping drifting sailing like a ghost, trailing her feet rather than stepping them down, trying not to creak the floorboards. She stopped by the entrance to father's study.

Light shone from under the closed door and she was careful not to touch it. No reason. Ghosts don't like light? Maybe so as not to refract herself back under the door. Avoid tearing cosmic light fabric. A rip might be sensed subliminally, her father might be signalled to open the door 'for no reason'. She would be standing there barefoot in her light pink nightdress.

Father's words were discernable now. A telephone conversation. A voice of stifled urgency.

'I've got nine hundred crates on the *Majesty*. Nine hundred... No! They've already been resold... Yes, the *Majesty*. No. It's a Calcutta Maritime ship. I need to know what the hell is going on with my tea... *That*'s right. I shipped with them because they said they would sail in *any* weather. Through hurricanes, sandstorms, hails of ice and hails of bullets. If Israel have invaded they'll just have to suck it up and sail on through. Nobody said anything about fighting at the Canal... Nobody *said* that! Yes. So perhaps you'll just go on now and have a word with our friends in... Don't tell *me* who needs what. I know what I need and I know what I've been promised. Tell our friends in Calcutta they're treading a fine line with me. Find out if other shipping companies have instructed theirs to divert. Find out now and ring me back as soon as you know.'

The door to father's study was the last one to the right in a terminating corridor, at the end of which was a great window. There was a large, bench-like ledge at the base of the window, an extended sill, and Clare, as she was listening to father being cross on the phone, hoisted herself up to sit on it. This left a gap of about one foot between her toes and the floor.

Fatigue had left her. She was alert with adventure, and intrigued by her father's late-night conversation. Sitting with her back to the window, she faced the full length of the corridor, her father's door immediately on her left. Studying the vertical wooden surfaces to either side of her in the window cove, she noticed an unnaturally straight grain running along the middle of the panelling on her left. There was no similar line on the wood to her right.

Inspecting more closely, she observed that the left side protruded slightly, extending beyond the limit of the window cove into the corridor, so that it was not quite flush with the wall. Again, there was no such irregularity to her right. The difference between the two sides was so minute, however, that one never would have noticed standing in the corridor, or even leaning onto the sill to look out the window.

Feeling this protruding lip of the left-hand panelling with her hand, she absent-mindedly applied a bit of pressure.

Pulling at it gently, she was astonished to find the whole panel swinging towards her, the straight grain revealing itself to be the axis on which half of the panelling turned. This cupboard-like door which she now held ajar was carefully hinged on the inside so that no metalwork was visible from the corridor or the window. Light poured into a space which had been dark for over a century, and a narrow descending staircase was revealed. Remarkable.

The phone rang again. Clare felt there was no option but to explore. She was a little frightened but it was too mysterious and enticing to resist. She knew where the servants kept an electric torch, and she glided back along the corridor and down another flight of stairs and then another, until she was in the kitchen. Beside the oven there was a shelf with matches and candles and a seldom-used, gleaming, steel torch. She appropriated it and flew back upstairs to the window cove, slid back up onto the ledge and reopened the secret door, stepped inside, flicked on the torch, and counted seven wooden steps.

Standing on the top step she felt a brick wall to her left (the exoskeleton of the house), and saw the rough unfinished side of the wall separating the staircase from her father's study to her right. There was a handle on the inside of the secret door, allowing her to pull it fully shut behind her. She wondered fleetingly if places like Narnia were true. Nan had read her a delightful book last Christmas about some children who went to Narnia through a secret wardrobe.

Here it was a secret staircase, and she descended to the bottom, the seventh step. The brick wall on her left continued to the end, and there was no way forward, but shining the torch revealed an open space to her right, an entranceway to a low-ceilinged chamber. It had more headroom than a crawlspace but far less than an ordinary room. An adult of average dimensions would have been forced if inside it to remain bent over, but it happened to fit Clare's height perfectly, as if the room, situated directly below her father's study, had been designed with her in mind.

She was startled to hear the floorboards creak over her head until she realised it was her father pacing in his socks. She was not in Narnia.

Under her own feet was a frayed reddish carpet with a faded oriental pattern, and the room appeared as though it had once been put to some human use.

She rested the torch on top of a small chest of drawers and looked about.

There was a large, comfortable-looking upholstered chair in one corner, and next to it a tea table with a glass candlestick, a half-used candle in it. Hardened wax flowed down its side and formed a solid white puddle on the tabletop. The edges of the carpet were littered with dead moths. Otherwise the place seemed empty. She opened the drawers and found them bare, then settled into the soft chair and remained there a long time. Normally she would have been quite frightened sitting all alone in a dim abandoned room, but her father's presence right above kept her at ease until fatigue again overtook her, and soon she slept. Her father's faded words drifted down to cover her.

By four in the morning her father had gained an assurance that his shipment would proceed through the Suez. He was wealthy enough to do his business as and when he pleased. He had agreed to a renegotiation of terms with his insurance agent, deferring to the latter's uneasiness about the proximity of the Sinai skirmishing to the shipping route. This was to prove an exceptional bargain on his part. The very next day the major insurance companies all doubled their rates for ships sailing via Suez, whereas his agent had bound himself to an increase of only sixty percent.

His affairs settled for the night, he switched off his lamp and left the study for his bed. Tired, he carelessly allowed the door to slam shut behind him, waking Clare with a start.

She was cold and felt unnatural and scooped up the torch for a quick exit.

At the top of the secret staircase she tapped the door open just a slit. She needed to peep into the corridor to ensure the coast was clear. It was.

She replaced the torch in the kitchen, then returned to her proper bed, her heart and nerves alert but her head leaden.

Bees buzzed in her brain the moment her head touched the pillow. Bees trapped in thick sleepy cobwebs. No escape. No trouble sleeping.

Profound grogginess when Nan shook her awake at daybreak.

War Room

ROPER'S NIGHT had also been lousy. Tortured, in fact. He slept at one in the morning, having toiled in his apartment all evening on the beer exporters' brief for Selling. The case was indeed hopeless, and over the course of the evening Roper developed the opinion that they ought to drop the client rather than make embarrassing arrangements for an impossible defence. What barrister would take it on, anyway?

He had hauled stacks of paper back with him from the office, to work in relative comfort at his dining table. His sheets spread out all over the place, his mind spread out all over the place, he had been unable to resist a trip downstairs to buy a case of beer. This was after scoffing down an appallingly greasy serving of halibut and chips with no accompanying beverage, then spending an hour reading about the beer trade.

Sipping a cold Belgian lager, he lifted the telephone handset. 'Mr Selling, Roper here. Sorry to disturb you at home.'

'Roper?' He sounded bleary, though it was only eight o'clock. 'Well, what is it? I'll have you know I'm entertaining a visitor.'

Roper imagined he must be entertaining only in the dubious sense of ploughing through a tedious monologue on the glories of his past, the profit figures of the previous year, the absolute uselessness of every last underling at the firm, the excitement of the proposed yellow carpeting, the hidden advantages of retiring to the Basque coast as opposed to the Riviera. He probably poured mediocre port out of an expensive looking decanter, a master of stylistic deception, of the subtle trickery of false detail. Roper already suspected the call was pointless.

'Mr Selling, I do apologise. I'll be brief. I've read all the material on the bungled warranty...' (only a minor stretch of the truth) '...and it is abundantly apparent to me that not only is the case hopeless, it will damage the firm for us to see the client through with this folly. Really, Mr Selling, the whole thing is a contractual abomination, and my sincere opinion is that we're in a position to present the client with a stark choice. Drop the case or lose our representation. We can't afford to hold onto them through such a shambolic exercise. We'll only lose export business if the case makes the newspapers. And we shall have to dredge the City sewers to find a barrister who'll go ahead with it. It's simply...'

'You said *brief*, Roper. I've not got all night. You *will* prepare the instructions. Use a pseudonym if you're ashamed. Call in sick the day of trial. The *week* of trial. We'll find a student to stand in for you when the phones start ringing. *I'll* find the barrister. Lord knows I've got favours to call in. Just write the bloody instructions! And don't ring me again tonight!'

Either it was a deliberate show to impress his guest, or the old man was finally, truly, losing his grip.

So he laboured until midnight, at which hour he felt ready to stuff a handwritten sheaf of instructions into his briefcase for Sarah to decipher and type up in the morning.

He slept in his underwear, not bothering to find his way under the covers, and awoke at half past one to wipe a slime of drool off his cheek. His body was hot and restless, couldn't settle comfortably in one position. Drifted off again. Deeper this time. Two unknown women fought over his groin. One slapped the other on the face and she died and he saw her soul fly away and her corpse fell on his head, making it an effort for him to breathe. The dead woman's hard nipples were poking into his eyes. The other one was laughing coarsely as she mounted him, pinning him to the wet muddy ground with her legs. Her tongue was hanging out of her mouth and it was so long it reached her navel. She licked her breasts and belly with it and little thorns poked out of its tip and she pierced her own skin with one of them and thudded her pelvis into him and into him and into him and into him and her eyes caught fire and she screeched like a wild beast and death spasms pulsed through him and he awoke.

He was suffocating under a pillow, his fingertips in his eyes, his underwear around his ankles, a mess spread across his belly and pubis.

Bloody hell.

He got up and fumbled for the light switch and missed it.

Took a shower in the dark, hot water streaming through the

hairs on his abdomen, cleansing away the sordid Lilith traces and the dank sweat of a demonic coupling.

His lower back ached, and night doom rose all around him with the hot steam.

He put on soft pyjamas, crawled under his blankets and slept til seven. Then breakfasted heavily at the greasy restaurant downstairs, the one with the androgynous toothless proprietor who kept the curtains half drawn, where the red and white checked tablecloths were never changed. The food was always delicious. Two sausages and baked beans. Fried bread. One boiled tomato. Toast with butter the ultimate satisfaction. Filling up some great gap in his belly.

Normally if there were instructions to submit that day he would glance them over on the underground journey. But he couldn't care less about these ones. Let Sarah point out his errors. He would fix them over lunch, give her back the revisions to type up, then throw them at Selling. So instead he bought a newspaper from a street vendor.

But the train was crowded and it would have been too awkward to read it properly. He satisfied himself with the front page offerings. 'Fighting in Sinai'. Subheadline: 'Tension High as Israel and Egypt Each Cite Other as Aggressor'. Details sparse. There had been a feint towards Jordan by the Israeli generals, who made a last-minute about-face and penetrated Egypt. Border raids by *fedayeen* the excuse. It was unclear what the official British reaction was. Perhaps they had not decided one yet (in fact it had been worked out long before the hostilities were staged). Surely it would be a matter of some delicacy given Britain's dealings in the region. The government had been wringing its hands over the Suez nationalisation, but had also recently cooperated with Egypt over the Sudan. And hadn't there been a pledge to defend Jordan against any attack? Could Britain go to war against Israel? But the column said Jordan had been left out of it for the moment. He was foggier on foreign affairs than he liked to admit. Moorgate Station. Work.

Penny was on the telephone at reception so he blew her a kiss to make her blush, and walked straight through to his office.

'Sarah, where's Selling? Actually, never mind. Could you do these up for me, please?' He handed her the manuscripted instructions.

'Morning, Jim. Selling's convened in the Baxter Room. All lawyers. He's been calling it the 'war room'. Better make yourself known in there.'

'Good God. Alright... Well, see if you can have those instructions done up by lunch. Look for errors, Sarah.'

He walked over and turned the Baxter Room doorknob. The door was locked. He could hear people talking inside. He knocked. Rounthwaite opened the door and he was looking strained. The windows were closed and Roper was assaulted with tobacco smoke and body odour.

'We've been here since half seven,' Rounthwaite whispered to him.

'Roper, you could have turned up a bit earlier.'

'It's only five past nine, Mr Selling.'

'Do you not read the newspapers when you get up, Roper? Or have you spent your morning blissfully unaware of the hostilities underway at the gateway to the Suez Canal?'

'I read about the fighting.'

'That's a start. Tell us, Roper, who is fighting whom?'

'Israel and Egypt, said the paper.'

'One point. Now, double your gains. Where are they fighting?'

'The Sinai.'

'*Very. Good.* Perhaps you could now tell us, Roper, what,' pause 'is at the western end,' pause ' of the Sinai Peninsula.'

Roper knew that if he didn't play along like a child, things would go worse for him.

'You said it yourself; the Suez Canal.'

'So you *do* pay attention. Goo-oo-ood.'

Selling bared his teeth in a morbid, joyless smile.

Rounthwaite was absentmindedly pulling on his nose hairs with the tips of his fingers, engrossed in this delightful exchange. Johnson was reading something while incessantly picking at the very top of his scalp, Pinsky was hovering at the window with his back to everyone and Bigby was staring at Roper with pursed lips and a stupid look about him. But his wobbly premature jowls always gave him a foolish, hen-like appearance.

A handful of lawyers were huddled around one of the other senior partners at the edge of the room, talking excitedly. Who, wondered Roper, would run the shop now that everyone was being herded into this zoo cage?

The doorknob jiggled and there was a knock, and Rounthwaite got up to usher in the next hapless soul, but hesitated at the door and looked at Selling. Selling waved his permission and Rounthwaite opened it.

'We've been here since half seven,' Roper heard him whisper to the new arrival.

'Ah, Martins!'

Wispy blond Martin Vandermeulen was the only person in the firm not a senior partner whom Selling referred to by something other than last name. He couldn't be bothered to learn 'Vandermeulen', so by way of concession he pluralised 'Martin' to give it more formality. If it infuriated Vandermeulen he hid it well.

'Roper was just giving us a lesson in geography, politics and business. Pull up a chair. Carry on, Roper. What is the significance of the Suez Canal?'

'Shipping route. Eliminates need to go round the Cape.'

Selling had made him into a robot spitting out data.

'Shipping route.' Selling tapped the table with his forefinger for dramatic effect. 'England's most vital link to Asian commodity markets. Most *vital* link. And *what*, Roper, do we deal in at this firm? What's our number one source of business? Shipping! Shipping, shipping, shipping! And so you read in the newspaper that there's fighting going on at the gateway to England's most vital shipping channel, and the possibility doesn't enter your brain, your sterling mind, your *Oxford* mind, that perhaps the obvious threat posed to the continuity of unfettered navigation through the Canal might have some bearing on the business of, oh, just a few of our clients? Doesn't set off some gear in your head to tell you you'd better drop everything and rush into work chop chop?'

'Nothing's happened to the Canal, I don't think, Mr Selling.'

'I've lectured you before on how our reputation; nay, our *prestige*; on how our prestige depends on all of us remaining two steps ahead of market developments. Well, this is a bloody market development, wouldn't you say, Roper?'

'Then we're wasting precious time, aren't we, Mr Selling?'

'Indeed we are, Roper. In-deeeeed we are.'

He swivelled to face the room head on, and stood up.

'Right! We shall have teams! Carruthers will be managing the clients. He will have Patterson, Arujo, and Barclay. You'll field all wires and phone calls and one of you will be in constant liaison throughout the day with the other groups to keep the information flowing. Set up a link with reception as well. The public face and so on.

'Brown will be running ship-to-shore communications. That is, hounding the shipping lines to keep up with their latest news and turns of fortune. We must know if any of them are instructing to divert so we can pass the knowledge on to Carruthers's team so they can call in the clients for advice. The shippers may have better information than the wire services, and this will be valuable. Collinson and Barclay, you'll assist Brown.

'Ritter-Jones will head De Quincy, Bartlett, Payne and Savage in file digging! Go through every active file and take a note of which have Suez interests. Work out exactly how each one might be adversely affected, and Ritter-Jones will decide how to proceed on a case-by-case basis. We must know the clients' problems before they do. Two steps ahead!

'Parkins will be our Lloyd's man. Simmons and Welsh will be general coordinators. The two of you will circulate continually to determine each team's needs and meet them as they arise, convey anything important between teams, and keep a general eye on the running of our war machine. Any team finding itself in need of additional help, another lawyer, another secretary, another telephone line, a book, let Simmons or Welsh know and they'll arrange it.

'And law. I shall lead the law team. Roper, Bigby, Rounthwaite and Martins will be with me in the library, learning everything there is to learn about the laws that pertain to our state of affairs. Legal questions relating to the files, to clients, anything to do with the situation, come straight to one of us. We shall reconvene at noon for an overall reassessment. Emergency session may be called sooner, however, by any team leader.

'The rest of you will carry on normal business to the best of your abilities, a skeleton crew to steer the firm as if none of this Suez nonsense is happening. If you can pull it off seamlessly, all the rest of us shall have to resign on account of superfluity once this storm has blown over.'

Roper was impressed for once. He had never before witnessed Selling's barking actually put to good use. Certain people were simply meant to take charge in extraordinary circumstances, though their natural manner was inappropriate the rest of the time. He thought of Churchill. He did feel Selling was overreacting, but at least this would make his day more interesting.

As they walked to the library, Selling turned to him.

'You know, Roper, I think we ought to forget about those instructions you were working on. I've decided it might be best for us to jettison the client. I know they're big, but after all, what good are they to us if they keep on breaking their contracts?'

Roper had no reply.

'No good at all, is what. Just a big hassle.'

The Address

THE ISRAELI Commander-in-Chief had orchestrated the Sinai manoeuvres to avoid engaging the Egyptians until air cover was provided by the British and French. The secret protocol, settled upon in that lush French suburb, envisaged an Israeli push into the Sinai in the direction of Suez on the pretext of one too many border incursions by Egyptian-sponsored *fedayeen*. Israel was to benefit by gaining passage for its commercial shipping through the Straits of Tiran, and by securing the elimination of the menacing, Soviet-supplied Egyptian air force. The Israeli attack was to be followed by an Anglo-French 'ultimatum' to both Israel and Egypt to cease hostilities or be forcibly separated by British and French armies. Egypt was (rightly) predicted to ignore the 'ultimatum', the Europeans would use the occasion to reoccupy the Suez, and everyone would be pleased save Nasser, the Egyptians and the Arab world. And the families of the boys who died in the crush of war.

The world soon turned against the revived *Entente Cordiale*, and it never quite got that far. But as the fighting began, such was the plan, though only a very few at the very top knew of it.

As the Israelis deployed in the Sinai, their diplomats were left in the dark.

The Security Council entered urgent session and the customary power alignments in that chamber were tossed into disarray. The Americans and Soviets joined hands to condemn the developments, and Britain and France cast their vetoes against them. Britain's first veto.

The Israeli Ambassador was thus compelled, in an atmosphere of exceptionally abrupt tectonic geopolitical plate movement, to operate in ignorance of the precise political underpinnings of the sandy conflagration in which his country presently played the visible spearhead. But it didn't matter.

An eloquent man of unswerving faith in the cause of his nation and the directions of his legendary masters in Jerusalem, he was

73

well capable of defending his country's actions no matter what the throes of circumstance. He assumed the floor in the General Assembly and spoke in heartfelt defence of the State of Israel with honesty, conviction and emotion, as only a deeply loyal believer could do. His words, those which lacked direct reference to the object of the week's fighting, were strong and true, and the effect was rapturous. He spoke without a script, drawing the paragraphs directly from the treasure troves of his head and his heart.

Stretching back far behind the events of this week lies the unique and sombre story of a small people subjected throughout all the years of its national existence to a furious, implacable, comprehensive campaign of hatred and siege for which there is no parallel nor precedent in the modern history of nations. Not for one single moment throughout the entire period of its modern national existence has Israel enjoyed the minimal physical security which the United Nations Charter confers on all member States, and which all other member States have been able to command.

Our territory has been subjected to constant encroachment. The frontier has not been for Israel a barrier against the sudden leaping forward of violence by day and by night. The toll of dead and wounded has been augmented by countless pipelines blown up, by water supplies demolished, by trees pulled down, by an inferno of insecurity and danger which has raged along peaceful farms and homesteads in the frontier area.

The Commander-in-Chief called in to visit his Southern Command headquarters at the desert city of Beersheba, where the general in charge had been ordered to stay put inside Israeli borders until instructed to advance into Egypt. They had to wait for the 'ultimatum' to expire and for Britain and France to engage the Egyptians accordingly.

The general at Southern Command was aware of the secret protocol restricting initial Israeli offensive activity, and considered it a ludicrous reason not to push forward immediately. Why bother with Europeans who cared nothing for Israel and might abandon her at their slightest whim? Better to descend on the

Egyptians like a whirlwind, sweep them away unawares, and maximise Israel's physical gains.

So the Commander-in-Chief walked through the halls of the Beersheba command centre to find them abandoned. All officers had moved forward in mobile headquarters. Only the empty echoes of his own boot heels rose to answer him.

He returned to his jeep and with his entourage sped along desert roads to the Egyptian border which could no longer be called a border.

He was furious, frustrated and sad that the general had disobeyed the directions of the General Staff.

When he passed through the dusty frontier outpost of Qussaima in pursuit of the wayward army, his depression was compounded by the spectacle of a few Israeli soldiers, those who had remained to hold the village, chasing chickens through the thickets, skirting the sorry carcasses of the camels they had shot without cause.

The recalcitrant general was subjected to the rage of the Commander-in-Chief through his radio receiver. The safest way. When the two met face to face minutes later, only the revised orders passed from one to the other, those refashioned by the Commander-in-Chief under duress of weighty circumstance as his vehicle kicked up a trail of sand along the barren Sinai road.

'Your brigade is supposed to be twenty-five miles inside Israel. You are twenty-five miles inside Egypt now, a day ahead of schedule. Our cover is blown and the entire war must be sped up by twenty-four hours. Your brigade will now proceed straightaway to capture the Jebel Livni - Ismailia axis.' But then he added, calmly this time, 'just know that our country, its young men, are now forced because of this advance to proceed without the diversion of the British and French and without their air cover. Remember this.'

Surrounded by hostile armies on all its land frontiers, subjected to savage and relentless antagonism, exposed to penetration, raids and assaults by day and by night, suffering constant toll of life amongst its citizenry, bombarded by threats of neighbouring Governments to accomplish its extinction by armed force, overshadowed by a new menace of irresponsible rearmament, embattled, blockaded, besieged, Israel alone amongst the nations faces a battle for its security anew with every approaching nightfall and every rising dawn. In a country of small area and intricate configuration, the proximity of enemy guns is a constant and haunting theme.

These fears fall upon us with special intensity in the frontier areas, where development projects vital to the nation's destiny can be paralyzed or interrupted by our adversaries from a position of dominating geographical advantage.

The Egyptian soldiers stood ready, crouched ready, lay ready, muscles tightening into spasms, elbows grinding into rock, awaiting the advance of the Israeli paratroopers and land reinforcements into their ambush.

The road wound through the rocks down below, the approach and the traverse in their sights.

Dominating geographical advantage.

In Cairo the Colonel was forced to interrupt a meeting with the Indonesian Ambassador, and the Egyptian leadership coalesced into anxious conference as the first British bombardment lost its way and demolished the international airport by mistake.

The 'ultimatum' had been allowed to expire at six that evening, and only as the British bombs dropped promptly from the sky at one minute past the hour did the Colonel and his men appreciate that the peculiar behaviour of the Israelis in the Sinai had been a ruse to draw their forces away from the Canal, leaving it open to unopposed seizure by the colonial powers.

'General, you must withdraw from the Sinai. It is a trap. We must concentrate on the security of the Canal.'

'The Egyptian army will *never* retreat! If they are to die, they will die honourably.'

'Never mind dying honourably. The Egyptian army must live to fight honourably. At the Canal, not in the Sinai.'

'Colonel,' said the Egyptian general to the Egyptian president, 'I ordered some time ago that withdrawal tactics cease to be taught at the academy. I cannot very well turn around and order my officers to withdraw. We will never withdraw.'

This zealous man, the head of the Egyptian military, could not be persuaded, so the Colonel himself began issuing orders over the telephone for redeployment to the Canal. Confusion was rife in the desert as commanders fielded conflicting movement orders. But whatever chaos swirled elsewhere in the Egyptian ranks, the men lying in wait at Mitla were pleased to find their numbers grown as a new wave of human support dug in alongside their hidden flanks.

Their strength was thus reinforced, new fuel poured upon the fire of their courage, an extra layer of human security to shield their rocky perch. But when, pray, the fight? Not long now.

So sit tight.

Every activity by farmers and citizens becomes a test of physical and moral courage. These are the unique circumstances in which Israel pursues its quest for security and peace.

On innumerable occasions the active defence of Israeli life and territory has been compromised in deference to international opinion. We know that Israel is most popular when it does not hit back and world opinion is profoundly important to us. So, on one occasion after another, we have buried our dead, tended our wounded, clenched our teeth in suppressed resentment and hoped that this very moderation would deter a repetition of the offence. But sometimes the right and duty of self-preservation, the need to avoid expanding encroachment, the sentiment that if the claim to peaceful existence is not defended it will be forever lost, prevail in the final and reluctant decision.

The objective was the gatepost at the southern tip of Sinai to the Straits of Tiran, a town called Sharm-el-Sheikh, where gently frothed sea waves lap sun-soaked sands, and pavements and sandstone houses reflect pure beating sun, artfully bouncing its light back and forth between each other while a slight warm breeze rustles the waving fronds of seaside palms. It is a town of reciprocated daylight, of sun down to sand up to sun. Capture this place, the bay of the sheikh, and Israeli shipping would be free to sail to Eilat.

But the Israeli paratroopers who landed near the town of Suez were not at the southern tip of the peninsula nor anywhere at all near to Sharm-el-Sheikh. They were camped a short hike from the battalion of Egyptians who waited nervously for them behind the rocks at Mitla, in the northwestern quadrant of Sinai. The paratroopers had been told to wait at their position without provoking combat, part of the great strategic ruse to confound the Egyptian military leadership.

But their eager young commander, a man by the name of Sharon, requested of his superiors that they allow his people to move in and capture the tactically appealing defile at Mitla, where Azim's section, minus Azim himself, lay in wait.

When permission was promptly refused, he persisted in supplicating. Allow me at least to send a reconnaissance patrol through the pass.

He was granted this indulgence on the condition his men avoided any heavy engagement. Remember, it's Sharm-el-Sheikh we're after, not repeat not Suez, nor anything needed to support an approach to Suez.

Fine. Understood. Just a patrol; just to have a look.

But 'patrol' he interpreted liberally, and insisted to his reconnaissance men that they carry with them two companies of infantry in armoured half-tracks, a modest accompaniment of tanks, and a trusty troop of heavy mortars to clear them a path. Just in case.

The men in this ensemble knew he expected them to try and capture Mitla.

Stones crunched under tank metal and the rumble of heavy machinery alerted Walid to the approach of the Israeli team. A whole day and a half lying fretfully in wait, but now it was time. His knuckles whitened around the barrel of his gleaming Czech weapon. Would its shiny glint make him an easier target? Someone quietly radioed for air support, and within moments a foursome of Meteor jets swept low over their heads, casting dark cross-shaped shadows over the enemy rolling towards them out of the gritty distance. They should have given reassurance, but instead their thundering swoop only reinforced the darkness of the task that awaited.

The Egyptian soldiers' hearts leaned over a common precipice, their bodies they imagined gripping the ground with tight reptile legs, stabilising their shaky adrenalined bodies, their spirits hovering over corporeal cliffs of mortal fear. The endless wait for the first shot, moment to moment to moment with pulse aflame, is its own special country, its subjects an exclusive assortment of men who have attended the swift shattering burst of live artillery after many hours of silent anticipation.

The convoy entered firing range and someone let loose an anti-tank gun below him.

The first shot. Defence of the fatherland.

A deafening and terrible firestorm was set loose. Walid was hit in the face with a chip of rock and blood dripped onto the outcropping he rested on, belly down. He shifted back a few inches, his eardrums assaulted with the explosion of mortar rounds. Why don't embattled ears have a mechanism for shutting themselves?

An enemy half-track was speeding ahead of the group below, but encountering heavy anti-tank bombardment, the driver skidded to a halt and jumped out his door. As the man tried to crawl behind the vehicle for cover, Walid took aim and held his finger on the trigger, his body vibrating gently behind the repeated shots of his recoil-free automatic weapon. The man was caught in Walid's shower of death and ripped in half by the concurrent arrival of an anti-tank round.

Behind the mottled corpse and his ruined vehicle an Israeli fuel truck was hit and it erupted into a ball of searing white flame. A column of black smoke drifted to cover Walid, as shots echoed with cacophonous steadiness from the two opposing hillsides and Israelis collapsed in piles, the wounded and the slaughtered not distinguishable from Walid's distance.

Then something terrifying began.

The Israelis swarmed out of their vehicles and dispersed along both sides of the pass, scrambling up the rock face and attacking his comrades below in hand-to-hand combat. The Israelis' mortars had been destroyed and they understood they were heavily outgunned and outnumbered and had driven into a position where victory by straightforward means would be impossible.

It became a fight of point-blank pistol shots, machine gun salvos released from the backs of caves in desperation. When the ammunition ceased to pour out of a given grotto the Israelis rushed in and slit throats. Blades in flesh, grenades at close range, limbs torn off. Quick muzzle flashes of execution. Walid's head filled with the screams of his compatriots and he pointed his gun down the rock face, hoping to slow the brazen Israeli foot ascent to his elevated position.

He and the men at his level succeeded in halting half a dozen enemy from scaling up to them.

Who was the predator now in this horror of tooth upon neck?

They had been shooting for twenty minutes now. The universe blazed and crushed and screamed around Walid for seven more hours. A hundred eternities.

In the second hour he became an automaton, reloading and firing, reloading and firing, casting up a barbed bullet fence to prevent any soul approaching him. In the third hour his senses died, he heard nothing and felt nothing. Only his eyes remained on duty to record the puddle of blood and urine around his body as his arms, locked in place, somehow held his gun steady. In the fourth hour his soul rose out of his body, rejecting it as acceptable habitation for the time being. In the fifth hour his forearm was snapped in two by a stray bullet from below.

He remembered nothing else after that except a flashed image of being carried at fast pace by four of his friends on a canvas stretcher toward a truck, then blackness, then a bumpy journey down a long road, then blackness. Then sunlight and the pretty face of a nurse with a white headscarf and long black eyelashes. An angel. She had kept his life. The Israelis had kept Mitla.

Classic acts of war by maritime blockade have been added to Egypt's land belligerency in the total pattern of Israel's siege. Throughout the development of this policy during the Nasser regime we have witnessed a constant sequence of aggravation. The blockade and interception have been extended, in the name of belligerency, from the Suez Canal to another international waterway, the Gulf of Aqaba. The State of Israel has had to distort the entire pattern of its economy, to bear illicit burdens running into tens of millions of pounds, in order to compensate for the impact of this piratical system which Egypt has established on a great artery of the world's communications.

Egypt fell under fresh imperial administration in the late nineteenth century, and its new British masters exercised effective control over the geography flanking this great artery. Their own country just recently industrialised and crisscrossed with railway track, they constructed train lines in Egypt.

By the 1920s they had linked both sides of the artery, the Suez, with a railway bridge. It was called El-Firdan, and it bore travellers in carriages from the green plains of the Nile over the Canal, whence they continued across the rugged Sinai wilderness, through derelict Ottoman lands to Europe's spired gateway, Constantiople, then onwards. Africa to Asia to Europe in seventy-five hours.

Lieutenant Hamid drove his Mercedes gracefully along the canal road from the compound where he had collected Azim in the town of Suez, a small encampment at one end of the El-Firdan bridge their destination. Neither one said a word as they made the journey. Azim was lost that evening in depressive introversion, and Lieutenant Hamid didn't care to interrupt his passenger's silent excursion onto the bitter waters of self-perpetuating gloom. He had not been sent by military intelligence to mother the small taskforce of technical men he was keeping by the bridge. Only to ensure they did their destructive work with precision should the order be given.

Had Azim been less focused on his own mental morbidity he would have marvelled at how beautifully and fluidly Lieutenant Hamid handled his vehicle.

They arrived at the bridge after the five others at the camp had retired for the night.

'I will sleep here. There is room in the third tent for you. Or you can sleep in the car also if you are quiet. I will brief you tomorrow. And please do not shit too close to the camp. If I smell shit I might want to kill someone. Personally, I prefer to shit directly into the water. It is more sanitary.'

Lieutenant Hamid rolled the window down for air and they covered their faces with their shirts and slept.

In the very early morning, the air a palpable darkness, Azim in impenetrable slumber, Lieutenant Hamid awoke to the deep groans and grunted panting of consensual buggery in the neighbouring tent, and lay there and did nothing. He knew the sound. A commissioned officer would have been under an obligation to punish the men. He was there only to employ their expertise, and frighten them a little. He had been trained to keep small groups under his control using psychological tricks. His knowledge of their carnality... If long-term secrecy of their operation became necessary, it was leverage he could wield to enforce their silence. He rolled up the window and went back to sleep.

Azim met the others in the morning. One he knew from engineering college. Another, a specialist in bomb fuses, had the contorted face of a leper. He said he had been cured by dapsone pills, but Azim was secretly glad he had chosen the car for the night. The other two were privates, brought along to assist.

Azim learned from Lieutenant Hamid that they were to crash the bridge into the Canal. The West could not trample on Egypt's sovereign rights, steal away her cloak of dignity, then expect her to keep her legs splayed wide open so their big ships could enter her opening with impunity. The artery supplying the oil that coursed through Europe's veins would be cut off right at this point. *Right here*. Azim would identify the essential structural joints that would have to be knocked out and then supervise the positioning of explosives. That would be his job in this war. The leper would light the fuse.

'When will we do this?'

'It may not be necessary.'

'How will we know?'

'Just practice. I will let you know.'

'When?'

'Enough! Do your work, your preparations. If it is time I will tell you. If you are not prepared when the moment comes I will shoot you and find somebody else. For now we will wait and see.'

'Wait and see,' says the Egyptian dictator, 'soon will be proven to you the strength and will of our nation. Egypt will teach you a lesson and quiet you forever. Egypt will grind you to the dust.'

I can assure members of the General Assembly that it is indeed a disquieting experience to live in a country surrounded by neighbours who bombard it by day and by night with predictions and menaces for its physical destruction. There is no doubt that these authoritative directives furnish the psychological and emotional background against which belligerency by land and by sea is organised, with growing intensity.

Her eyelids drooped. She had been wakeful enough when Nan took her to school that morning, but leaning her elbows on her stout wooden classroom desk, she had to battle the soft white waves of drowse. And why fight off nice soft white waves? Why resist being carried away on driftwood down a lazy swelling warm river? Because a long wooden ruler would be smacked against her knuckles if she were seen to be sleeping. Because mother and father would be informed. Because sleeping in the classroom was a crime. Her teacher had said so.

Father had not been at breakfast and she knew why but didn't say. She was already far enough out of favour with her parents and ought not to risk sinking into the pit she had dug for herself any further by revealing her nocturnal exploits in secret passageways. Even Nan had been unusually stern with her this morning, signalling without actually saying it that she knew of the dinner incident involving the coins. At least she didn't know the whole story behind them or she would have turned red as beetroot and possibly exploded all over the place.

She had already turned red as beetroot four times as far as Clare could remember. She mentioned this to Nan once and Nan had warned her then that if it happened six times she would explode and be Nan no more.

Clare became unsure whether there might have been a fifth instance when she was very little that perhaps she had forgotten, and so Nan might actually be primed to explode the very next time Clare made her turn red. If it happened now Clare would have to mop up mushy wet red bits of bloody flesh and gather up many little bone chips from the taxi floor and wipe spaghetti veins and chunks of brain off the windows and collect Nan's eyeballs carefully; Nan said she was quite particular about having her poor old eyeballs preserved in a tin if she ever exploded; and it would have been all Clare's doing.

A large part of her didn't believe Nan's dire warnings, but there was always that nagging doubt, those seeping irrational thoughts, acidic pollutants eating away at the foundations of her edifice of sensible thinking. So a thin layer of terror often informed Clare's day to day behavioural calculations to some degree, especially when she was in the presence of Nan.

In the schoolyard the cold air restored her wakefulness as she conferred with her group.

'I'll not be able to give you any money for ribbons.'

'But you said you would.'

'Mother and father are punishing me. I'm forbidden from spending my money. I am sorry.'

'Whatever did you do, Clare?' asked Anne.

'I spoke with a stranger on the bus.'

'Oh, you mustn't speak to strangers Clare, they could mean you harm.'

'I shan't do it again.'

'You cause us such a lot of trouble, Clare,' said Maxine. 'It's a wonder you're still part of our group.'

Ellen interposed. 'Shall we play tug of war?'

'That's a boys' game.'

'The fourth years are playing it.'

'The fourth years? We're not strong enough to play against them!'

We are not unaware of the limits of our strength. We are among the half-dozen smallest members of this Organisation. Being a democracy, we work under the natural restraints of public opinion, which compels us to weigh drastic choices with care and without undue precipitancy. We are in short a government which determines its actions by the single exclusive aim of ensuring life and security for the people whom it represents, while safeguarding the honour and trust of millions linked to it by the strongest ties of fraternity.

There is perhaps no member of this Organisation more sensitive to all the currents of international thought, more vulnerable to the disfavour and the dissent of friendly world opinion, broader in the scope and extent of its universal associations, less able to maintain its life on any principle of self-sufficiency or autarchy.

It was with a full knowledge of this fact that we have been forced to interpret Article 51 of the Charter as furnishing both a legal and a moral basis for such defensive action as is applicable to the dangers we face. Under Article 51 of the Charter the right of self-defence is described as 'inherent'; in the French translation it is 'naturel'. It is something which emerges from the very nature of a State and of humanity. This 'inherent right of self-defence' is conditioned in the Charter by the existence of armed attacks against a member State.

Article 51. Chapter 32. Section 87. Roper tossed about in bed, unable to rid himself of the lines of legal text jigging before his eyes. Where any right, duty, or liability would arise under a contract of marine insurance by implication of law, it may be negatived... He rolled over and buried his head under a pillow, only to be invaded by Section 49. Deviation or delay in prosecuting the voyage contemplated by the policy is excused... where reasonably necessary for the safety of the ship or subject-matter insured. What was reasonably necessary? Insured. Would *Rickards v Forestal Land* apply? Probably not. Reasonably plus necessary. He felt like crying. Why couldn't he sleep? Did the wording cover impromptu judgment calls by ship captains who lacked substantial knowledge of the extent of hostilities ashore a canal stretch? They were statutorily excused from performance of the warranty. Negatived. Positived. He had been assigned the Marine Insurance Act of 1906. Neutralised. Selling had gone to the lunch-hour meeting and told him to stay in the library to keep on reading. Neuralised. Sarah brought him a jacket potato with cottage cheese and it had sat in his stomach all afternoon along with the breakfast sausages that had already taken up permanent residence in his gut. Sarah with soft balloons for breasts. And the smell of baby powder when she leaned over him. In his mind in his bed he buried his face in her bosom between his two pillows. Baby powder. He just wanted to sleep. Gunpowder. Lower down he was tightly painfully erect and it refused to soften. Think blackness. Think falling. Unclench the body. Give up grasping for womanish phantoms. Systemic release. Breathe... Sleep.

He slept, and slept, and the olive woman came to him from the party. She didn't touch him, only stood in his doorway and brought hope and devotion into the room. His devotion. He was utterly in her sway. She had only to ask and he would bear the earth on his shoulders, want no reward but to know he had done her will. Should she smile on him he would sail the sky in final fulfilment. Her presence tamed his sexuality and he felt no primal urge to do her violence. Awash instead in tenderness. Sacred distance the rule; serenity, not beastly concupiscence. He belonged to her as to no other.

How many other nations have had hundreds of their citizens killed over these years by the action of armies across the frontier? How many nations have had their ships seized and their cargoes confiscated in international waterways? How many nations find the pursuit of their ordinary tasks to be a matter of daily and perpetual hazard? In how many countries does every single citizen going about his duties feel the icy wind of his own vulnerability? It might perhaps require an unusual measure of humility and imagination for others to answer the question how they would have acted in our place. Nobody else is in our place and is therefore fully competent to equate the advantage and the disadvantage of our choice.

'Now you can rest easier, Chief Officer. The choice to enter is proven correct.'

The Captain waved a transmission in front of all the bridge officers. It was from the Company and it instructed the Captain and officers of the *Majesty* to join the ship in the next Suez convoy as planned.

They were now one ship among more than twenty, a great floating train, muddy Suez waters the track. Their autonomy of navigation was gone, in the hands now of the Canal Company pilot who sat in the wheel room with a plate of Indian sweets on his lap courtesy of Calcutta Maritime, issuing the obvious directions to the helmsman every few minutes.

The monotony grew thick upon Naveen, blanketing his consciousness like a pernicious black mould. He had been given extra bridge duty for the Canal transit, 'as an instructive experience.' Surely the usual four-hour shifts would have sufficed. What can you learn in six hours watching a pilot munch on sticky desserts that you can't learn in four? He leaned both elbows on a table covered in charts, chin in hands, and tried not to let himself doze.

Suddenly he was jarred to alertness by the wrenching sound of scraping metal. He looked up to see shards of ceramic fly across the floor. The pilot's plate. The man had jumped to his feet abruptly at the noise, heedless of what was on his lap. The scraping screeching sound had come from afore and Naveen and the pilot reached for the same set of binoculars at once, their hands colliding.

'So sorry, sir.'

Naveen stood back to let the pilot take the binoculars. The Second Officer found the time to give him a searing glance.

'It's stopped! The ship in front of us has come to a full stop!'

They were on an imminent collision course with the rear end of a Finnish steamer.

The Chief Officer sounded the general alarm while the pilot sized up the situation and issued his order.

'Hard astern!'

The Captain rushed over. 'Belay that, seaman!'

'Aye, Captain.'

'Cut to dead slow and steer us three-three-five. Hurry!'

'Dead slow. Three-three-five.'

The pilot was gripping the railing in a rage. He had been superseded in a crisis by the ship's master. That was not permitted.

Everyone except him and the helmsman now ran to the starboard window, to see a great turquoise-painted hull of a ship looming next to them. They were drifting very slowly alongside the vessel which had suddenly run aground. They had avoided it by mere feet.

'I will have your Suez permit revoked, Captain.'

'Pilot, sir, my apologies. At our speed steering was the only option. We were following too close to avoid collision without changing our bearing.'

'Why did you not warn me of this?'

The Captain looked at the pilot and said nothing.

You should have known. It's your job. We resent pilots. Maybe we're always secretly hoping for you to cock up.

They were near the tail end of the convoy, and the two ships behind them had also managed to avoid collision. The radio's emergency channel came alive with multiple voices, then the heavily accented Suez traffic controller took priority and instructed them to drop anchor and await further directions. All crew had taken emergency positions, and the Chief Officer began making phone calls to the various stations to advise of the situation, telling some to stay at their posts and others to go back off duty.

Naveen got the broom and pan and began sweeping up the plate shards. Better to start cleaning of his own accord than be ordered by the Second Officer.

As he worked, the deck began to vibrate. A rumbling in the sky with a whistling overtone drew everyone's attention to the front window. Four military airplanes flew low overhead. Grey with green and white stripes. Egyptian airforce. The Chief Officer cast an ominous look at the Captain.

The pilot too looked worried. He paced over to the radio and switched it to an obscure channel and spoke into the handset in a worried tone. But none of the officers understood his Arabic.

The Government of Israel is firmly convinced that it has done what any other nation would have done in our place, with the reservation that many would have done it earlier and with perhaps greater impact of resistance. We hold it as a self-evident truth that the lives of Israeli men, women and children are not less worthy of international protection than the lives of the hired fedayeen *groups, which are the main instruments of Nasserism in its assault upon the peace and decencies of Middle Eastern life.*

Across Africa and Asia, wherever Nasserism spreads its baneful influence, it works actively to subvert all peace and progress and to establish an ambitious and insatiable hegemony. Now, having considered that he has humbled and defeated the international community and the maritime Powers, Nasser returns to his first target, Israel, which is to be swamped from three sides with a new wave of fedayeen *violence.*

'What about Israel? Perhaps Pinsky has some inside knowledge.'

Roper and Bigby were in Selling's office and the three were bouncing uninformed theories off each other about the possible intentions of the combatants.

Roper had arrived that morning to find Selling in an apocalyptic mood. No longer the commanding but sensible man of yesterday's marathon, he had now turned entirely to political speculation, and the floor and desk of his office were papered with maps of various parts of the world, the chairs strewn with the morning's newspapers.

'I think the way forward will be for us to establish a foothold in Israeli government circles. Wait, Roper. I know what you're about to say. They wouldn't have time for a commercial outfit like us at a time like this. Well, I think you're mistaken. You're often mistaken, I've noticed lately, Roper.'

'Mr Selling, I hadn't voiced an opinion on the matter, though I was going to suggest some friends of mine at a newspaper as potentially useful contacts.'

He thought of Percy and Helen and how they would have a wealth of information at their disposal.

'Roper, you must never underestimate the reach of a Jew. I told this to myself when deliberating over whether to invite Pinsky to the firm. It did not take long for the conclusion in my mind to become a resounding yes. As long as he keeps away from the public face of our business and is content to manipulate his network of dealers in the shadows, he is a huge asset. A Jew always has ties to money, and ties to government. Don't forget that, Roper. Bigby, see if you can find Pinsky. Ask him to come by my office as soon as he can.'

Roper was astonished at Selling's indiscretion. It was not as if they were at Selling's club, where they could be sure the society would be sympathetic to such expressions. But then it occurred to him that Selling saw nothing objectionable in what he was saying. In fact, thinking about it, Roper could picture him uttering the same to Pinsky's face, or on a radio interview.

Pinsky arrived and stood in the doorway. Bigby was stuck behind him, and peered into the office over Pinsky's shoulder, his eyes darting beneath stupid drooping eyelids. His jowls were obscured behind Pinsky's frame, and only two thirds of his face showed.

'Ah, Pinksy! Our resident expert on the Israelites. Roper and I wondered if we could prevail upon you to tap into your network of Jews and let us know just what the hell is going in the Middle East. We must keep two steps ahead. Imagine what gods we would be to our clients if we rang them up with news of the next battle or diplomatic manoeuvre before it happened! Pinsky, tell me you can patch us through to the right people.'

All the unoccupied chairs were covered with newspapers and Pinsky remained standing. Roper had never seen him smile, but now there was a flicker at the corners of Pinsky's thin mouth. They passed in an instant and Roper thought he might have only imagined them.

Bigby was shifting back and forth from behind one of Pinsky's shoulders to the next, trying to get a better view into the office, and Roper hoped Pinsky would turn around and slap him.

'Very good, Bigby. Go away now please and thank you,' said Selling.

Bigby quit his shifting, but didn't leave.

Pinsky had a soft, almost feminine voice.

'I'll see what I can do.'

'Splendid, Pinsky, see what you can do.'

Selling winked at Roper, then called after Pinsky as the latter walked away.

'Post haste, Pinsky, post haste.'

There is aggression, there is belligerency in the Middle East, but we for eight years have been its victims, not its authors. That is what I mean when I say that world opinion as here represented should decide whom to trust. Shall it be the small free people establishing its homeland in peace and constructive progress or shall it be the dictatorship which has bullied and blustered and blackmailed its way across the international life of our times, threatening the peace in many continents, openly avowing belligerency, placing its fist upon the jugular vein of the world's communications, bringing the Middle East and the world ever nearer to the threshold of conflict, intimidating all those who stand in its path; all except one people, at least, which will not be

*intimidated; one people whom no dictator has ever intimidated,
the people which has risen up against all the tyrants of history, the
people which knows that the appeasement of despots yields nothing
but an uneasy respite, and that a Government which allowed its
own citizens to be murdered daily in their homes would lose the
dignity and the justification for which Governments are instituted
among men?*

A fisherman drifted lazily in a bright blue, red and yellow painted
wooden boat. At his feet there rested a tangle of net and rope, a
bailing pot, a pail half filled with lampuka fish, some of them still
thrashing desperately. There was a kapok life vest covered in
green canvas, a box containing crusty white bread and tinned
sardines and oranges and drinking water to see him through his
day as he rocked gently in the sun.

But for the last few weeks he had also carried with him,
wrapped in a sheet of plastic and buried under an innocent-
looking pile of empty jute sacks, a black metal radio transmitter.

For two years now he had attended secret meetings in a third-
storey flat in Valetta. Of those in his village, only his wife knew
where he went twice a month when he left their quiet house in
Marsalforn and took a bus and ferry from Gozo to Malta. A few
fishermen from other villages attended regularly, but there were
also farmers, quarrymen and students from the university.

About a month ago they had received a special guest to one of
their meetings. He came representing a secretariat in Kaliningrad
of some unintelligible description, and he came with a bag of
money, which he handed over to their treasurer on the condition
it be used for the publication of information leaflets.

He was short and blond and spoke to them in accented
English of the pride the working people of the world took in the
secret dedication of stalwarts such as themselves who undertook
to assemble covertly in internationalist gatherings.

British-style imperialism, he said, had been finally and totally
decimated in the last war. So then why was Malta still a stomping
ground for British navymen? Why should the virtuous young
women of the islands be corrupted by boozing sailors who cared
nothing for their language and culture or their dignity? Why

should hardworking farmers tolerate these lazy imperialists who lived in immorality and decadence on the backs of the people of Malta? Why was English the language of officials and not Maltese?

Though they all identified with international socialism, many in the room disagreed with him about the British. Some were proud to be part of the collective which had received, en masse, the George Cross, for the bravery and endurance displayed by the entire population of the islands during the German and Italian assaults on Malta in 1941. They saw no contradiction in associating themselves with military steadfastness against the Nazis and supporting communism at the same time.

But *this* fisherman had no love of the British.

He had lost his only son in their war, and that experience for which he could not find a sensible justification had set him thinking about politics, and about his country, and about why the British were really there.

Malta was just a convenient stepping stone for the Royal Navy, a way for them to dominate the Mediterranean. The blind loyalty of his compatriots to their imperial masters disgusted and saddened him. People here expressed an inexplicable allegiance to the Queen, a foolish and blind political traditionalism. If only they would stop to think!

He agreed with everything the visitor said, and he made this known by grunting his approval throughout the speech.

As the meeting was dispersing the man pulled the fisherman aside and asked him if he would like to do something more than just attend these meetings. What was the use of talking secretly with like-minded people but following up with nothing more? Was he convincing anyone to join the movement? No. He was in league only with the converted. Would he like to make a tangible contribution to the international struggle of the working class against capitalist imperialism? A *real* contribution?

What, he wondered, could a simple man like him do?

The visitor put his arm around the fisherman's shoulder.

The group was dispersing and the two of them went downstairs and took a walk down the residential street.

The blond man gazed at him and spoke in a tone of friendship tinged with veneration. The world, he said, was run by simple, ordinary people. They were the gears and levers and grease and motor of the great machine of global production. The sophisticated ones simply pushed the buttons and looked at flickering lights and other claptrap. It was all a big phoney display. They used their corrupt methods of coercion, their great theatrical performance of power, to harness the produce of this mechanical dynamo for their own greedy and idle purposes. But any idiot could push buttons. One day soon all those idiots would be overthrown and the components of the machine would realise they could operate without controllers.

Until that day, it was enough for him to know that being a simple fisherman did not bar him from contributing profoundly to the internationalist cause. In fact, he was better placed to do so than nearly anyone else.

Come, let me give you a task.

He had been given the radio and shown how to operate it. He was to tell no one. Not even the members at the meetings. Some might be capitalist spies. Maybe even Americans. CIA. Incredible. He had never thought of such a possibility.

You will carry on fishing as you always have. But keep this radio with you on your boat. If you see any warships passing through Maltese waters you open up the designated frequency and send us a message. Clear your throat twice into the microphone to begin a transmission. Follow with eleven short taps of your fingernail if you see one ship. Four taps if you see two. Two taps if you see three. Seven taps if you see between four and ten. Nine taps if you see between ten and twenty. You will not see more than twenty. Then you indicate their bearing by heavy breathing at the end of the transmission. Blow once for north, twice for north-northeast, thrice for northeast, four times for east-northeast, and so on. Blow nothing if you're not sure.

If your boat is approached by a patrol, throw the radio overboard before they come near enough to see what it is. If they question you about it you tell them regretfully it was a smuggled case of dutiable liquor. The information you transmit will be verified using secret Russian technology. But your eyes are the most valuable to us.

You are the man in the front line.

The 'case of liquor' had just sat in his boat. He'd not had an opportunity to use it once. He was told by his neighbour last week that the British sailors had been running through the streets of Valetta. War exercises. But he had not yet spotted a single warship and worried that he might be missing them, so he began spending longer hours out at sea, telling his wife he was trying out a new technique which took longer but yielded more fish. But still nothing. Just drifting.

Drifting lazily. Today he napped. The rocking lulled him to sleep, his arm crooked over his head to keep out the sunlight. Barred thus from his brown eyes, the sunlight instead reflected a partial rainbow off his brightly painted boat onto the water. It also reflected the military grey of a great armada. He heard distant motors and woke up and sat up. The boat was rocking too regularly. The waves were patterned. He looked to the south and rubbed his eyes. Perhaps he was still sleeping. As far as the eye could see there were military boats. Not one, not two, nor four nor ten nor twenty. He counted seventy and then ten more and then ten more and it was simply not to be believed. He could only estimate. Between one and two hundred military vessels stretched out into the blue distance. A few were giant islands of grey metal like he had never seen before. Many were smaller. Destroyers, aircraft carriers, troop carriers, frigates, and many unrecognisable types.

You will not see more than twenty. Nine taps if you see between ten and twenty. He crouched down and engaged the radio.

All he could think to do was send the maximum nine taps, then wait, then send them again, then again, then again, then again, until he had lost count of how many transmissions he made. Sending little flotilla signals to the Soviets. How many flotilla signals to make up an armada signal? For it was a veritable English armada which sailed out of Malta that day.

Israel and the Arab States, the region in which they and we must forever live, now stand at the crossroads of their history. An aggressive dictatorship has for the first time encountered successful resistance. Some elements of its pride have been broken. Those whom it has outraged with impunity have stood up and asserted their rights, and the hope of freedom burns brighter in the Middle

East today not only for Israel but for many others in our region who have found ways of communicating to us their deep apprehensions over what Nasser's encroachment means for their own cherished sovereignty.

If the power of this tyranny is not artificially revived, our region will again become a place where men of all nations, including Israel, can live and work in peace, where legitimate universal interests will be respected under the sanction of law, where contracts with other lands will be held in respect, where all those in Asia and Europe whose fortune is linked by history and geography with the Middle East will receive justice and respect for their legitimate interests. It will be a region where the great maritime nations will not have to suffer the indignities which they underwent in this building last month, when they had to hang with exaggerated deference on every wave of the hand, on every nod of condescension from the representative of the territorial Power which had converted the unconditional right of navigation into an act of grace or privilege to be conferred or withheld at will.

Our signpost is not backward to belligerency, but forward to peace. Whatever Israel is now asked to do for Egypt must have its counterpart in Egypt's reciprocal duty to give Israel the plenitude of its rights. Egypt and Israel are two people whose encounters in history have been rich and fruitful for mankind. Surely they must take their journey from this solemn moment towards the horizons of peace.

Thus concluded the Israeli statesman his address, the sublime symphony of word he had whipped up from out of the ether. He had left his mark and could sit down. The room was drowned in deafening global applause, an admixture of admiration at his unbelievably spontaneous verbal deftness and newfound if passing empathy with the ideological, emotional and political motivations of his people. The surprise of his own unblemished performance, and the thunderous, engulfing reaction it engendered in the chamber, stirred him to a state of sober elation. For a time it enabled him to ignore his complete physical exhaustion.

III

Descent

THEY WERE piloting onward once again, but not without some delay. Inspectors had to verify the Finnish steamer's turquoise-coloured hull was not unsafely compromised before tugs had come to force her back into the convoy and painstakingly to coax her back into service. There had been no word as to why she had run aground, collided in a great clamour with the rocky edge of the Suez.

Their vessel anchored right alongside the casualty, but without enough clearance to carry on forward, the officers and crew of the *Majesty* could only wait, secretly suspecting an Arab pilot to be at fault. In fact, the pilot had been Greek, and matters had been out of his hands due to a mechanical failure. But this was not known on the *Majesty*. Since the Egyptians had nationalised the Canal and there had been a mass exodus of most of the foreign pilots the previous month, the new lot were still highly suspect in the eyes of many people in the sea business. This was despite their nearly impeccable record of seeing ships through the waterway.

Everyone was irritable, though the Captain was the calmest of them. Probably he had experienced something similar in his seafaring past. But the Chief Officer was becoming less and less easy, more prone to fits of exasperation, more easily set on edge by the innocent speculative remarks of his colleagues as to the state of the convoy.

At the fore of his mind even before the delay was the fear of being trapped in a war. He had worked himself into a private panic while off duty in his cabin, and prayed only that God conduct them through what he perceived to be their dire straits, trapped in a maritime traffic queue with no alternate route, battles probably blazing around them on all sides just out of earshot of the Canal; that God see them through this constriction with the greatest possible despatch.

The incident with the Finnish steamer had only compounded and aggravated his growing anxiety. Thinking back, he realised he had always hated the Suez. Now it was rearing up to taunt him with the spectre of calamity. He opened his Bible for consolation, but by chance his worry was heightened as his eyes lighted on a verse in Proverbs.

'A prudent man foreseeth the evil, and hideth himself; but the simple pass on, and are punished.'

They should never have entered the Canal.

He reached for a bottle of cherry brandy and took a deep gulp, and a reassuring fire warmed his core.

'As a bird that wandereth from her nest, so is a man that wandereth from his place.'

He should never have started out on a career at sea. He should have remained with his family in India.

Another sip.

It was too sweet even for him.

He reached further back, behind the banana liqueur and the orange daiquiri and pulled out his Irish whiskey.

'The wicked flee when no man pursueth: but the righteous are bold as a lion.'

Surely this labelled him a sinner, and he longed for the confessional.

His telephone rang and he let it ring, sounding the knell of his perdition. And how many knells it sounded. It wouldn't let up so he threw it on the floor, ripping the cord from the wall.

'He that passeth by, and meddleth with strife belonging not to him, is like one that taketh a dog by the ears.'

Whatever that was supposed to mean, it told him they were passing through, meddling, where they shouldn't be. They were sailing into war.

He lay down on his bed, and there was a knock at his door. He got up laboriously and trudged to open it. It was the Cadet, to tell him they were again setting sail.

Cadet, my son, let me be for now. The Captain has determined our path and we have no choice.

Naveen didn't like the sound of choicelessness. It bothered him more than it bothered him to see the Chief in such a state.

Is there anything I can do?

Just leave me be, Cadet.

So he returned to the bridge and reported to the Captain that the Chief Officer was resting with flu. He did not want to expose the much loved man to ridicule in his time of weakness.

*

The order was given and the vessel shuddered into movement, and again they drifted forward under the direction of the Suez pilot. The latter had been behaving oddly, pacing, sweating, sitting quietly for long stretches, then bolting up suddenly to look out at the skies through the binoculars.

Was everything alright?

Oh yes, of course, he would smile at them. There has been some aggression against Egypt, but this is being handled easily by the well trained Egyptian troops and the Canal is in no danger. We are entirely safe.

No sooner were the words of reassurance uttered than a low thundering was heard in the distance to their starboard.

But after a minute it died away and no further signal of live engagement was detected at their position.

The pilot had taken to chewing on his fingertips incessantly. His nails wore down and Naveen watched the ends of the man's digits turning red. The sight disturbed him and he turned his attention to the weather station to keep busy. There had been a thick fog the previous morning, delaying the convoy's departure from the Canal entrance, but since it had lifted all had been clear.

The Second Officer kept glancing at Naveen, but he held his peace, the Captain being present. Had the two been on the bridge alone it would have been one of those moments when the Second Officer had loose at him, but presently Naveen was under the unwitting protection of superior company.

*

The Chief Officer was down below, rolling in his bed with his bottle and his Bible, alternating between tears and bouts of emotional relief.

Even in his miserable state he recognised that he was reacting not only to the stress of the present, but to months of built-up frustration. He had been fighting off the grip of some evil spirit

101

for their last eight voyages, and he did not know why. He had increasingly been seeking comfort in food, sleep and alcohol, and in his Bible, though it had been a gradual process and he had been mainly unconscious of it.

He recognised, now that his floodgates had been cranked open, precipitated by the pressure of the day, that he had privately been permitting Satan to feast on his soul even while he kept up a kind face to the officers and crew in public, pretending all was well.

Minerals

'NOW, CLARE, would you please explain to us the difference between an element and a mineral?'

The eyes of the whole class were trained on her. There was never so much collective satisfaction to be had as in watching another student stumbling for an answer.

Clare had been daydreaming again, and had absorbed none of what the teacher said all morning.

While she was lost in flights of fancy, the classroom had been a delightful place to be, crawling with magic vines and populated by talking flowers planted in neat rows, their heads turned to face the tree of wisdom swaying at the front of the room. Butterflies camouflaged as the books of humans rested beside every flower.

Now that the tree had spoken to her and become a schoolmistress once again, the class was a stark place. The blackboard loomed over them all, a great forbidding wall. The stares of her classmates pierced through the back of her head and made her neck tingle.

'Are you with us, Clare?'

'Yes, Miss Berkhoff.'

She heard someone behind her trying to suppress a snicker.

'I'm not sure you are, Clare. Did you even hear the question?'

'What's the difference between a mineral and an element, Miss Berkhoff.'

'What's the difference indeed.' The teacher walked with a slow, ominous step down the aisle towards Clare's desk. Her classmates stopped their shuffles and giggles. Fun was fun, but when the teacher left her territory, passed the neutral zone that was the empty space between her desk and theirs, and entered the students' ranks, there was no such thing as fun. Punishment was approaching like a shark after blood, and the slightest murmur would draw its attention away from Clare's blood towards the blood of another. Heads would be devoured.

She came to a halt next to Clare's desk and towered over

Clare, casting her shadow across Clare's face, obscuring any rays of hope she still entertained of being rescued by a brave volunteer.

The teacher grabbed hold of her right ear and yanked her up from her seat so she was standing, then turned her around to face the class.

'Repeat after me, Clare. Ignorance is fettering.'

'Ignorance is fettering.'

'Sloth is sinful.'

'Sloth is sinful.'

'Now tell the class that you have been ignorant and slothful.'

'I have been ignorant and slothful.'

'Tell them that your progress is fettered by your ignorance.'

'My progress is fettered by my ignorance.'

'Tell them that you have sinned by sloth.'

'I have sinned by sloth.'

'Sloth means not keeping up with the discussion in class on account of laziness of mind. Let this be a lesson to any girl who thinks she can make her way forward in the world by losing herself in daydreams.'

Clare had been let off easily.

At break Anne and Maxine were talking together in a corner of the schoolyard, and Ellen had not come to school that day.

When Clare approached her two friends, they walked away to a different corner. Now they carried on conniving, glancing in her direction every so often. Why had they turned against her? Clare was sure it had nothing to do with what had gone on in class, but must instead be linked to the recent tension between them over the stupid ribbons. She tried joining them again, walking more determinedly this time.

'Can't you see, Clare, we're trying to talk,' said Maxine.

'Privately,' said Anne.

'What would you want to hide from me?'

'Oh, nothing,' said Maxine. 'Not everything is your business, you know.'

'I thought we shared all our discussions in our group.'

'Are you in our group? We're not sure, Clare.'

Clare didn't know how to respond to this.

'You're not the same as you used to be, Clare. You're always dreaming.'

'You're slothful and ignorant.' They laughed. 'And you're disloyal. You care more about yourself than about the group.'

'Of course I do. Who doesn't? I'm sure you're the same.'

'Friends come first, Clare.' They laughed again, and Clare, rather than feeling hurt, just felt like she was wasting her time.

'What about Ellen?'

'Ellen is too kind for her own good. My mother said one mustn't ever be too kind or people will walk all over you.'

'Is she still part of the group?'

'You've no right to talk about the group. You have nothing to do with it now. We've decided.'

'No we haven't,' she heard Anne whisper forcefully.

'Yes we have,' Maxine reaffirmed. 'At least Ellen doesn't betray us or forget about us.'

Clare walked away.

When she sat down on her carved stump at the other end of the schoolyard she could tell they were talking about her. They kept stealing glances in her direction, chattering on about something, then laughing to each other. It was just as well. She didn't need friends. Besides, if she did, Ellen was her friend. And Nan was her friend. And she had more fun sitting alone and imagining anyway.

An element was a pure substance, and was solid, liquid or gaseous. A mineral could be made of a combination of pure substances, and was normally solid. People needed minerals to nourish their blood and plants needed minerals to grow. The teacher had made sure she knew this before class was let out for break. Clare wondered now as she sat whether she was a mineral. Whether her parents were minerals. Whether her house was a mineral. And if she were mineral, a thinking being, could other things that were more obvious minerals, like stones and trees and fences, be capable of thinking like she was? She concluded it was likely they could. But they lacked mouths and hands with which to make their thoughts known to the world. Clare felt lucky to have been created a human.

Later, at dinner, her mother and father pointedly reminded her of her ongoing punishment for engaging in deception. She then thought that maybe it would have been more lucky to have been made a mineral without hands and a mouth. No hands, no handling stolen money. No mouth, no lying about it.

'The gravy is superb this evening.'

'Sublime.'

'Such a shame Clare has to subsist on dry bird meat.'

'Yes, a shame.'

'Well, as a wise man once said, the truth will set you free.'

Clare chewed her chicken many times. When she finally swallowed a mouthful, it descended in her throat all dry and unsatisfying. But rather than incline her to confession, her punishment was only stiffening her resistance to any notion of cooeprating with her parents' demands for information. It also diminished the urgency she felt earlier about having to return the money to its rightful owner. Being put on the defensive was gradually swaying her to internal self-justification. Her new sense of being wronged rather than being in the wrong was helping convert this self-justification to self-pity.

She went to her room and sat on the floor and finally began feeling sorry for herself. Sorry for herself and unappreciated and unwanted. She felt uncared for.

Maybe, she brooded, they all needed to be taught a lesson.

Scabbard of Danger

THE PILOT left suddenly. The man charged with seeing them safely through the Suez had sidled off on a motorised dinghy, leaving them adrift. He had received an Arabic transmission and promptly collected his associates from their various stations on board, and the six of them had disappeared.

Half an hour later the bridge officers were informed by radio in accented English that all shipping had been forced to a standstill in the Canal due to foreign aggression. Officers and crew were instructed to lay anchor and invited to come ashore where they would be welcomed as guests of the Egyptian people.

'Go and check the tea chests, Cadet.'

The Second Officer's obsessiveness shone through in tense moments.

Naveen decided he ought instead to take the opportunity to check on the Chief Officer, being the only one who was aware of his true state.

'Aye, sir.'

He went downstairs and knocked gently on the Chief Officer's cabin door. No response. He knocked again and heard a shuffling from inside, but the door remained shut. He bent down and tried to peer through the ventilation grill at the bottom of the door (imagine the Chief Officer had opened the door just at that moment), but it was designed to prevent a straight line of sight through from one side to the other. He stood up and banged his head against the cross.

After recovering from the bright flash of pain, he called through the door.

'Sir? Are you in there? Are you alright?'

There was no answer, so he tried the handle and the door opened.

He leaned his head in and was met with the spectacle of the Chief Officer lying face down in the middle of the floor and the smell of alcohol. He slipped inside and quickly closed the door behind him. The air was thick with trapped humidity and vaporous ethyl, and the Chief Officer groaned.

He tiptoed over to the window, though he needn't have been concerned about rousing anyone, unscrewed the six bolts and swung open the porthole for air. He then approached the supine Chief Officer, knelt down next to him, and tried to roll him over. Not as easy as it looked, but applying further force he was eventually able to rotate the unresisting body onto its back. It opened its eyes, which were an alarming and sickly shade of yellow, crisscrossed with too many red squiggles.

'Cadet.'

It was a weak squeak, a statement to himself, an acknowledgment for the register. It's the Cadet. He has rolled me over. I'm not presently capable of any more sophistication of thought.

'Sir, why don't you come to the bed?'

He sat the man up, and shoved a chair behind him to keep him upright.

'Sir, can you get onto your hands and knees?'

After a quarter of an hour of tentative limb manoeuvring by Naveen, the Chief Officer found himself seated on the edge of his bed. His gut churned and burning poison rose to his throat and he suddenly found the energy to get up and sway to his toilet, where he promptly discharged the contents of his large stomach, his head leaning over the bowl.

Naveen brought him a glass of water, which he took and sipped slowly.

'Ah, that's much better. Thank you, Cadet.'

'Perhaps you had better sleep, sir.'

'Cadet, nobody must know.'

'Of course not, sir. Would you like anything before I go?'

The Chief Officer put his hand up for silence and cocked his head.

'The engine is not running. Why not? Are we through the Canal? Why are we stopped?'

Despite his worry, he lacked the inclination to get up and look out the open window to see their situation.

Naveen faced a moment of indecision. Tell the man in his state that they were sitting ducks for any passing bombardment, be it from land or air? Or purposely deceive him. The latter act would involve casting definitive judgment against the fitness of the Chief Officer for duty.

'Sir, for the moment we have stopped. It is probably the safest thing.'

'Stopped! Cadet, our Captain is a madman! He is the one who must be stopped! Do you know there is a war blazing around us?'

For the moment the distance was silent. No rumbling of ordnance nor crackling of guns.

Naveen would rather not have heard the impulsive words just voiced by the Chief Officer.

'Sir, perhaps now it is best for you to rest. We are safe. Perhaps you would speak with Captain tomorrow morning, when you are in more presentable state.'

He wished he had used a word other than 'presentable.'

But the Chief Officer, rather than object to the description, showed the apology and bashfulness, the easy agreeability and abrupt shift from aggression to passivity, of a chronic drunkard. He sighed and sank into his bed.

'Yes, when I'm more presentable I shall go. Now I shall rest. Probably it is the safest thing. We are doing the safest thing.'

'Yes, sir.'

'Cadet, I do not normally drink so heavily. I... I don't know what possessed me today. When I was a boy...' He trailed off.

Naveen waited for a minute until it was evident no more words were forthcoming. Then he took his leave.

'See you in the morning, sir.'

He shut the door gently behind him and wandered down the corridor, wondering if they would accept the offer of Egyptian hospitality, an invitation card brushed with a stripe of the unknown and unforeseeable and highlighted in his mind with a Middle Eastern scabbard, concealing vague danger. He had never been out of India before.

Now he had ceased dreaming of misadventure. They were near enough to death and destruction for his craving for excitement to be more than satisfied. Their predicament was a low but steady dose of electricity through his nerves, keeping him fully alert without overstimulating. Ready to act but not on edge. There was already enough fodder in his last day and a half of experience to sustain the awe and admiration of his family and friends and children and grandchildren and their children and children's children when they repeated his tales after he was gone from the world.

'Years ago, when I was just a cadet, I was on board a Calcutta Maritime ship. As we passed through the Suez the area came under fierce attack. Of course I kept my cool and helped steer us to safety. Yes, I carried out my duties without flinching.'

'Uncle Naveen was once caught in the crossfire of a great war in Egypt. All the officers were paralysed with fear as rockets and bullets flew past the ship...'

'No, you have it all wrong, the ship was under direct attack. They hit the ship! It was on fire!'

'Yes, you are right. Rockets and bullets slammed into the hull and crashed through the windows. Only Naveen, young and confident and handsome, retained his presence of mind throughout the onslaught. He single-handedly steered the ship to safety and risked his neck rescuing lowly able-bodied seamen who were caught out on deck during the firefight.'

'He was the best sailor the merchant navy ever had. He was a technical genius at the same time as possessing the character of a true leader.'

'Great-uncle Naveen was a Captain in the Indian Navy shortly after independence. His ship was caught in an imperialist war and by his quick thinking, diplomatic spirit and clever use of nautical flags, he effected a cease-fire on the ground and was instrumental in helping bring the conflict to a speedy end. He is an unsung hero to this day.'

Presently Naveen decided there was not enough time to check the tea chests after having spent half an hour ministering to the Chief Officer. He would return to the bridge and if he were lucky the Second Officer would be caught up in something else and be distracted from asking for Naveen's report; although preferably he would not be caught up in crossfire, which Naveen hoped would be confined safely to legend.

Bravura

TEACH THEM all a lesson, and get away from all the pointless fuss. She would worry her parents to death and give her 'friends' cause to feel sorry they had turned their backs on her. Give everyone a good long chance to ponder their recent interactions with her. Remember that she had feelings too, which ought not to be trampled on. The bad things she had done were not her fault. The crimes committed by her hands and the lies uttered by her tongue had been those of an automaton. They, the malfeasances themselves, had seized her and propelled her into their maelstrom of evil and she had been unable to resist. She had not sought them out, not purposely mingled with bad company, not intended to act wrongly.

Not intended.

But the mental element of a crime is not always the same thing as intent.

She would now take a step on her own, free from the clutches of blackness and not as a sleepwalker stumbling through dark passageways and saying yes to every visiting urge. And urge was not even true. She had felt no urge to take the coins, no desire to lie, no wish to shun the path of good. Compulse yes, impulse no. She had been thrust by an invisible hand that lived behind her spine, her words ground out by a foreign motor in her head with mechanics and a driving force all its own.

Or perhaps the evil was without her, a transparent cloud of venom which her body was forced to avoid. It surged under her arms and they rose to its bidding, it swirled round her ankles and she lifted her feet to walk, it floated by her right side and she was reined to move left. It brushed the back of her neck and she spoke words to satisfy it.

Stop.

She was another person now, escaped from the skin of her previous ensnared self by taking charge of her own affairs. Automatism giving way to autonomy. Maybe that was how life was, she thought. People shedding skins like snakes. Only the skins people shed were metaphorical. Only Clare did not know the word 'metaphorical.' Only she had better move forward with her plan or she would sink back into the quicksand of passivity.

So when all was dark and the house noises had ceased and only the clock ticked a sound into the stiff air, Clare set about collecting provisions for her disappearance. She took bread, cheese, apples and chocolate sauce (to sip), and wrapped them in a towel and of course took the torch. The kitchen a general shop. Then shuttled them to the secret place down the corridor up the ledge through the swinging panel down the steps light the torch enter the carpeted hideaway. Drop the things on the table and realise drink would be required, and a chamber pot. More complicated than she anticipated. A blanket also necessary.

So she completed a second round of shopping, taking a woollen cover from the very bottom of the linen store to avoid notice of its absence. As they stocked no chamber pots in the house, she took a saucepan from the kitchen. And she filled a pitcher with water there to take, then went back to her hideaway and closed the panel behind her, shutting a door on the rest of the world.

She was in the house but in another country; in a room on a voyage. She might as well have been afloat at sea.

She wasn't scared.

She switched off the torch to prove it.

She walked around the room tentatively, brushing the furniture and feeling around and around with her hands.

This was Clare country, and she ought to know its geography with her eyes closed.

She looked up and no light shone through the floor cracks. Father was away asleep in his bedroom. She was alone, the master of her own conduct in a land not hers. Occupied territory, but then again her own house. The composer and conductor and performer of her own new music.

So let the walls listen spellbound and dead moths get up and dance.

*

And they raised anchor and sailed through the Bitter Lakes. And

112

the crew murmured against the Captain, saying wherefore sail we forward into certain battle? Better we die ashore, even as prisoners in Egypt, than meet a silty watery grave in this wilderness. And the Captain heeded them not, for the last words of his masters echoed strong in his ears.

And the Chief Officer made forth from his quarters unto the deck to seek the glory of the Lord in a cloud, but he sought in vain. The vista was cloudless and not even a haze of dust stirred the morning on the Sinai horizon. The air and sky were clarity, and neither physical nor metaphysical nuage was presented to satisfy the Chief Officer.

Anything now set him into anxiety. Before it was their stationment and now it was their movement. There was an Amalek in his head and it made everything hopeless. He leaned against the railing in despair and the Canal surface beckoned to him but he turned his head away. His legs weakened to jelly and he dropped to his knees and tried to pray but no prayer came.

A spirit sickness was growing on the bridge. The men's minds felt war around, but their senses returned no true signs of it. No sight, no sound, no smell, no touch of war. And a battle might have snapped them free from it, pitched them face to face with their fear. Instead the stillness and quiet told them they were already inside the eye of death. Floating meaninglessly within the black pupil. As they reached its outer circum it would dilate and dilate and they would never leave it.

The Captain stood firm at his post and was oblivious to the surreality of being on a watery treadmill.

Soon they reached a constriction, where the Bitter Lakes channel back into the Canal, and nerves were tightened like strings on a violin when another formation of warplanes roared overhead, hitting the pitch to which their bodies were strung and causing them to reverberate to the tune of these jets. They were MiGs, and they made a fearsome noise.

The Captain made a general announcement.

'This is the Captain. We are under instructions to attempt to pass through the Canal, and we will follow these instructions. Radio messages as to the state of fighting in Egypt have been contradictory, and there is no use trying to decide which report is accurate. It is enough that we see and hear no signs of live combat.

This means we are safe for the meantime, and we will take advantage of this opportunity to make as much forward progress as possible. Staying anchored is no assurance of safety, and going ashore would be the same thing as abandoning ship. I am not prepared to abandon ship. This morning we have successfully navigated around other anchored ships and we will continue that. With any luck we will be the first ship ever to sail through and out of Port Said with no pilot.'

Bold words, and they shook the men from their trance and many began thinking rationally.

Reason, however, when fed with variables and exercised severally by a multitude, is bound to yield different results depending on the values chosen by each individual. Some reached conclusions concurring with the Captain's message and others reached contrary positions. Still others couldn't be sure. There will be fighting here so better we proceed there. There will not be fighting here so better we remain. There may be fighting here or there so there is no knowable better. The thinking, rational at one level, was based on uninformed predictions at a more basic level.

Discord thus began.

'We do not know if it is safer to proceed, and you do not know either.'

Naveen watched silently as arguments broke out. The Second Engineer stormed onto the bridge from out of the belly of the ship and demanded information. The Captain refused him permission to use the radio and ordered him back below. The engineers normally spoke with one voice and thought with one mind; the Second Engineer would be representing the will of all the engineers, and Naveen saw the seams of cohesion between wheel room and engine room beginning to stretch.

'Where is the Chief Officer?' The Captain glanced at the clock.

'Sir, I believe he may still be ill.' But Naveen was unsure.

The Captain lifted the telephone handset and flicked the switch for the Chief Officer's quarters. There was no answer and he set it down.

'Go and check his quarters.'

Naveen did as he was told, descending to the Chief Officer's cabin, knocking, waiting, knocking, pushing his way in, finding the room deserted, leaving quickly. Where to find the Chief

Officer? He returned to the bridge to inform the Captain the search bore no fruit.

The Captain sent him to look more broadly, preferring not to cause further alarm by using the general speaker to summon the missing officer. Naveen checked the mess, the toilets, the lounge, the kitchen, and telephoned down to the engine room to ask if the Chief Officer was there.

No.

Then he began checking the deck outside.

He climbed metal steps and smelled the coarse exhaust and felt the breeze of motion down the Canal.

On the third level he found the man standing at the rail.

They were leaving the stretch of Suez which connects the Bitter Lakes with Lake Timsah, and entering the latter calm body of water that is roughly halfway along the Canal. On a map, it is a rat swallowed by the Suez snake, part of the way down its digestive tract.

Surveying their situation just then, it occurred to Naveen that the helmsman would have quite a story to tell one day, steering his way along the Suez with no pilot and no radio contact with the traffic controllers and circumventing anchored vessels, sailing on the left at a couple of points as though he were back on a road in India and driving a car. But a giant steel car with a propeller and a rudder and thrusters and no wheels.

Naveen approached the Chief Officer and the two stood together in silence.

After some minutes Naveen recalled his mission and informed the Chief Officer he was requested by the Captain on the bridge; that it was, after all, his watch.

'It is my watch?' He glanced around absently. 'I am watching.'

So they stood and watched. Looking to the northwest, they watched an injured ship being tugged south towards the resumption point of the Canal at the bottom end of the lake. The two ships would shortly pass one another. Naveen and the Chief Officer stood in silence and observed in amazement as they drew alongside the vessel and saw it to be sinking. The ship appeared to have been damaged by aerial bombardment, with a great gaping hole and twisted metal where there should have been a deck. Black soot was spread outwards from the point of rupture.

Naveen thought that if they were towing the boat where they appeared to be towing it, it would sink at roughly the south end of Lake Timsah and obstruct the only navigable passage for large freighters at that part of the waterway. If this estimate were to prove accurate, they would not be able to turn back should they encounter difficulty further up the Canal.

Then again, if there were other anchored ships ahead from the southbound convoy, which undoubtedly suffered the same paralysis as their own northbound convoy, the passage would be narrow and it would be an extreme and testing task for them to reverse in any case.

'Sir, let us go up to the bridge. We will have a better vantage point. And my orders...'

This time he stopped short of mentioning the Captain and his directive to retrieve the Chief Officer, and the man looked at him blankly for a little while and he felt a butterfly in his stomach. But then the Chief Officer nodded vaguely and turned and started a slow march along the deck to the corridor. Naveen followed a few paces behind, as they made gradual progress and then met the internal staircase to the bridge, where the Chief Officer again paused.

'Sir, the bridge.'

Yes, the bridge.

Right foot up and left foot up and the Chief Officer hauled his frame achingly up the steps and his mind was grim and he had leanings in his head to disobey the Captain who had put them in this foul place.

The staircase to the bridge was lit with a low red bulb, and the feel was like a light shone into the mouth through the flesh of a cheek.

There was a door at the top of the steps. The Chief Officer stood before it and Naveen three steps below, handling the railing for support though they were in a calm place on the waters and no rocking was felt.

The Chief Officer unlatched the door and let it swing. He walked into the bridge, stopped, and looked about him. There was dead quiet and all eyes were upon him. He turned his head to meet gazes, and they did not affect him, for his mood was set against accepting influence from the behaviour of others. He felt immune to stimulus, his body and mind a clod of moist dirt from the ground.

But he was in a potter's kiln and didn't know it. Even his

steady form could be hardened into a definite shape under the heat that was to come. Now he would stand immovable, just a bulwark against the Captain's own stubbornness of purpose and nothing more invasive. But soon he would find that even mountains of earth can be shaken into motion.

They approached the final narrows of the Canal, and walked to the rear windows to spectate with binoculars as the Egyptian ship they had passed heaved and tilted and began its final rapid descent to the bottom. But the bottom was not far down and it came to rest with its top well visible. The significance of the sinking and the blockage only then percolated through the sedimentary layers of the Chief Officer's awareness and he recognised their entrapment, their compulsion now to travel only north or sit stranded.

His head throbbed with old drink and his mouth was sour and bitter and his fingers felt fat and swollen. And then he finally let the anger barrel through his trunk and transform him. It was enough. They were in the hands of a fool, and fools were a breed the Chief Officer did not suffer, no matter the sometime closeness he enjoyed with them.

Hardened rock now, a stone age blade, he purported to assume command.

'The Captain is clearly unfit. Until further notice he is relieved from duty.'

There are few kinds of statement more in need of immediate supporting action and a quick and forceful show of initiative than this. But the Chief Officer did nothing. And everybody did nothing.

The Captain had imagined many times, as captains do, the unfolding of such a scenario. He had always been resolute with himself that he would step down gracefully and not resist the will of those who must have good reason to see him removed. But now it had actually happened, he knew there was too much egoism in his resolution. It was about him and not about the ship. He must sacrifice his aspiration of dignified humility and instead think detachedly of what really was best for the vessel, its officers and crew, their cargo and the interests of the Company. The extremity of the Chief Officer's action caused him to pause and ponder whether his course was as correct as he had hitherto assumed, but it did not prompt the instant resignation he had always planned. He did not yet have reason, as Naveen had through his recent experiences, to doubt the psychological integrity of the Chief Officer.

The Second Officer's response? He knew this was the end of their long-lived trio of friendship and felt a sorrow grasp his core but he said nothing, because everything stops one day and he was never one to stand in the way of endings. He let them take their natural course and sturdied the structure of his life with the stiffening sadness they provided.

Nobody did anything.

Then the Chief Officer, finally acknowledging the need to follow through now that he had committed himself, trudged over to the general address speaker and lifted the handset. No eye contact between anyone, and still no action by the others.

The Captain was just then admitting to himself that he had been in error to take them into Suez, but at the same time asserting in his mind that now the damage was done, it would be worse for the ship to suffer a change of command. What, after all, could the Chief Officer do that he could not? There was a blockship barricading their southern escape, so they could only move forward. Better the Captain move them forward than the Chief Officer. Now was not the time to precipitate instability among the crew.

A double voice on the bridge, direct from a larynx and also over the loudspeakers: 'This is the Chief Officer. The Captain is presently unfit for duty and I am assuming command. All officers and crew now answer to me. As you know, we are in some danger. I will do my best to get us out as quickly as possible. Carry on your duties as normal.'

The Captain made his decision, too late, that he ought to remain in charge. He stomped over to the Chief Officer, intending to wrest the handset from him (and precipitate by his own new announcement over the system even more of the very instability he had hoped to avoid), but now the Second Officer stepped forward and tried to restrain him.

'Sir, it would not be wise.'

'You must not call him 'sir'!'

'I will call my Captain 'sir' if I please,' he said of his brother-in-law's uncle. 'You,' he pointed at the Chief Officer, 'have overstepped your authority. But Captain, sir, it is a done deed. You must consider reaction of crew before you speak. What were you going to say to them?'

Naveen decided he ought to speak up.

'Sir, the Chief Officer is in no state to captain the ship. I have seen him these last days and he has been drinking and simply not himself and we cannot allow him to take command.'

The Second Officer looked as though he would attack Naveen physically.

'Keep silent, Cadet! Nobody spoke to you!'

'I'm sorry sir, but under these circumstances I feel I must say...'

'Cadet! You have no experience! What do you know of these circumstances? You know nothing. This is first. Second, you may not suggest such treachery of *any* officer without solid evidence and I am sure you have no solid evidence and I am even more sure it is a product of your overactive imagination. Third, if you *did* have evidence, *why* did you not bring it to us sooner, before it was too late? Now it is too late!'

Hindi replaced English. The Second Officer was counting on his fingers and he was truly, frighteningly furious.

But Naveen felt emboldened, the thin tense sheet of ice between him and the Second Officer already shattered, and spilled on about the Chief Officer, whom he had now in any case also alienated. He even spoke over the voice of the Second Officer, drowning out his words.

'I did not tell you earlier because...'

And he justified himself, shouting to them his account of recent events. And the Second Officer tried to blame him for their present sorry state, and Naveen rebutted, righteously indignant.

The Chief Officer said nothing, waiting for the match to lead to some final judgment and hoping for exoneration, and the Captain said nothing, waiting for the judgment and hoping for reinstatement.

These were mad times.

*

In London, they did not know exactly what was happening in the Canal.

Ways In

THE PREVIOUS morning, Selling whisked by Roper's door without stopping, calling into the air as he passed.

'In my office, Roper.'

Yes Captain *sir*, thought Roper. He got up from his desk and followed the trail of Tabac Original musk down the corridor to Selling's office.

'Sit down, Roper. There are a couple of things I want to discuss.'

The musk was unusually strong and it tickled Roper's nose. He tried hard to suppress a sneeze, and failed.

'You're not catching cold on us, are you? Because I can't afford to send you home if you are.'

'I think it's just allergies, Mr Selling.'

'Allergies are for girls, Roper. Stiffen up.' He tapped his desk with his pen. 'Right. First thing: who have you found to do the carpets?'

'The carpets... Er, well, you see, with the stress lately on Suez, I thought you would prefer for that sort of thing to be held off until afterwards.'

There was an uncomfortable silence.

'Yes, I thought so,' Selling eventually said, and frowned. 'Roper, you had *days* before Suez kicked off to get the carpeting arranged. Besides, just because there's a war going on over a thousand miles from here doesn't mean the office in London can be neglected. Now that the Royal Air Force are involved, you ought to leave the war to them and look after your own back garden. Am I wrong, Roper?'

Roper shook his head, but attempted a sour look at the same time. It didn't suit his clean face.

'What did you do during the Blitz, Roper? Did you cower away in the cellar or did you carry on with your affairs, sticking up two fingers at the Huns and marching proudly down the streets?'

Roper had been thirteen at the time, and living with his

mother and sister in Kesteven.

'*Get* the carpets done, will you?'

'Of course.'

'Good. Now for the important thing. We've got to get a handle on this Suez business. I've got a client who has a shipment of tea with Calcutta Maritime and it's gone into Suez and they've lost contact. It may not do any practical good, Roper, but I think we would be making ideal use of our Israeli contacts if we put on a show of good connections for the client.'

'Which Israeli contacts?'

'Pinsky is a gem. He says he can arrange a meeting, probably just one, but you never know once you've got your foot in the door...'

'A meeting with whom?'

'Roper, I want you to take my client to the Jewish embassy. Pinsky has a contact there in the trade division. Said something about weapons, but never mind that. We've our hands in more benign things like tea. Sugar and spice and all things nice, Roper. Go to the embassy and show the client around and have him shake some hands and make sure whoever it is you meet over there gives a few authoritative words on the conflict. Preferably some reassurance about the shipment. Perhaps the Israelis will even protect it for a sum.'

'When?'

'Here are his details. Ring him up once you've set a time with the Israelis and let him know. Give him the impression it's quite important. We do want him to turn up.'

Roper looked at the index card and recognised the name. He hadn't known Selling had been keeping such a prominent client. He had been hoarding his business secretly. Perhaps they had a personal connection. But then why would Selling ask *him* to make the call?

'I've spoken to him, Roper, and he's expecting your call.'

Ah.

'So off you go. And get those carpets done. *Just* get them done.'

He started whistling idly as Roper left.

As he walked away he heard Selling muttering to himself cheerfully.

'Sugar and spice and all things nice. Dee-dee-dee. Dum-dee-dum. Sugar and spice...'

*

Clare slept through the night in the soft chair, waking numerous times to adjust herself. It was comfortable, but nothing like a bed, and her limbs grew tight every so often and caused her to stir. Her neck would then bend over the armrest and rub against the hard wood frame and she would open her eyes. These frequent waking intervals kept her from being disoriented. The memory of each stirring would carry through to the next and prepare her for her situation when she sat up and looked about and saw the strange place around her.

At dawn some daylight shone through the cracks in the ceiling, and also, more brightly, through a small hole in the brick wall by the bottom of the steps. She got up, stretched, and felt aches in her joints, and awkwardly used the chamber pot, then went over to the hole of light to try and see through it. But all she saw was sky.

She noticed that a square area of bricks at this place in the wall had a definite border and that the bricks were of a slightly different texture than the surrounding ones that made up most of the wall. Standing back, it appeared to her as though there had once been a proper window, which had at some time been filled in with brick and mortar. The peephole was at one of the corners of this now solid brick window, where the replacement mortar had eroded away.

When she moved back from it she saw the hole projected a beam of dust into the shadows. Quite thick dust. Probably that was what happened to things that stayed in this room forever. They turned into dust. *She* might stay here forever and turn into dust. Then nobody would ever find her.

She sat still on the old carpet for a very long time. She counted even numbers from two to four thousand. Then she counted the odd numbers from one to three thousand nine hundred and ninety-nine. She always found the odd numbers more difficult for some reason.

She counted and counted and got lost in numbers, so that

when father entered his study at seven o'clock she took no notice other than to count his steps. Five from the door to his desk, and for some reason only four back to the door. She rubbed her eyes and felt tired, and pulled the woollen cover over her and slept on the carpet.

Until she was roused by a frantic sounding conversation between her mother and Nan. But it was far away in some other room and she could make out no words. No doubt they were talking about her and she realised they must be worried stiff, but suppressed the guilt that washed over her momentarily. Leaving her hideaway now and giving herself up to the two women would be a full waste. The impact of her absence would not be felt deeply enough if she emerged after only one morning of being missing. It would only bring about worse punishments. Besides, hearing their blurred voices reassured her and made her feel safe, causing the room to lose its slight spookiness.

When their voices faded away into a different part of the house and her chamber bore no sound again, she got up and padded around and around. She followed the symmetrical pattern on the oriental carpet with her toes, and became a ballerina for a time. A dainty dancer in the soft contented quietness of a grand house in the morning. Then she worried about being detected by her step, and stopped. She ate some of her rations and drank some water. Strangely, she had no inclination to have the chocolate sauce. Maybe she was becoming an adult living here on her own.

Then she noticed something she hadn't noticed before, and it was a major discovery, though it didn't seem so to her. Entering this place from the bottom of the steps, one looks immediately into the room and sees the carpet, the chest of drawers, the chair and the table, all at the further end away from the steps, deeper into the house from the street, which is to the east of the room. Coming into the room, one's eye lights upon the west, south and north walls, and sees the east wall only when sitting in the chair and looking back towards the entrance side. Then the focus of attention is the area by the base of the steps to the far right, by the hole and the extinct window, and not the wall that runs along the greater part of the east side of the room.

But now she noticed a door built into the ignored east wall. There was a hole where a knob should have been and she put her finger into it and pulled, but it wouldn't budge to open. She threw her body against the door a few times to loosen it, and when she pulled it again it creaked and swung out, and there was nothing much of interest inside, as far as she could tell. It was a cupboard built into the space under the steps.

There was just a contraption of poles and a board, which she did not recognise as a painter's easel. And there was a draped cloth which she lifted, to uncover several large paintings leaning on each other and against the brick wall under the steps. She did not want to stir up the dust and she left them be.

The painting facing her had a scene of meadows and trees and sheep and a young man with a staff. But she knew all about such places, and did not need pictures to recreate them for her. Though it *was* a pretty painting.

Perhaps this place had been an artist's studio. If there had indeed been a window, there would have been natural light to paint in. But it must have been a very short painter, or he would have developed a stooped back and a sore neck in the low-ceilinged room.

But who really knew?

The answer was lost, deeply buried beneath old layers of time.

Flight

THE CAPTAIN rushed forward, seized the handset, and reasserted his command over the vessel by an announcement. The chaotic argument that gripped the bridge had not gone decisively in his favour, though it had also failed resoundingly to exonerate the Chief Officer.

There came a moment of pause when everyone was red faced and out of words and ready to shift to physicalities, and the Captain saw it as his chance to regain control via the general address system. He was breathless as he acted, barely conscious of what he was doing. It was as though he were deciding upon each step after taking it, his reflexes operating ahead of his thoughts.

The Chief Officer turned to Naveen and Naveen saw the look of a bull in his eyes and for a split second he considered relying on the other officers for support, but thought better of it, and ran.

The Chief Officer left the bridge in pursuit of the cadet.

Unknown to Naveen, however, the Captain, once he had recovered his wits from the astonishment of the eruption on his bridge and his own resumption of command, sent the Second and Third Officers after the Chief Officer to apprehend him.

'Use reason with him, but if he does not yield to reason, remind him of the rules.'

He spoke with a voice of confidence, but inside he could not be sure if these two were for him or against him, or wavering. There was nothing he could do to ascertain this. He could only hope for their loyalty. He would have to assume it existed. With the Second Officer he was fairly sure.

'Captain, what about the cadet?'

'First find the Chief Officer. He is the danger. The cadet is above his head, but he is a good lad and not any threat. We can speak with him later.'

After all, it was the shouted testimony of the cadet against the sanity of the Chief Officer that had finally solidified his resolve to take back his command. Still, the boy could have warned them sooner, and ought to endure some nominal punishment for arrogating too much responsibility to himself with respect to the state of the Chief Officer.

*

There's not far to run on a freighter, and various alternate courses of action flashed through Naveen's head as his boots clamoured against the metal deck and the railings rushed by. Swinging through openings, undoing latches and kicking open doors in single fluid motions.

On the jildi. In a hurry.

He would have to hide or fight as flight could not go on for long. It was too late for diplomacy at this stage. But for now he ran and ran, even though he had left the Chief Officer far behind, because the rush of escape was wired through his sinews.

When he was halted, it was not by the Chief Officer, but by two crewmen, able-bodied seamen, who themselves were shouting anxiously at each other in the corridor and blocking his path with their gesticulations. He could have pushed by them, even smitten them with impunity in those days, but he was out of breath and it was an excuse to stop. Besides, there is something daunting about encountering two full-grown men in a narrow and low corridor on a ship of burden.

The mind must even in normal circumstances overcome an instinctive hesitation to bypass two stationary male presences crowding a narrow passage in a hard functional setting, no carpets nor pretty designs nor dim lights to set the softer tone of, say, a cruise ship. And these were far from normal circumstances.

So now Naveen stopped and watched, panting, as one declared faith in the Captain, the other in the Chief Officer. Yet another heard the ruckus and emerged from his cabin and yelled at them both that neither commander was any good and they ought to mutiny. A fourth and a fifth joined them from out of nowhere. One was grey-haired and he stood aside and listened silently, but his younger companion urged his own good sense upon the group vociferously. All seemed oblivious to Naveen.

So it had happened, he thought. The crew had been divided,

and not just into two. There were two leaders and there were sailors loyal to one, sailors loyal to the other, and sailors loyal to neither. Still other sailors didn't care, and would carry on their duties, which would be the same regardless of the identity of the man at the top. As long as they got their pay and their shore leave.

*

All the while the ship was moving on up the waterway, the throttle set at dead slow.

A ship in a war on a Canal in a halted convoy with no pilot and a crisis of command, and disorder through the lower ranks, and yet displaying to the outside observer the illusion of united resolve by its forward movement. But in fact it was for the moment a renegade carriage with no conductor, broken away from its train and rolling down slim slippery tracks of trouble into the bright but menacing unknown.

The propeller spun its rotations loyally, answering only to the caring touch of the engineers on its controls, once removed from the chaos of the command centre topside. The combustion cylinders pumped in succession and oil churned through filters and water vapours steamed through pressurised pipes; and the gears continued their long spinning kiss.

Drums beat in Naveen's head.

He turned his back on these arguing men and regressed down the corridor, going back the way he came. There would be a diversion ahead; he would not have to retrace his steps exactly and thereby inevitably meet the Chief Officer. Instead, he could and did turn off the route, into the internal staircase.

Down or up?

Down would be further away from the Chief Officer, but he always felt easier in high places. Being low made him feel hemmed in. Being up allowed for a rapid descent. Being down meant an arduous climb to escape a pursuer. Where was the flat land, with no up nor down?

Being on a ship in a sea was being trapped. You could leave if you liked but you couldn't really. If you did you left food and drink and bed and the barrier between your legs and the mouth of

127

Leviathan, between your skull and the razorteeth of sharks. Even a lifeboat was no answer. You would run out of provisions after a time and be slowly devoured by the elements, an agony. But then being on dry land was also a confinement. It was just a matter of perspective.

IV

Concentration of Moments

THERE are a handful of extraordinary moments that punctuate the ordinary lives of most people, moments which can be recalled by those who have experienced them not only as abstractions, points recognisable for their pivotal significance or profound symbolism in a person's history, but also as physical parcels of eternity, pockets of reality which can be lived, heard, spoken, smelled, over and over again, for as long as there is sense left in the minds of those recalling. These are moments of sharply carved perception, with all faculties engaged. The sound archive of the brain is set to record; nostrils are primed to grip an everlasting scent. Pure, unblotted pages are hastily spread open in the memory book to meet the occasion, ready for indelible inscription of the exceptional, to be read and reread for decades to come, sharp and clear and powerful as the day they were etched. Naveen's and Azim's and Roper's experiences would all soon contribute a concentration of such moments to the great rippling agglomerate of remembered human existence.

*

Roper's day began with bright light.

He was lifted awake by the rays of the sun through the gap in his blinds on the lids of his eyes. His sleep had been sound, he remembered no dream.

His clock showed an early hour.

He had anticipated his alarm and was up in time to shut it off before it began its daily assault. Normally it rang for twenty minutes before he got out of bed. He smiled at the healthy feeling, stretched, and resolved to make good use of the extra minutes he now had. He would read the newspaper on a bench in Finsbury Circus and stroll to work a master of his own time, not rushing into the office, not panting nor ill humoured. Maybe he would lean over the reception desk and kiss Penny, maybe ask her to dinner. Or maybe Sarah. His imagination was briefly ensnared, aswirl in the capricious tidepools of early morning ambition.

A brisk shower washed away these thoughts.

He put on a starched white shirt and freshly pressed suit and went out to meet the morning. He appropriated a crisp copy of the Daily Mail and kept it tucked under his arm for the underground ride to Moorgate. A light breeze had picked up by the time he reemerged into daylight, but he felt warm. The Metropolitan Line was always stuffed at the rush hour, and the heat of cramped humanity remained with him on the open streets as he made his way contentedly to a bench, knowing he was five minutes' walk from work. He could relax.

He had a meeting scheduled for a quarter past nine with the beer exporters, during which he was expected to make clear the firm's position on their hopeless case. He was not to negotiate, just to present the stark options to the client, so that meeting should be over in a shot. Later he was to lunch with Selling and the tea merchant and then travel alone with the client to the Israeli embassy for what could only be an interesting meeting. He had never before dealt in a professional capacity with diplomats.

Now he rested one leg over the other and spread open the pages of the paper, and enjoyed the fresh businesslike scent of grass and newsprint and autumn leaves, blended with the wool of his suit and the morning traffic air. He scanned for details on the war, so he could discuss the latest with Selling and the client and the Israelis and feign some degree of confident familiarity with what was going on. But he got bored and just closed his eyes and leaned his head back and let the leaves play tricks with the sun on his face. He would see orange and red through his closed eyes, then grey and black, then orange, as the branches swayed back and forth above him.

Suddenly he felt cold wetness on his ear and neck and opened his eyes, alarmed.

An elderly couple were sitting across from him, scattering feed to the birds. What were *they* doing in Finsbury?

The park was seething with a mass of pigeons. Pigeons huddled in boisterous conclaves around piles of feed, pigeons fending off their competitors, pigeons taking overflights, doing reconnaissance. Kernels were being tossed back with seriousness and precision, important affairs being transacted on the grass and gravel stock exchange floor of Finsbury Circus. And the processed residuum of this feeding business, the funny smelling detritus, was being jettisoned willy-nilly, a negative externality, meaningless to these City traders with great round midriffs as it slid unnoticed out their bottoms... and onto Roper's hair, into his ear, down his neck, seeping into his starched white shirt, a light splattering also on the shoulder of his suit.

*

Not one to run, the Second Officer walked quickly through the corridors, looking for the renegade Chief Officer. Thorough and methodical, he used his authority to gain access to every cabin along his search route, making sure no sailor was harbouring his quarry. He had sent the Third Officer to do the same on the lower decks.

But the Chief Officer did not consider himself a fugitive. He was pursuing Naveen in a peculiar combination of fear and rage, and was unaware he was himself under chase. He rambled steadily from deck to deck on his search.

All three senior officers witnessed what appeared to be rampant disorder among the crew as they went. Some men had taken over the kitchen and were feasting on ice cream. Others had a flinging match in the officers' lounge, and paperbacks were strewn everywhere in large piles. Portholes were ajar and outer doors propped open and there was a breeze in the halls. Yet the ship chugged forward. The engineers had decided to behave themselves and keep their machine running, and the mayhem that seemed to have overtaken the craft was in fact caused only by four or five of the eighteen men on board. And they could be brought under control. The real crisis had been at the top of the chain of command.

Finally, after disturbing a number of sleeping crewmen in their beds to make sure none of them was really a masquerading Chief Officer, the Second Officer encountered the real one out on the deck, and approached him quietly from behind.

He felt pity for his old friend and regret that he was charged with apprehending him, but he also felt the call of order. It was a biting disappointment to have to face the Chief Officer in this way, but rules were rules.

He spoke to the Chief Officer's back: 'you must come with me,' but then stopped as the latter started visibly and shuddered violently, his nerves frayed.

The Chief Officer, himself in a mindset of nervous belligerence, sensed predation all around him.

The Second Officer had only an instant in which to watch him swivel about, and to register the Chief Officer's large, beefy right arm swinging towards him with invisible speed, controlled by instinct and reflex. A fraction of a second before it connected with the back of his jaw, he saw the surprise and belated regret in the widening eyes of his assailant, as the Chief Officer realised just what he was doing and whom he was striking.

Then impact.

He heard a loudness in the side of his face and saw daggers stabbing lines of light across his field of vision, and felt an overwhelming pain and then colourless faintness.

*

Roper didn't touch the bird dropping, but strode briskly to Crossley & Broke and confronted Penny wordlessly. She couldn't hold back a laugh when she saw him.

'You're a fine sight this morning, Jim. What happened? Call in at Wrench Merryfield along the way?'

'Penny, I don't suppose you have any helpful suggestions. I've a client in twenty minutes.'

Friendly but appropriately insistent, he thought, given the mess and the rush.

Actually, she *could* think of a few helpful suggestions, and stood up, smiling secretly to herself, liking his helplessness. Normally *he* was teasing and tempting *her*, but this morning she was in bold form and was minded to take advantage of the turned tables.

'Come with me,' she requested, and took him by the arm and led him into the ladies' room.

She locked the latch and wet a towel and pushed him against the door and started to clean him off.

'It's just birdshit, Jim. It comes off with water. Barely has a smell.' She liked using a coarse word with him.

She kept her face two inches from his as she worked.

She was shorter, and he felt her breath on his chin. She inclined her head and her hair tickled his cheek and he didn't brush it away. Yet his incorrigible British superego was burdened by the impropriety, and he effected some half-hearted resistance.

'If that's all it takes then I can do it myself,' he said.

'No, I'm sure you're useless, Jim.' She made a show of fussing. 'Here, let me get to your neck properly.'

She undid two of his shirt buttons, and felt inside with her hand, turning her face up again to his, now just an inch away.

Invisible bolts of texture filled the gap between their bodies and the feel was ripe for more, though she knew this readiness could slip away in an instant. They would shy away from the dappled verge of bodily entwinement, and he would go back to his business. Her hands, which were trembling now, would steady, and she would return to her desk, a wounded nymph concealed in office garb. Or perhaps, just possibly, they would seize, captivate and harness this passing heat; or maybe it would captivate them, hold them long enough and fully enough to burn off their inhibitions, then carry them away, taking them where it would take them.

So she paused, waiting, her heart beating so loudly in her ears it frightened her.

Surely, he thought, this was an invitation, her eyes sparkling and her mouth an inch from his, very slightly parted. But he wished she would make it more clear, less ambiguous.

Meanwhile she wondered how much clearer she could be, worried he would not respond and that this would indicate disinterest. She would be humiliated and silently disappointed, but of course with a brave face and professional cheer, and no tears. She was a big girl.

Yes, perhaps this was a great mistake. Her hormones had got the better of her good sense and she ought to pull away, pretend she had never offered herself. Perhaps he was too thick to notice.

But no, he had. He was perceptive, clever, witty; partly why she wanted him, why her body required him. Surely he'd not thought this the ordinary behaviour of a receptionist. Or had he?, she wondered fleetingly with incredulity.

But no, he hadn't. And all the uncertainty was quashed as he moved his head only a fraction and his lips and her lips were magnets, drawn together in spite of any hesitation by their owners. It lasted just an instant, and he stepped away from the door, his pale bared chest against her tightly bloused breasts, and pushed her gently to the tiled wall. It was cold on her back and a thrill went through her at being pinned between two firmnesses, one stony cold and one muscled warm and attending to her. She was kissing him actively, with earnest application, and it kept him breathless. Their heads, joined at the mouths, their lips and tongues jousting for dominance, his hands on her hips, and hers on his chest, feeling with her cool palms his warm beating heart. He was further unbuttoned.

He stole a glance at his watch.

He had just ten minutes, but then so did she.

Of all days.

*

And of all things. Naveen in his earlier daydreams had never contemplated himself in flight on his own ship, his own home. Desperate times, he told himself, and continued his (redundant) efforts to evade the Chief Officer. He did not know of the latter's engagement with the Second Officer out on deck.

He waded through the disorder when it was at its height, books flying through the air and men shouting at each other. Only one thing was certain on the boat, he reckoned, and it was that the Captain would be on the bridge, guarding his command.

Desperate measures could be forgiven in such desperate times.

The locks were not real locks on the ship. They bolted out intruders, but not persistent ones, and were designed to allow access in emergencies. Mainly they were intended to confound stowaways or slow the progress of pirates, and the officers all knew how to force them open in case of trouble.

He used two thumbnails to slide the catch-pin outwards, aligned it with the thread inside the mechanism, unscrewed the part that remained inside, clockwise to confuse, and eventually the latch slid free. He glanced both ways to ensure his entrance would be unseen, and then stepped forward, trespassing under the lintel of the Captain's doorway.

The Company furnished its captains with a handgun each and a small stock of gold sovereigns. These were reserved strictly for emergency use, and it was expected that most captains would never have to resort to either resource throughout their entire careers at sea.

Naveen had no desire to bear a lethal weapon, which he did not know how to use anyway. But he did want some gold. It was just a feeling he had, something premonitory in the back of his psyche suggesting to him that he might need it. The restlessness on board was unsettling, and he convinced himself he would feel safer if he possessed the means to buy himself out of a compromising situation, a confrontation with the crew, perhaps. Or perhaps buy *all* the officers their freedom should there be a seamen's mutiny. Surely he would regain their esteem and confidence if he pulled off such a feat, demonstrating the foresight to have taken out the gold version of a collective health and safety insurance plan.

He did not recognise that conduct informed by such alarmist calculations was unwarranted in the face of the mild disorder on display in the halls. This was because he was ill equipped to ascertain the degree of its severity.

The working men of the ship wanted job stability and pay. None of them was about to spur a revolt. They enjoyed the chance to argue ship politics and welcomed the excuse to behave freely for a short while, opportunities provided them by all the recent fooling about of the senior officers over the intercom. The crew knew the instability would not last, and simply wanted to get the most out of the confusion while they could, then settle back into their routines once they were out of the war zone and all was calm again.

The life of an able-bodied seaman on a freighter is monotonous and lonely and gives rise to an odd, melancholic sort of accumulated energy that vents itself in bars and brothels when the men are in port, or in random displays of mischief when pent up too long in the boat, especially should an unusual development arise such as this, distracting the disciplinary attention of their superiors.

Nor was the situation outside the ship of great concern to them. Most had witnessed major political strife in a more direct and traumatising form than they were seeing now. Those who were from Punjab had lived the sectarian massacres in 1947.

War a few miles away as they sailed through the Suez? They had seen violence and death in their *homes*, in their ditches, in their railway stations. This was not remotely as awful. Frightening when they heard the distant rumble of battle, to be sure, but it did not instil the bloody terror, the hellish insanity, of mob brutality in the streets, of the cries of children whose families had been bludgeoned to death before their eyes at the hands of their neighbours while they cowered under a scrap of metal on the street.

The impersonality of armoured vehicles and the deserted, cold fear of warplanes and bombs streaking silver from the sky did not compare with the heart-stopping glint of murder and blood vengeance in the reddened eyes of a man with a knife on your doorstep. Nothing would ever approach the sheer wrenching horror of learning that your sister impaled herself to avoid being raped. And the crewmen couldn't care less about the risk of damage to the ship from stray ordnance, so long as they weren't hurt. Only the officers had to answer for such things.

But Naveen lacked the exposure to their sea life, lacked familiarity with the men themselves, which he would have required in order to perceive that they posed no grave threat to order. So he shut the cabin door behind him and made for the Captain's safe.

He had learned from his friend who studied in the technology institute in Calcutta that safes of any reputable brand had their locks set to standard combinations by the manufacturers, usually 100-50-100, and were meant to be changed by the owners upon purchase. Many owners, probably out of laxity, never reset the combinations when they bought the safes, relying solely on the deterrent effect upon the mind of any would-be thief of the forbidding metal box with a large dial of many numbers. Or perhaps some thought that 100-50-100 was a combination unique to their own safes. Whatever the case, a young man in India with any sense of mischief at all does not forget such a pearl of wisdom. Now was Naveen's opportunity to put it to good use, and he rotated the dial accordingly.

As he manipulated it with his fingers, they approached the El-Firdan bridge.

Azim and the men had been encamped several days at the western end of the bridge, where it had taken them only one morning to work out the most promising method of despatching it into the Canal.

Afterwards they waited, and snacked, and napped, and drew water from the Canal in a pail to wash themselves, and dripped sweat in the sun off their mudwater-rinsed skin, and yawned, and reclined in the fullness of boredom. There was not even the tension and stretched mood of waiting a long while for a looming battle. But this was no cause to complain. They were glad to be out of the action and with the benefit of a patriotic justification for their absence from the zones of carnage, even if it was information they could not share. They were enjoying a vacation from death, and thus did not really regret the delay and uncertainty of sitting on rocks and staring at the water.

Things were very still. The last two days there had not even been any passing ships for them to observe. Lieutenant Hamid informed them that the convoys had been suspended.

'It is a punishment to the West.'

'Then why would we still have to blow up the bridge?'

'Why do you think?'

'Is it to stop the Israelis from taking vehicles across?'

'Ha! No. The Israelis have been obliterated. They have been slaughtered like sheep in the Sinai, and our forces are progressing towards Tel Aviv.'

'Then what is the purpose? Why do we stay at the bridge?'

'So that we are ready to destroy it immediately if the order is given. Because it is also a punishment to the West.'

So they waited. Even had they wanted to act, their fear of the terse and enigmatic Lieutenant Hamid would have held them back from any rash movements. He had by now found an occasion to threaten each one personally with execution, always with a quiet and frightening geniality. His threats were matter of fact and almost friendly.

'If you speak of this, you will probably die.' An emotionless prediction, but spoken directly into the eyes, delivered with a steady frozen gaze, and then, as though the words had not been uttered, he would continue the conversation in an ordinary tone.

He hinted at a vast knowledge of methods of torture, and suggested he knew people who would be more than pleased to have test subjects for their freshly learned interrogation techniques. Never mind that there was no cause to interrogate them. They would be fodder for experimental new procedures, useful human samples.

At other times he was unreservedly warm, fraternal and charming, resting his arm on someone's shoulder, laughing together with the group, confiding a sexual anecdote. They feared him and respected him and at times even loved him. It was a gift he had with people. The gift of persuasion, they once told him. It had been well honed by careful instruction at a secret foreign training centre.

Now, abruptly, he ordered them all to get ready. He must have received some signal, though they did not know by what medium. They had been authorised, he said; commanded, in fact; to proceed with the demolition.

Azim set about laying charges in eleven locations on, under and about the structure with the help of one of the privates.

Under the direction of Azim's acquaintance from engineering college, the others lay out the wire, affixing it to both sides of the bridge. The leper had already prepared the fuses and fastened them to the charges which Azim was deploying. It needed to be a controlled series of explosions, and the sequence would have to be just right, otherwise some of the blasts could be wasted and portions of the bridge not collapse precisely as intended. The meticulous preparation of appropriate fuses had therefore been crucial.

As the men laboured, Lieutenant Hamid watched their rapid progress with one hand in his pocket, a cigarette burning slowly in the other. Anyone looking carefully would have noticed that he never actually put it to his mouth. It was just another part of his act, having a stub of something burning in his fingers, issuing up mean columns of dry, merciless wisp. A costume fixture.

Then, when they were finished their work, when the bridge had been strung up and made ready for its appointment with oblivion, the men stood in the middle and leaned over the edge on the south side, their heels resting on the outer rail of the train track, brazenly confident that no accidental spark would cause them to be torn to pieces along with the bridge. *They* were the fusemasters. They and not a maverick spark would complete the task. And if they pleased, and they did, they would pay a final silent tribute to the benevolent sturdiness of the concrete construction. A tribute of closeness and touch, one final gesture of reliance on its support.

As they readied to leave its surface for the last time, Azim spotted the distant outline of a ship sailing north in their direction.

*

He'd had astonishing love with Penny, unconcealed hate from the beer exporters, lunch and fine wine with Selling and the tea merchant, and now they were in the back of a cab, he and that wealthy client, rushing round turns and cutting off buses in a dash through early afternoon traffic as they escaped the square mile and headed vaguely west.

The client was silent most of the way. Roper had tried some small talk but found it led nowhere.

The man pulled some files out of his briefcase and engrossed himself in them studiously.

So Roper had a few minutes to reflect.

He thought about the episode with Penny, which only came to him as dark flashes. A confused slide show, it was not a seamless chronology but a rapid whirl of motions. Kissing and shoving and pressing of skin and the clatter of his belt on the floor. It was roughness applied hastily, and it had been satisfying. Or had it? Surprising, maybe, and exciting, but now he wasn't sure it had been what he wanted.

What *did* he want?

They careened perilously close to a bus as lanes merged but his mind was elsewhere and he didn't blink.

He became sure he wanted something more. Perhaps just more of the same, which he knew would in the long run become impossible.

He felt tired suddenly and rested his head against the window.

*

Azim rushed off the bridge to find Lieutenant Hamid.

141

'There is a boat coming, Lieutenant. What shall we do?'

'What kind of boat?'

They went to find a set of field glasses, and discerned that it appeared to be a commercial freighter.

'I don't care what you do. We were not told of any traffic on the Canal. If there is a mistake it will be somebody else's responsibility. If you like, let it through before you blow up the bridge. Maybe it will be better if it is out of our sight. It is not our problem.'

Azim nodded and set off to inform the others, but stopped when Lieutenant Hamid called after him.

'Or trap them if you prefer, Azim. Maybe it will give you satisfaction.'

Yesterday he was Husseini, today Azim.

'I don't even care if you blow it up the moment they pass under the bridge. Crash it on their heads.' He was yelling now, stirred by some rage. 'It will send a strong message to the West!'

Then his voice reverted abruptly to its usual dismissive tone, lacking emotion.

'The choice is yours. Do as you please with them.' Words spat out with carelessness and disdain, as though he suddenly considered their whole mission a waste of time.

So Azim decided for himself what they would do, and told the others of his decision as though it were Lieutenant Hamid's own.

As they were making their final preparations, Lieutenant Hamid informed them he would not be staying.

'Now I drive up the road and watch your explosion from a distance to be sure it works. When it is done, I will drive away, and you will forget you ever met me. If you do not forget, maybe one morning you would wake up to find your ears being sawed off. Maybe your balls will be crushed. I don't know. Maybe your son will be hit by a bus. It would be tragic. It is out of my control, and in your hands only. Some of my colleagues are very powerful and very brutal, and I am not able to hold them back if you make mistakes.'

Then, as an afterthought, 'when you are done this you may leave also. Find your own ways home. May God reward you.'

He stepped into his Mercedes and without a smile, a wave or even a backwards look, he drove slowly away, gravel crunching under his tyres and exhaust spouting back at the men.

*

The dull charcoal taxi passed through the stone gateposts to a private road and pulled up at the kerb opposite the embassy. The driver did not get out of his seat to open any doors, so the two passengers alighted on their own strength, and Roper paid the massive fare through the window. The sum would eventually make its way onto the client's bill in some unobtrusive guise.

The sun of the morning was now obscured by puffy clouds with dark undersides, and a brisk wind blew their hair out of place and chilled the skin on their necks as they opened the metal gate and walked up the stone path to the building, which would have been a house of impressive stature somewhere else, but was dwarfed in this neighbourhood by white mansions all around. The flagpole over the main entrance was bare, though the plate at the door said 'Embassy of Israel'.

Roper pulled and pushed the ringer, but it only made a mild thud inside its socket, and gave no impression of triggering any bells inside. So he waited a few seconds and then followed up with a knock. They must have stood there in awkward silent anticipation at least a minute before the client spoke up.

'Not much of a welcome. I thought we had an appointment.'

The thinly concealed impatience in the client's voice communicated more than the bare words. Not much of a welcome. I'm degrading myself already, spinning about town with a novice lawyer in a taxi, dirtying my suit on soiled vinyl seats and soaking up central London pollution when I could be overseeing large shipments from the warehouse office, or romancing a promising new purchaser in Dublin, or bargaining for a better arrangement with the advertising firm. I'm standing here as a reluctant indulgence towards Selling, a man becoming greasier and more irritating by the week. The very least you lot could have done was ensure this ludicrous affair ran smoothly and not cause more aggravation than it already has by its mere existence.

City solicitors are such halfwits. Most think they know a thing or two about conducting big business, that they navigate the ins and outs of finance with skill and panache, but really they're

143

hopelessly amateur. If only somebody would tell them to stop pretending they had commercial sense and start concentrating on finding clever legal solutions to facilitate the operations of real businessmen, for instance the seamless expansion of one's own enterprise. That does *not* include standing like a banging fool on a doorstep, knocking our foreheads pointlessly against a shut door that won't open. Probably the Israelis are having a siesta. Or maybe they've all flown back to the Middle East to take up guns against the Egyptians. Or against my tea shipment.

He did not like to admit to himself how much was really at stake in this particular cargo. Even if there were an insurance payout it would not cover the cost of business that would certainly be lost on account of his diminished credibility as a reliable merchant. He had made unreserved guarantees to a couple of promising new customers, and their budding relationships were sure to be sabotaged should this shipment not arrive at least vaguely on time.

He began physically to sense the urgency of this concern and it was an itch in his legs and he had to begin walking. He turned away from the embassy and paced down the path to the street.

Roper strode after him, embarrassed and worried for the success of their exploit. What would he tell Selling if it went wrong?

'Let me ask the gatekeeper,' he called after the client.

He half-jogged to the entrance of the private road, cutting across an unfenced lawn, and approached the uniformed man in the gatehouse.

'Excuse me; we have an appointment at the Israeli embassy but we've knocked and there doesn't seem to be anyone about.'

The gatekeeper chuckled.

'They don't use the front entrance to let in visitors. Unless you're the Queen.'

He smiled, baring tobacco-blackened teeth, then suddenly lost himself in an exaggerated fit of raspy coughing, and Roper inched back from him very subtly, ever polite.

Finally, the evil vapours evidently expelled from his lungs for an interval, he leaned over to Roper and lowered his voice to a confiding whisper.

'Try the side entrance, mate.'

Roper thanked the gatekeeper as the latter began laughing again, and escaped just as this cacophonous performance threatened to merge into a prolonged, deathly wheeze.

The client appeared to be at the end of his tether. He was pacing restlessly back and forth on the pavement and looked as though he was trying to decide whether to leave, or if it was worth his while to remain the extra seconds it would take to give Roper a piece of his mind, and then leave.

Roper pre-empted hastily to avert either disaster by leading the client authoritatively to the side entrance, with an assurance that they would find someone this time, and saying he was dreadfully sorry for not working out this slight logistical complication beforehand.

'Suppose I ought to have read up on the entrance habits of *homo sapiens Israeliens.*'

His weak attempt at levity was not received by an appreciative audience. The client pointedly avoided giving any acknowledgment.

The door opened.

'Ah, hello, I'm James Roper from Crossley & Broke, and this is our client. We have an appointment.'

The young man looked at them doubtfully. 'An appointment? The consular section is closed.'

'Ah, no, ah, it's actually with your Trade Representative. He's a friend of Isadore Pinsky, at our firm.'

'The Trade Representative?'

'Yes.'

'Just a minute.'

They stood there for five, and the wind began scattering raindrops onto them. The door had been shut in their faces and they were at the mercy of the elements as the weather grew steadily more miserable.

Suddenly it reopened and the young man ushered them in.

'Sorry to keep you waiting. Can I see your passports, please?'

The client had known from prior experience at various embassies to bring his along, but Roper, after making a show of fumbling through his pockets in a huff, had to admit that, well, actually, he didn't think he'd brought his, and was it really strictly necessary? They were welcome to telephone his firm for confirmation of his identity.

The client exhaled through his nose in amusement.

'Just a minute.'

They were left in the antechamber with one smallish couch and closed doors barring their way in all four directions.

After a couple of minutes, the man returned, and said, mysteriously, 'it is alright. Please follow me.'

They were led down a corridor and into what looked like a small boardroom, but without any of the usual trimmings. No paintings and no chandelier, and the table had metal legs. And there were no windows. Just a dual-bulb overhead fixture above without a shade.

'Please wait here.'

What else would we do?

So they sat down and stared at the table, and every few seconds the client made a show of drawing back his jacket sleeve to look at his watch. After no more than two minutes, he rose to his feet abruptly.

'I've had it. Who do these clowns think I am? I have far more useful things to do than sit on my backside being kept waiting by some hooknoses.'

He picked up his briefcase and made to walk out.

'God save us,' he muttered, 'from the perils of leaving them to attempt affairs of state.'

Roper stood up, alarmed, and the client looked at him over his shoulder as he placed his hand on the doorknob.

'This outing was a royal waste of time, and you can tell that to Selling.'

In fact, it had worked out perfectly for him. He didn't want to be here in the first place, but felt some gentlemanly obligation towards Selling, with whom he had close ties in the 'old boy' network. Had he stormed out any earlier, he would have appeared unreasonable. But now any observer would agree that he had been put out unconscionably and that the inconvenience was the responsibility of Crossley & Broke. He would see to it the story was spread, and the other firms would now begin queuing up for his custom. A businessman of his stature had a character reputation to maintain in the City. He had to cultivate and project the aura of a valuable client, and not be seen shuffling between firms disloyally. That was how he ensured for himself the highest standard of service. This was his long-awaited safe excuse to switch firms.

Roper struggled for the appropriate response.

'Well, I'm sorry it hasn't worked out. If you must leave... well, of course you know best. I, er, of course I'll stay and wait for the Representative and try and discover what information I can. Of course we'll pass on to you anything of note straightaway.'

The client left, and Roper sat back down, feeling light-headed.

*

The ship was now fast approaching the El-Firdan bridge, where Azim and his companions were making their final preparations and Lieutenant Hamid was rolling away down the Canal road to establish anonymous distance between himself and the impending blasts.

This was still unknown to Naveen, who was sweating with anxious haste in the Captain's cabin, caught up with the safe and concerned to get the gold and leave before he was discovered.

He was disappointed to find the Captain had used more prudence with the combination than he had hoped. There was no sound of tumblers magically falling free inside the lock, and it did not release when he tried the presumed numbers of the factory setting.

Quit and leave while he was still undetected? Not yet. He felt too much self-appointed responsibility to accomplish this task he had conceived for himself. So he resorted to looking for a record of the combination. If it's not a birthday or something similarly familiar, then it's written down somewhere. Everyone writes it down, his friend had told him. Everyone. Such little faith we put in our own memories when it comes to arbitrary strings of numbers, even very short ones, if they happen to be the keys to important things like treasure.

He rummaged through the drawers of the Captain's desk, trying, he was not sure why, to leave everything just as he found it. He came across a spiral-bound notebook of names and addresses entered on lined pages in blue ballpoint with pen strokes that were just slightly too rounded and fluid to be described as decisive. Instantly recognisable as the Captain's own handwriting. He flipped through the book's coarse greyish pages, blemished with unevenly distributed flecks of brown fibre, and sure enough, at the last one, inhabiting the bottom left corner in isolation, were the numbers 246102. They spoke volubly to Naveen and he rushed back to the safe with excitement.

He tried 24-61-2. No luck.

He fumbled through various other permutations, his fingers becoming slippery with cold sweat, until, entering 42-16-20, the safe door clicked open.

The view inside was not spectacular. A wooden box with 'Enfield' printed in black on the side, presumably containing the gun, a stack of passports (entrusted to the Captain under Company rules by every officer and crewman) tied together with a string, and a small purple felt bag, which he reached for and opened by loosening its yellow drawstring. It contained a paltry ten gold sovereigns. Nothing compared to the fabled gold-stuffed chests on the merchant ships of yore.

He pocketed seven of the coins and left three in the bag in the safe, and shut it with a click. Spread around the risk. As an afterthought he opened the safe again and extracted his passport. He would feel easier in these conditions carrying it on his person.

Quickly he exited the room after having a deck about to make sure evidence of his intrusion was minimal.

If his plan was for the benefit of the officers and ship, why was he worried about it being detected? Because it had been executed solely on his own initiative and without authorisation from above, an abnegation of the hierarchy. But the chain of command had been shaken, its links unclasped and refastened. Surely its integrity had been injured and its moral authority diminished. Sufficiently to justify so brazenly independent a feat as Naveen, an inexperienced cadet, had just performed?

The answer is arguable, and we lack enough information to judge definitively. But if it is 'yes', then maybe his act was attended by trepidation not because it was wrong for him to have committed it (when did doing something wrong ever instil much trepidation in the ordinary person purely because it was wrong?), but because it would if discovered invite retaliatory or exemplary punishment by those who pretended to the highest offices on the ship, regardless of their moral claim to those positions. How else to repave cracked authority than by fear?

Or perhaps it was just a matter of habit for Naveen. His minor acts of disobedience had until now been surreptitious so that he could keep his neck out of trouble and preserve his future career. Visiting the Chief Officer and witnessing him in his fallen state instead of checking the tea chests as ordered may have contributed to the achievement of just the opposite. His practice of selective disobedience had backfired from an instance in which he probably *was* doing the morally right thing in disobeying. An irony. In any case, now that he was (he thought) in trouble, and his reason for stealth was evaporated, he had already been well habituated to tiptoeing his way through the tunnels of insubordination. Now seemed no time for any experimental new boldness.

Seemed.

*

Meanwhile the curtains of destiny were fast closing on the present incarnation of the El-Firdan bridge. Earlier editions, bridges carrying the same name, had been destroyed at the site before, once under uncertain circumstances at the end of the Great War, and once during the conflagration that blazed around Israel's declaration of independence.

Eleven years after Azim saw it to its third death, it would be obliterated yet again. And decades on, in a vastly altered global power dynamic, it would be rebuilt with high technology and financial assistance from the Japanese.

Today it was in the hands of Lieutenant Hamid's band of demolition men, plucked from their ordinary routines and styled as engineers of mayhem by the security apparatus of the Colonel's brazenly defiant regime. Now, uncoiling the two hundred feet of wire which was the link between their fingertips and the fate of the bridge, they backed away, a retreat of fear and respect, from the terminally charged structure. They had situated the explosives to prevent (they hoped) any serious chunks of debris flying in their direction. Still, they preferred the dubious protection of huddling behind a family of palm trees at one of the isolated green patches on the otherwise arid west bank of the Suez.

The verdant lushness of the Nile delta does not extend fully to the Canal. God coated the famous river valley with a wide paintstroke of humid green, but only a few wayward drops sprayed from his brush to bless the zone of the manmade waterway, an area once home to the mysterious Hyksos, with subtropical abundance. And all those splattered green blots by the Canal, textured with vertically oriented tufts of stiff-backed halfa grass and swaying with proudly benevolent date palms, had settled only on the west side of the Suez. The largest of them is concentrated at the nearby city of Ismailia, though smaller patches are spread and scattered elsewhere, all along the Canal between the town of Suez and the Mediterranean Sea.

The east bank, however, the beginning of the Sinai wilderness, is sand and stone, with only the odd lonely shrub. Here a rock, a jagged mountain, a slinking desert fox, there a burning bush.

The detonator box rested in the hands of the leper. It had a T-shaped handle on the top that was to be pushed downwards, the way they set off dynamite in Westerns.

Now the long body of the boat floated before them. The *Majesty*'s name printed on the bow was legible from their position. The front of the ship loomed as it passed, then the middle, then the end, a stretched out display of welded steel, the mark of twentieth-century heavy industry on the face of yielding waters. Progress along an artificial incision in the sand which bridged oceans.

A man stood alone on the deck, a small dark silhouette up above, and the flag flapped gently in the imperceptible breeze of the ship's languorous advance. Another figure could be seen slowly descending a staircase.

The ship came to the bridge and they let it pass under. Once the stern was visibly clear of the structure by at least fifty yards, Azim nodded at the leper. Bring it down.

But the poor man could do nothing.

'What is wrong? Push the handle down.'

'I cannot.'

He inclined his ugly head sadly.

'You cannot?'

'I cannot destroy the bridge. It is like tearing off a limb of Egypt. It is the technical pride of my very own teachers. No, I cannot.'

Azim looked to the other men. One by one, as he made eye contact with each, they shook their heads.

God help them. He was hunched behind a tree with a group of forlorn soldiers with downcast eyes, putting on despondent airs. Hamid would kill them.

'Move out of the way.'

He took hold of the control box as the leper stepped aside. The handles were melted into the grip of his fists.

A lone sandpiper dipped and coasted over the bridge, blissfully senseless of the perturbation that was seconds away.

In Azim's mind the instant future had already happened. He saw the big concrete slabs and their myriads of little stone chip children projected skywards in a magnificent thundering burst of fire and ash and smoke. The vision made him dizzy and he looked at the ground. Then looked up again, and the bridge was yet whole, though it shimmered behind the distortion of heatwaves.

The air was still and hot and soundless.

Then he closed his eyes and pushed down the handles.

Azim's moment.

They felt the sky fall on them and their ears rang with softness, but they could stand. *They* were yet whole. The bridge was not. A series of rapid shockwaves were released as the air around the explosives was compressed to the order of ten pounds per square inch in the space of a second. The smoke was minimal, but the water had been mightily disturbed. An empty space breathed at them where the bridge had stood, but when the men looked hard they could still trace in their minds its invisible outline.

Azim, feeling like a statue of heartless rock, gazed at the ship he had spared. As the dust was just settling he could have sworn he saw a human body plummeting from its deck into the shaky waters below.

*

Armed with some gold, his passport, and his inflated instinct for self-preservation, Naveen set out down the halls once again, unsure what to expect of the Chief Officer. Had enough time now elapsed for his fury to have dissipated? Naveen remained on edge, his readiness and responsiveness heightened, his flesh aprickle. He made his way outside.

151

Staircases and platforms hugged the lower white tower which rose above the main deck and contained the collection of upper decks where the officers and crew lived and ate, and which was topped off by the bridge, the command and navigation centre of the ship. It was on one of these outside stages that the Chief Officer recently served his regretted blow upon the Second Officer, some three levels above the main deck where Naveen now wandered.

The Chief Officer was unsure what to do with his unconscious colleague. He hadn't meant to strike him. He hadn't meant to strike anyone. It was just a reflex action, and he was reassured to hear the man breathing, a high-pitched whistle emanating from his nose, and to detect a pulse in his neck.

There had been no witnesses, and he began thinking of a story to justify the incident, but had difficulty conceiving a reason that was both vindicatory and plausible for his punch. Perhaps if he simply quit the scene he could pretend he had no knowledge of the Second Officer's injury. But it soon occurred to him with a wave of alarm that the Second Officer himself knew what transpired, and would inform the others when he awoke. Damning testimony could mean the end of his days at sea. He might even face a trial in India. Striking a crewman for insubordination was winked at, but never another officer. He was ashamed that for an instant he entertained the thought of dropping the unconscious man overboard. Or of giving him a second good wallop to the head.

He loathed himself for those thoughts, and sunk into a deep, depressive self-hatred, until his mind wandered to what few facts he knew about amnesia, and he consoled himself by the possibility that the Second Officer would not remember the encounter.

Looking forward, he saw a bridge growing large ahead of them, and was instantly certain with no rational cause that it would in a minute fall on his head as punishment for his misdeeds. He was seized terribly by the impulse to descend, to distance himself from the underside of the bridge before they passed beneath it, to spirit himself away from the accusing body of the second officer lying prone on the metal floor. If the structure were to come crashing down on them he did not want to be high up on the ship, one of the first to be crushed. If he went below he could cower in one of the cargo holds among the tea chests. The Second Officer would remain above. Maybe his injury could be explained away if he were a casualty of a falling bridge.

But nothing of the bridge fell upon the *Majesty* save its shadow.

The Chief Officer, descending the external staircase, unaware he was holding his breath, exhaled with relief from the bottom of his big belly when his section of the ship drifted clear of the overpass. Maybe God in his mercy had forgiven him that day his trespasses.

But when a mind is afflicted with persistent anxiety, its occasional spots of relief are fleeting things. One crisis behind him, his thoughts returned, panicky, to the other problem. The Second Officer had not been disposed of. His cloud of despair was becoming too thick to endure with any dignity, and he felt bereft of his humanity. He thought he no longer wanted to live. It was a death ship they were on anyway. They were enduring a floating purgatory here, and it was taking too long. They should have been in the Mediterranean, the precious celestium, by now, but he had the idea they were to be suspended in this in-between place for an eternity longer.

He felt cosmologically responsible for the sluggish torment of their predicament. He was not a Jonah to the ship, but rather something far worse. For every sin that was purged from his soul, he was driven promptly to commit another. He was Pharaoh, and the Lord kept hardening his heart. And what happened to Pharaoh? His chariots and his host were cast into the sea. The chosen of his captains were drowned. The depths covered them. They sank like a stone into the waters.

Naveen, meanwhile, had paused to observe with appreciation the bridge they were approaching, a welcome distraction from his worried wandering. He marvelled at the way people could come together in elaborate cooperation to produce works that were of practical benefit to their communities and at the same time wonders to the eye, and there was nothing like a bridge to symbolise the tangible good that could come from civic coordination. Surpassed perhaps in functional elegance only by an aqueduct. He thought about the railways in India, and admitted in his mind that the perfidious British had been good for something.

His rumination was invaded by thumping and he turned up and saw the boots of the Chief Officer percussing down the steps over his head, took a last admiring glance at the bridge, which was now behind them, and moved on, confident his greater sprightliness would safely afford him the brief hesitation.

Then he was spotted and his pursuer picked up his pace of descent.

And so there they were, yards apart, one not knowing what he would do when he reached the cadet, only that he had to close the gap between them and grab the boy and teach him a lesson; the other sure he would be subjected to grievous bodily harm if apprehended. The atmosphere took on unreal serenity. Sounds faded away into some invisible absorbent padding in the sky. Sweat beads dripped in slow motion from the fat man's brow, and the flesh rings of his neck enfolded the dankness of spiritual anguish.

The cadet stopped and pivoted, hit with indecision over which way to turn.

The Chief Officer drew nearer and still he hadn't resumed his flight.

It was a muffled deceleration towards bodily encounter, punctuated only by the resonation of the boots upon the steps, upon the deck, almost at the end, accompanied by the light, indifferent flapping of the flag at the bow.

When the bridge exploded, time accelerated rapidly and the shock ripped the last marble of sanity from the being of the Chief Officer and he howled like a jackal.

Naveen was stunned, his heart racing and his mind disbelieving. Had he really seen and heard what he thought he had? A deposit of blackened cement dust settled at his feet and said yes. Still unbelievable. The wind carried the smell to him and it was sharp and acrid, and irritated his nostrils.

He collected himself in time to realise the rotund man he once knew as 'sir' had reached the deck and was charging at him, his head bent forward, mad as a bull provoked. What he had known somewhere inside since his first days on board but not acknowledged to himself suddenly became clear to him.

He loved the idea of a life at sea, but he hated the life of this particular ship, with its politics and compromised friendships and dubious loyalties and the evidence that the happy, interdependent familiarity between the senior men was more brittle than it first seemed, that it was badly overworn, and had been strained by circumstance to the point of snapping.

What was it he had recently thought? Being on a ship in a sea was being trapped.

The Chief Officer was closing upon him.

Being on *this* ship in a sea was being trapped.

But they were not in a sea.

He stood up on the ledge and looked down at the water. And he was not trapped. Naveen's moment.

He jumped...

Suspended. Old layers of time. In Clare's secret room, time lost its meaning. She no longer was sure if she had been in hiding for hours or days. Maybe she had been there for weeks, and had fallen under temporal delusions encouraged by the falsely soothing cabal of quietness and dimness and stillness acting together to confound her perspective and to coax her ever deeper into the black, deathly comfort of the timeless room, to develop a dependency on its sandwiched isolation inside the neglected subconscious of the house on Melbury Road. Perhaps the place contained in its atmosphere remnants of something that had been on the site many ages before. Perhaps the walls were bathed in the conspiring shadows of ancient spirits. Perhaps the room was a way to transcend the binds of chronological progression, less a stratum in the pile of time than a vapour enstirred in the floating and shifting and sometimes coalescing clouds of existential perpetuity.

...and plunged into the waiting waters with a whack and a splash and a great burning on his skin from the impact. He had never been much of a diver. But he could swim, and as soon as he surfaced, spitting and thrashing, he motored away from the hull of the ship with all the strength he could muster, his arms rotating in fast strokes and his feet kicking rapidly.

The ship was still moving forward, and he did not want to find himself face to face with the giant propeller. He could not trust the Chief Officer to sound the 'man overboard' cry and have them turn the bow in the direction of the side he had leapt from, which was the standard procedure for protecting a body in the water from the cut of the spinning blades. In any case he wanted nothing more to do with the ship.

He reached the shore, and hoisted himself up onto the dry land of the west bank of the Suez Canal. He was standing on Egypt, dripping himself into the beige-orange dust, feeling for the first time since Calcutta the dull sturdy feel of hard ground underfoot. It seemed to him that he was swaying slightly.

He had forced open a new chapter in his life and planted himself on some very foreign soil, leaving behind his livelihood. But it was not a livelihood, it was a craft carrying caged madmen that had to be escaped. Maybe the Company would understand. Maybe not. Now he had to work out what to do. The sole responsibility for his direction was now his.

He saw a group of men by a cluster of palm trees and set off towards them.

*

Now Roper's moment. The door opened and his head reeled and the world tilted and his stomach dropped and he gasped sharply, and tried to conceal it as a tickle in his throat.

His motions on autopilot, he stood up from the seat where he had been waiting, straightened his suit jacket and walked round the table and shook her hand. A minute ago he had been aware of his palms being warm and dry. Now he was regretfully conscious of having made a cold, moist contribution to the handshake. In any case, she received it professionally.

'Jim Roper, Crossley & Broke,' he said, though in the circumstances he probably ought to have allowed her the first word. His voice faltered on the 'o' in Crossley, cracking dryly.

She smiled only a little, but with a devastating intensity he knew in his experience to be incomparable. Just the slightest parting of her naturally red lips at the very middle to display a tantalising crescent sliver of teeth, of pearl bared behind bolts of red velvet. She was unmistakably the woman from his dreams, from the party. The soul behind those dark eyes that were emblazoned in his mind was deeper than anyone's. And now it was just him with just her in a room all alone, a chamber of paradise, where fear and pleasure and awe and excitement were blended in a terrible mix. He smelled for an instant the fragrance of Eden, and sensed also the forbidding whir of the revolving sword.

'My name is Gefen.' She spoke, and her voice was both sharp and soft, incising but warm. 'I think you have met my brother.'

Even were he not already fully dumbfounded, which he was, and climbing up a steep rocky bank from the base of some deep valley of the mind, knocked to the bottom by a sudden gale, blinded by the bright light of another presence and prickled by thorns from the thickets of absolute and unremitting distraction, struggling along a clumsy ascent to reestablish his normal balance of cognition and perception in the rectangular room of two bare bulbs; even were he not undergoing this ordeal, he would not have grasped an inkling of what she meant.

'Shall we have a seat?'

She directed by example, pulling out a chair, and when he just stood there, she gestured with her hand for him to follow suit.

He sat, gradually regaining his stability, and she talked.

'We regret that the Trade Representative is not able to join us. I'm sure you are aware of our engagement with Egyptian military forces. Our senior staff are called away, unpredictably, to attend to related matters. I work closely with the Trade Representative, and have the same knowledge as him, so rest assured you are receiving the same information by speaking with me.'

'Of course. And I must apologise myself. Our client wasn't able to stay for the meeting. I believe he had some urgent business to attend to. He's left me here in his stead.'

With no effort at all, just sitting across and looking at him while he spoke, spiny with confidence but graceful in her pose, she confounded his fluency of thought. Formulating and spitting out his last sentences had been a serious endeavour.

Now she spoke again, and he fought the disjointedness it was causing in his concentration.

'How can I be of assistance?'

Her words were a bite on the nipple.

How can you be of assistance? Let up. Reduce your intensity. Close the tap just a few turns.

157

'Well, actually, I suppose we were wondering about a shipment, actually.'

He saw her raise a bemused eyebrow, but otherwise remain serious.

'Our firm,' he stumbled on, 'that is, Crossley & Broke, we deal in shipments. And our client is affected in the Suez, you see.'

She did begin to see.

'You are concerned about the safety of a shipment through the Suez?' She smiled broadly. 'There are a few things to say to that. Firstly, we pride ourselves on skilled military planning, but even we cannot know how the outcomes will be. I am in a position to assure you that Israel has no territorial ambitions with respect to the Suez.'

Now she must be repeating something they told all the staff in the briefing room, he thought.

'But, that said, we cannot guarantee the safety of the Suez. Our armies may be drawn there without the expectation in the course of the operation. It is the responsibility of Egypt, and the responsibility of the Canal authorities. Israel has entered the Sinai as a reaction to Egyptian hostility, and has no legitimate responsibility for the ships in the Suez. But we would always try our utmost to avoid civilian casualties, including ships.

'Secondly, I am in the position to tell you that none of this matters anyway. You will be able to read in the London newspapers tomorrow that any ships still in the Canal right now will be trapped there for a long time. This is because the Egyptians have sunk at least six of their own ships, in order to block the Canal. This does not have anything to do with Israel. They have chosen to stop the Suez traffic in response to the British and French attacks. I think if your friend has a ship in the Suez, he will have to start making other plans.'

'Yes, well...' He trailed off.

'Do you have any other questions?'

'No.'

But he shifted in his seat, trying to think of a way to buy more time here.

'Then I thank you for...'

'Well, I have a question. What did you mean about your brother?'

She had been sending body signals that she was about to leave, but now she settled again in her chair and relaxed her posture and laughed.

'Of course, you would not know what I'm talking about. But I think at least you remember me. Or am I so forgettable?' Her voice was a blend of sarcasm and accusation and humour.

'I certainly remember you.' Although, at the moment, he fought to recall her name. He had been so lost in the visceral overload of the first seconds of their encounter a few minutes before that he had barely registered her words. But thankfully it sprang to him. Gefen.

'Gefen.'

'Jim.'

'Yes, at the party on Brook Street.'

'My brother was the man you were speaking with.'

Which man? I was speaking only with you at the party. Silent words. Nobody else was important. You communicated with piercing clarity. Everyone else babbled incoherently. Incoherently. Oh, *that* man. The don. Your brother? You look nothing alike. You're olive and he was a freckled redhead. He searched his mind's eye, which kept images photographically for him sometimes. The facial features *were* similar. The same tight, bold positioning of the eyes as though they suspended the nose. Semitic noses, he thought, but not over-pronounced.

'Oh, I see. A fascinating chap.'

'He is a reader in philosophy at King's College, London.'

He nodded, a bright look on his face to express interest. But just as he was beginning to gain some ease with the woman, they were interrupted by a knock at the door, and the young man who had brought him there with the client popped his head in and spoke to the woman in Hebrew.

She got up. 'Please excuse me, Jim. I am needed upstairs. It has been nice to meet you.'

'And you.'

'Shimon will see you to the door. Good luck with your shipment.'

And she was gone.

On the way out, the young man interrupted his thoughts with some information.

'The Ambassador will hold a press conference tomorrow. Gefen must help him prepare the statements.'

Then he was out on the street, standing alone and bewildered, the wind flapping his collar and the leaves rustling strongly overhead. The road seemed deserted of human movement. He walked to the nearby high street to find a taxi, his heels clomping emptily on the pavement.

A streetlamp glowed overhead even thought it was still day, and the gatekeeper smiled seedily at him as he passed.

The Client's Business

STEPS SOUNDED above Clare's head, and they were steps of disturbance. Her father had arrived home that afternoon from his abortive outing with Roper to be met by his weeping wife, and Clare's nanny looking white as a sheet, and the household staff frantic and pacing to and fro and wandering the house, behaving strangely, peeking into the same corners and glancing behind the same doors, over and over and over again.

'Where have you been?' his wife wailed at him hysterically. 'I've been trying to get hold of you all day,' her voice quavered under the pressure of constrained emotion, and then she broke down altogether and rushed at him. 'Why weren't you in the office?' she sputtered and dribbled and grabbed a handful of the skin at the front of his neck and dug into it with her nails.

He grabbed her wrist and twisted her arm around until she felt a wracking pain in her elbow and she screeched.

He slapped her face.

'Collect yourself!'

But she wouldn't. She just sank to the floor in a puddle of tears and sobbed.

He turned to one of the servants, angry.

'Would someone mind telling me what's going on?'

'I'm sorry, sir, but Clare has gone missing.'

Come again? Clare has gone missing. Missing? She's not here, not at school. A stone was catapulted into his chest, knocking away his breath. When he recovered his bearing, he asked, 'since when?'

'Her absence was noticed when she didn't come down for her breakfast.'

'Have the police been called?'

'The lady said we were not to call them without your knowledge; that you had warned her once about the risks... of...' The servant looked down at her feet, now almost whispering. 'The risks of...'

161

'Of what?!' he shouted.

'Of kidnapping, sir.'

He let out a long, slow breath, and reached down to lift his wife from the floor, but she fought him away viciously and he withdrew, leaving her there in a heap. He did not like to demean himself expending fruitless effort on an emotional woman.

'Go back to your normal chores. I'll make some phone calls. Stop scouring the house for traces. We'll leave that to the detectives.'

He entered his study, his steps abnormally restive to Clare's ears below, then sat down to make his phone calls. First he called his criminal solicitor, then, on the lawyer's stern advice, the police.

Of course, the dispatcher said, they would send officers to the house without delay.

He got up and paced some more, unknowingly making a rhythmic auditory connection with his lost daughter, the top of whose head was just three feet below the soles of his feet.

The police arrived within twenty minutes, and took statements, and asked if they might have a walk through the house, and took notes, asking more questions. You're quite sure nobody has contacted you since she disappeared? Only we have to know or we won't be able to do our job. We've already said we're sure. Well, has your daughter behaved unnaturally recently? No. Was it her habit to disappear for short periods? No. Have there been any warnings from the school about slipping performance lately? No. Who would you say spends the most time with her, Mr or Mrs? Neither. Neither? Ah. The nanny. So they started their questions afresh, this time with Nan.

But Nan had noticed nothing strange at all.

After scribbling more notes and making a show of pondering and nodding knowingly to themselves and looking very serious indeed, the officers retired with Clare's father into his study for some whiskey and a private chat.

Just underneath them, Clare hugged the blanket around herself and closed her eyes and heard everything, staying dead still and trying to breathe ever so softly.

'We're going to begin a search of the area immediately, but we imagine you want it kept quiet...'

'It's imperative.'

'Yes, so we'll be sure to keep it at a very low profile. No uniforms, no dogs. We'll start with Kensington, but if we turn up no leads...'

'Yes, I know, you'll have to expand the search perimeter and...'

'...and if we have to do that, it will only be a matter of time before it becomes common knowledge. Then you might think it best to go full out with a newspaper advert, to show you're not shy of publicity.'

'You can leave my publicity decisions to me,' he answered brusquely. 'In any event I trust you'll see to it she's found before I have to make any.'

'We'll be doing our best.' They rose to leave. 'And if you *should* be contacted, we cannot stress how important it is that you let us know before taking any steps.'

He rose after them.

'Goodbye, officers. Someone will show you to the door.'

*

For a deal between two parties to be enforceable in English law as a contract, it must, among other requirements, be evident to the reasonable observer that the bargaining parties were, at the time of its formation, of one mind with respect to the full scope of their rights and obligations under the agreement, including being ad idem as to the allocation between them of the numerous risks associated with the execution of the contract (for example, the risk in a contract to buy a consignment of flowers that they will be ruined by a freak hailstorm before the harvest, or the risk in a contract requiring for its performance the use of telephones that an attack by Martians will wipe out all wire communications).

This union of minds by the bargaining parties gives birth, in forming a valid contract, to a creature that lawyers sometimes refer to as though it has a consciousness of its own. The contract must have 'contemplated' at the time of its formation (expressly or otherwise) the possibility of the occurrence of any given unexpected event that might render impossible or at least impinge heavily upon the performance of one or both of the parties. Otherwise, should such an unexpected event occur, it could suddenly become evident that there never was a contract in the first place. The parties could not have been of one mind vis à vis the allocation of risk, a crucial part of the agreement, if, at the moment they purported to enter into legal relations, neither of them had envisaged the chance of that particular event taking place. If the event was so vastly inconceivable at the time of the supposed agreement that the parties could not reasonably have intended for either of them to bear the risk of it transpiring, and serious enough that it renders any central object of the contract impossible to achieve, the contract is frustrated and the legal effect is that it is rolled back into nothingness. Void ab initio. It never existed. It might have looked like it was a contract, but it was an illusion.

One way for parties contracting by written instrument to demonstrate to each other, to the reasonable observer, to the courts if necessary, which risks of which unexpected but remotely possible events are contemplated and voluntarily borne by one or both or neither of them, is to include a force majeure *clause as a term in the agreement, setting out an exclusionary list of the unlikely events contemplated and declaring in the text precisely their effect on the continuation of the parties' obligations to each other under the agreement.*

It was concerning this type of clause, *force majeure*, that Roper was asked to refresh himself when he arrived at the office the day after his adventure at the Israeli embassy. It seemed, on careful scrutiny of the client's contract with the suppliers in India for the sale and carriage of tea by sea, which the parties had agreed was to be governed by English law in the event of a dispute, that the client might be entitled to relief from his obligation to pay. The relevant phrase in the contractual term was 'due to closure of the Suez Canal'.

Earlier, it had by no means been certain that the client would be protected under the contract. If Calcutta Maritime had instructed their ship to divert on account of hostilities even while the Canal remained open to traffic, the disruption would not have been due to the closure of the Suez Canal and the client might have been forced to make an insurance claim (always a reluctant last resort) for the money lost on account of the delay.

Armed, however, with the knowledge he had gained yesterday from Gefen that the Canal was definitely blocked, and the confirming report from Allied headquarters in Cyprus, published in the morning newspapers today, that there were six Egyptian blockships preventing passage through the Canal in both directions, Roper was able by midday to declare with confidence that the *force majeure* clause would operate in the client's favour *if* the ship was indeed in the Canal. The last word from Calcutta Maritime was that they had lost contact with the vessel and could not confirm absolutely that it was stuck in the waterway, but were assuming that it was unless and until they received contrary information.

Not good enough for the clause to operate.

'Well then bloody find out if they're stuck in there, Roper! And don't go back to the Israelis. You'll be wasting your time. They've been useless.'

Roper had passed on to Selling the small amount of relevant information he gathered at the embassy, but had not yet reported about the client's abrupt and aggrieved departure. And the latter had been too caught up in a family emergency to ring up and complain of his thorough dissatisfaction with the embassy trip.

Roper wondered, if the Israelis were out of bounds, how he would see Gefen again and how he would find out about the fate of the *Majesty*. In that order. His existence had now been irreversibly altered by the woman, he was well beyond the point of no return, and he knew deep inside that he had to connect with her further. It was a question not of whether they would meet again, but of how he would orchestrate it.

As for the boat, perhaps the Egyptians could be of help. But no, they were at war against Egypt. No real chance of finding a credible and obliging Egypt contact in London since diplomatic relations had been severed.

Perhaps, then, the Canal Company would be able to advise him. As far as he knew, they had an office in Paris. But when he rang the number listed in Sarah's address book for the Universal Company of the Suez Maritime Canal, he was told by a young woman at the other end that the Company's Paris operations had been suspended indefinitely. When he rang off and realised belatedly why this was the case, he felt like a complete fool for having tried the Paris office, and hoped Sarah knew less about Suez developments than he. Control of the Company had shifted to Ismailia four months ago, when the Canal was nationalised.

He was also unaware that less than a week ago, the day the bombs fell on Cairo, nearly all the foreign contractors who had chosen to remain and work alongside the Egyptian employees of the newly nationalised Company had been arrested and interned by the Colonel's authorities. Two men, brothers, escaped that unpleasantness. They had the prescience to get into a car and make a dash for Libya just hours before their colleagues were rounded up. They rolled their way across more than a thousand miles of desert and reached Tripoli, free men, the only foreign Suez contractors to avoid two months of captivity under Egyptian guard.

Roper considered himself thwarted. The Canal was Egypt, and Egypt was officially the enemy. There would be no speaking with the Canal people. He walked over to Sarah's desk and leaned wearily against her filing cabinet.

'You alright, Jim?'

He sighed, and smiled half-heartedly. 'Yes, Sarah, fine.'

She let him stand there in his own thoughts as she carried on her work. He hadn't given her much to do the last few days, so she'd been assisting a secretary who sat a few desks over from her and who was presently overburdened by the volume of work generated by her lawyer. Better to help someone else with their work than have none at all. A legal secretary with nothing to do could easily die of boredom at her desk. It was just something about the dry staleness of mood inside law offices that made idleness within them a dreaded curse.

'Do me a favour, Sarah, will you?'

'Course, Jim.'

'Find a good carpet supplier and have him come in for an appointment with me sometime next week. Tell him we're looking to redecorate.'

The Moths

THE DAY dimmed around Clare, a spear of twilight casting itself through the hole in the bricks, and she braced herself against the coming darkness. She resolved not to turn on the torch, to conserve the battery. If she remained here for any length of time she would have to accustom herself to manoeuvring without illumination.

She would have to be brave.

The room had not felt truly sinister until now. She concealed her whole body under the blanket, hiding her head to avoid exposure to nifts, the invisible floating beasties that hovered in her room over her bed on blacker nights. They hummed a low vibration and disturbed the air with their fleshy wings, and though she could never see them, she had no doubt they were scrutinising her with foul jealous eyeballs, poisoning her slumber with their bad hopes, brushing her face with their fetid breeze, desiring her suffocation. In her bedroom it was an escape to bury her head beneath the duvet. They couldn't get to her under there, because their sneakish thoughts got deflected off the surface of her cover.

But in this place she felt uneasy not being able to look around. She would glance about for shifting shadows before shrinking beneath her blanket, and no sooner would she slide under its supposed protection than she was washed in a wave of vulnerable fear, mizzled with gooseflesh, obsessed with the suspicion that one of the shadows was slinking towards her in her blindness. Every time she hid her eyes she revealed them again in a hasty flash only seconds later, to peer and be reassured that she was not encircled by nasty hobgoblins, that no devious lurker was towering over her with raised hand, and that she was not beset by demonic inhabitants of the underworld come to claim some nightly entitlement. Perhaps an allotment of one child's soul to be sucked from a dusty little dark space, this in-between stage she was inhabiting that was a portal between the land of the living and the misty, seething domain of the ghosts, where a person shouts forward in terror, and the distorted screeching echo of what was once her voice is flung back at her from behind, to wrap around her brain in clenching, strangling torment.

Somehow she blinked herself asleep, too tired to carry on battling the phantoms generated by her own edgy nerves. But her consciousness was trapped within the four walls of her hideaway and would not be carried elsewhere.

In her dreams the old candle burned on the tabletop.

She floated about the room, bouncing gently off the walls and drifting into corners, sweeping the carpet with her toes, always mindful to avoid the closet door, behind which she knew there was a heaving vortex that would suck her violently into a realm of swirling evil if she went near enough.

She allied herself with the moths, which were not dead after all. They chittered and hopped and swarmed together in a flittering jumbled dance, and landed on her shoulders and on her face and on her eyes. One tried to wriggle its way inside her mouth and she pulled it away by its wings and they popped off, and she bit down on its flaky little body and she knew she had done something very, very wrong. The moths at that instant gathered themselves away from her in a handkerchief-pointed cloud and spread out into a buzzing sheet, facing her in opposition, then slowly closed in so she had to step backwards. And backwards and backwards until she could feel the suck of the closet door and she tried running away but her limbs were leaden, stuck in thick molasses and unable to locomote. She could not get forward and a silent scream ripped through her head and she awoke with pins and needles, and all was very still and deathly quiet.

The house was now in a fitful sleep, and it was her chance to wander about. She crept out of the room to empty the pot and replenish her supplies, making sure not to leave any obvious traces.

When she returned to her sequestration, she felt much emboldened by the excursion and no longer afraid of demons. The room began to feel like it was home.

Pretending

ROPER spent his weekend mainly wandering the streets in the vicinity of the Israeli embassy, sitting on park benches scouring newspapers for the latest on Israel, and not eating very much. He had not felt such spiritive mobilisation since he was sixteen and smitten with the vicar's daughter. Back then, he'd spent the entire summer volunteering to assist with church events, from laying out tablecloths at charity lunches to tacking up concert posters. Anything so she would notice.

It did cross his mind as he walked past the embassy road and glanced at Gefen's building in the distance that he was behaving like an obsessive schoolboy, and that now he was in his twenties such conduct might more readily be condemned as unseemly prowling, sinister and by no means a way to gain any positive recognition. But he brushed the thought aside. Nobody would know. And *he* knew he was not a menace.

First thing on Monday morning he made himself another appointment with the Israeli Trade Representative's assistant.

'She was very helpful last Thursday,' he told the accented voice on the phone, 'and my firm would be most grateful if she could spare another few minutes for a meeting today.'

'Today? She is very busy. It will not be possible.'

'Just a quarter of an hour.'

'I'm sorry. It is not possible.'

'I see. Well, what about tomorrow?'

There was a long pause, and Roper lost himself in the irregular crackling of the telephone connection, then started to fear they had cut him off.

'Hullo?'

There was no response, but he heard incoherent voices in the background, reassuring him he was still connected. Then he heard rustling and breathing in the other person's handset.

'Hullo?' he asked again.

'Yes.' Pause. 'Crossley & Broke?'

'Yes, hullo, that's right.'

'She will meet you for fifteen minutes today...' more voices in the background, discussing. 'If you are available at five o'clock?'

'Yes, I am.'

'She is very busy, but she will meet you.'

'Oh, that's splendid. I promise I shan't waste her time. Thank you *very* much.'

'You're welcome.'

*

He straightened his tie and waited for an answer at the door. She opened it herself, and stood facing him, looking quite tired and quite serious and causing him by her stance to fear he was making a mistake. She really did have important work to do, and here he was waltzing in like a joker, putting on a play and jeopardising his firm's reputation with this charade, just so he could soak up the emotional nourishment of her presence.

But quickly she cast off her unwelcoming bodily expression and smiled warmly and ushered him in. He had brought his passport this time, but now no one asked to see it.

'You are back so soon.'

The fatigue in her voice somehow made her all the more wonderful. He wanted to see her into bed and cover her with a soft quilt and watch her sleep, to worship the rise and fall of her breath and to learn how she looked with her eyes closed and to arrange her hair on a pillow and inhale the air that she exhaled. He would stay awake by her bedside all night just to have the precious knowledge of her sleeping form. He would leave the room for her to undress. She instilled in him only sensations of virtue. But he was quite happy to practice deceit in order to come by her, to come by the virtue. A minor thing when there was such heavenly bounty to be reached.

They sat down at the same table as before.

'How else can we help you, Jim?'

He had rehearsed the pretence many times over the last couple of days, and now he felt able to speak to her with self-assurance, unlike at their previous encounter. Funny how pretending now seemed to come to him easier than asking his *bona fide* questions of last week.

He settled into a comfortable position in his chair and leaned his elbows onto the table.

'We're concerned about the effect of the hostilities on...' He was about to say 'on the secure transportation of cut diamonds,' knowing that one of their clients relied on an Israeli company for their diamond security and having overheard Pinsky saying that the company's directors had been called up as reservists to fight at Sinai. But several problems occurred to him just then, all at once. The Israelis might wonder why he and not Pinsky was asking, since Pinsky was the one who dealt with the Trade Representative on such matters. If word got back to the firm that he was interfering in Pinsky's business, the consequences for the future of his career didn't bear contemplating. Hell, they could probably even sue him for some kind of tort.

It also occurred to him that it was simply a stupid question. What could the Israeli government do? Pluck the security company's directors out of a parachute drop so some law firm in London that was too interested these days in current affairs and not interested enough in practising law could assure a client that they had preserved their security company from destruction in a war by backroom political manoeuvring? It was ridiculous.

So he caught himself. The pretending was not so easy after all.

'We're concerned about...' Then struggled to come up with a legitimate sounding concern on the spur of the moment.

She was fairly sure she knew why he had come. She leaned her own elbows on the table, and looked directly into his eyes, paralysing him.

'...about making fools of yourselves?'

Heat rushed to his face and she leaned back and laughed.

'You're red,' she said happily.

He had rapidly entered a nightmare of shame, but she was merciful and ended it quickly.

'I think I understand,' she said. 'I think what you want to discuss is better to discuss outside my work hours. I can get away probably around midnight. We are permitted six hours to sleep.'

Hugely relieved that she had taken direction of their meeting, he was suddenly very exhausted.

'Oh, no. I wouldn't want to deprive you of your sleep,' he replied. 'How about lunchtime tomorrow?'

'I cannot. We are too busy.'

'Couldn't you just slip away for a few minutes? Say you're going for a sandwich and some air?' He was back on the offensive, grasping.

'I have responsibilities, Jim...'

'Of course.'

'...but I'll try. Without promising.'

He grinned at her over the victory, but continued to feel like a fool, now for being so persistent. Had she been British he would have given up after the slightest hint of her reluctance, imposing being anathema to the imposer even more than to the object of the imposition. But with her he got the sense that some bargaining and cajoling was almost expected, that her 'no' really meant 'yes, but what do you think, it's as simple as asking once?'

'I'll be at the south gate of Holland Park at one,' he said, and did a lot of awkward smiling as he made his way out.

But she was smiling too.

*

Even Clare was smiling. It was morning number two in hiding, and the longer she remained, the easier it became. She amused herself for hours watching the goings on in the street through the peephole, and it was this link with the outside world, the visual fodder it provided for friendly flights of fancy, which had made yesterday bearable. She watched men and women and children and dogs walking along, the milkman and postman going about their business, and she told herself their stories.

The woman with the round bulb for a nose who was pushing a springy pram with big wheels was the mother of a hero. The baby was a boy who would grow up to conquer darkest Africa and save British children in the civilised outposts from being stewed alive by cannibals. During childbirth she'd had a vision of her son's future, and since then had kept her house stocked with books about savannah, cannibals and the jungle, and had already assembled a complete explorer's kit suitable for a full-grown man. It hung on a hook inside the front entrance hall of her house, and it was all she spoke about to anyone who would listen.

And the postman, he was really a lost tourist. He had woken

up on the ground one day without any recollection of who he was or where he lived. He forgot that he was on holiday from his home in Gloucester. Tormented by his memory failure, he was obsessed with finding his true abode. He assumed it must be in London, so he had taken a job delivering the post all over the metropolis in the hope that he would one day deliver mail to his own house and the memories of his life would come flooding back to him. In the meantime, he had constructed a giant bird's nest of a dwelling at the top of a dense leafy tree in St James's Park, where he lived among the squirrels and pigeons. When he got bored up high and chose to wander at ground level, he was particularly friendly with the swans, who would bring him bits of food. He took his baths in the little lake.

This morning a group of uniformed schoolchildren bustled past noisily, their cheerful chattering and youthful exuberance skipping up at Clare from down below, triggering thoughts of school, her friends, her teacher and her parents, and her frustration with them all, and the coins.

She no longer felt any guilt whatsoever. The self-pity had gone as well. She was (so long as she was not afflicted by the dark) a picture of calm. She felt that in the time she had spent in seclusion she had become another person. By taking firm charge of the direction of her affairs, by acting dramatically and unilaterally in sequestering herself, she had bolstered her general confidence of action. She considered that *now* if she were confronted with the pressures of friends or strangers or circumstance to do something wrongful, she would have the self-possession to step back and think and say no. Never in her present frame of mind would she do what she had done on the bus. Instead she would maintain the momentum of her own moral volition and shout 'thief' after the boy, not be sidetracked, diverted and caught up in the smoke and mirrors of his cunning and devious performance.

But then maybe he would not have targeted her in the first place. Maybe it was the evidence of her emotional vulnerability that had identified her to the boy as a likely partner in crime. The only way to have reached her present state of clarity was to have learned from the real experience of moral error and its sobering effect on her intensely sensitive conscience.

So she had changed, but was she really another person? If she were, would the new 'her' still possess the merit of having grown in character with experience? Or would an analysis in such terms be meaningless if 'self' is really a chronological sequence of multiple identities?

Hollow Bones

JUST ANOTHER man in a trilby hat, he stood at the park gate and heard distant bells chime the solitary hour of one o'clock, the sound mainly hidden behind moving cars and standing bricks and determined heels clomping on humble sections of roadside pavement. He faced the direction she would be coming from, if she would be coming at all. 'Without promising.' She had disclaimed liability, assumed no responsibility for the pounding of his heart or the flutters in his tummy, or the light, weak feeling in his limbs as though his bones were hollow reeds.

What would he say when he saw her? Something extremely simple or something more witty? He decided that any attempt at cleverness would sound contrived and probably stupid.

At ten past one he sensed that she wouldn't turn up, and this calmed him somewhat. He had rushed over the top of the ridge and there was only London on the other side, no bayonets, no piercing arrows of a soldier woman's gaze. Just the confidence and competence and busy direction of a leading city going about its tasks, people running the world and running market stalls with equal detachment, women driving prams with reckless abandon as though pushing wheelbarrows, everything done briskly and with importance, inhabitants participating purposefully in the adventures of life but somehow without complete investment, without the binding commitment of full corporeal engagement. Always in the middle of moving on to the next thing.

But not Roper. He was a waiting fixture, planted into the ground, another of the gateposts. She wouldn't come. He scrutinised the distance for her posture, not yet familiar with the pattern of her gait, but knowing very well in his mind the shape of her form. Figures that might have been hers drew near and weren't. Far away angels came closer and were everyday women. Necks and breasts and waists and hips and thighs and ankles they had, but not any flames projecting from their faces. Some were beautiful. All were beautiful, actually, each in her own way, but none had the crackling electrical spark fountain of his deity. None killed with a glance.

At twenty past one he turned to leave, and she was beside him. He started, his chest compressed all over again.

'I am sorry if I startled you.'

'Gefen. I thought you wouldn't come.' He spoke with gentle accusation, almost mocking himself with the tone of his words so as to say he wouldn't have been devastated, smiling lightly to indicate that actually her lateness was nothing to him at all.

Where had she just sprung from so genie-like?

'It is not easy getting away in the middle of a war. We are separated by much distance from Israel, but inside the building I feel like I am in Israel.'

She didn't say just how difficult it had been to pry herself away. He wouldn't have understood.

It was important to her to leave and meet with him. She carried herself with such self-assurance and abrasive overconfidence that he would never have known she was touched by his interest in her. She felt she owed it to herself to be receptive, if just this once, to the attention of an Englishman. She felt she was learning things about another part of the world that nobody back home would understand. About the mentality of uprightness and the values of gentility and tradition. England through the eyes of an expatriate Israeli woman of coupling age, moulded in Palestine, for all intents a native product of the Holy Land.

A few months ago, before she had left Israel, she would have laughed if someone spoke of such old-fashioned characteristics as having any social value. Great Britain in two words embodied an Israeli's idea of pompous silliness. The better side of Europe. The Queen of England was not the brutality of Ukranian pogroms or the evil of Hitler or the echoes of the Roman Catholic cruelties of past centuries, but was still highly laughable to an Israeli, and in more serious terms there was still the raw nerve of Anglo-Jewish tensions in Palestine before Israel's independence.

But Gefen was coming to have some appreciation of English proprieties and ceremony. Dealing with English businessmen was exciting and educational. They were so polite and deferring and self-effacing. And now there was one who obviously liked her. It made her feel happy and free and she wanted to allow herself the chance to see where it would lead. She did not know if she would ever be away from her country again, at least not with this much independence. At least to get to know him on a personal level, if nothing else.

'Let's walk in the park.'

'Yes, of course.'

'I don't have much time.' She felt the pull of heavy responsibility.

'I have all day. All week if you'd like.' Was he sounding over-obliging? Would his attempt at romantic effusiveness turn her off?

'You are not working for the people I'm working for.'

'Why do you work for them, then, if they're so demanding?'

'You would not understand.'

He found that a bit insulting and arrogant, but a wound inflicted at her hands was better than the kiss of anyone else.

'Wouldn't I?'

'Israel is special. Let's talk about something else.'

'Alright. How 'bout can I take you to lunch? Surely you're famished from all the hard work.'

'Famished?'

'Starved.' Like I'm starved for you.

She was about to laugh and say no, out of nothing more than reflex. But she remembered why she was here with him, and altered her reply. 'I would like to come, but perhaps another day? I am greatly needed at the embassy.'

They passed an affectionate couple strolling arm in arm, and Roper was aware of the footlong space between Gefen and himself like it was the searing bright gap of an arc light.

'I've no doubt you're indispensable, but surely your country can wait an hour. Half an hour.'

'I...'

Seeing she was going to refuse, he turned the creeping tension into a joke. 'Surely they can put the war on hold for more important things, like us getting to know each other.'

She didn't laugh. 'If we are lucky it will be over soon, and then I would be happy to come to lunch with you. Will you walk me back to the embassy road?'

'Wouldn't miss the chance for anything.'

The walk back took less than two minutes, and it was entirely silent between them until she stopped and stood facing him on the pavement, squinting up at him against the sun.

'I hope we can meet soon.'

'How can I reach you?'

'Don't call the embassy again. It will become obvious. Let me call you.'

He didn't bother to protest, and scribbled his home number on the back of his business card and gave it to her.

They parted ways before they came within view of her building so nobody would see the real reason for the absence she had begged of her superiors. They hadn't touched once the whole time, not even a brush of their sleeves, but she sent him rocketing into exhilaration when she turned back and waved, flashing a brilliant warm smile that wrinkled her cheeks and the corners of her eyes and revealed beautiful white teeth for biting his heart in two. Her beaming countenance could have melted arctic ice in those two seconds.

A Non-Combatant

BROKEN FREE. Naveen looked back at the *Majesty* and saw the Chief Officer still standing on the main deck, though it was impossible to tell where the poor man was looking or what he might have been thinking. The ship was still rocking from the explosion, and it appeared now to have come to a stop. They must have just cut the engine, though there was no anchor in evidence. They would have found there not to be much way forward anyhow. Blockships obstructed the Canal further ahead.

He mustn't look back to his previous shell of a home anymore. The way for him was onward into the fold of unknown company, though their sufferance of aliens be untested, not backward into the society of the confirmedly damned. So he proceeded to the road, and made a cautious approach along its edge towards the huddled collective of bombists, who were now beginning to pack up their gear and looking like they might be readying to disperse. Secretly adrenalised from a mix of fear and excitement, he nonetheless ambled lazily to avoid projecting any stridency, hoping to seem as unthreatening as possible.

If you don't appear quick, they won't be tempted to slow you with a shot to the leg, or to the head.

He was unsure whether to worry about the chance of a hostile reception from these people who were just men like him. How dangerous could they be? Still, in this unfamiliar setting he would exercise a bit of prudence. There was, he understood, a war going on somewhere around here, and he wanted to make it clear to anyone and everyone that he was not a combatant. Just a cadet from a school in Calcutta who'd jumped ship within Egyptian territory and scrambled hastily ashore, as one does.

When they caught sight of him approaching they looked nervous, and he could see them conferring about what to do. One of them shouted at him in Arabic, and he didn't understand the words. He opened his arms wide in a gesture of friendship and continued to advance slowly, and saw with sudden alarm that one of them was raising a rifle to his shoulder and pointing it straight, there could be no mistake, at him.

No mere scabbarded scimitar.

He stopped dead in his tracks and raised his arms. The men did not move. They just stared at him.

The one with the rifle didn't lower it. But he didn't pull the trigger either.

After a few seconds Naveen thought it best to try and communicate with words. 'I am not your enemy,' he projected slowly in English. 'I am from the boat.'

No reply. No movement.

He didn't know what else to say. He didn't know if they understood. He didn't know if he would live much longer, whether this was to be the sorry end of his first voyage, the end of his life, the end of the adventure game.

The silence wrapped him in its thin, suffocating film, shortening his breath and weakening his legs.

'I know you are from the boat.' The film was punctured. The man with the rifle stepped forward tentatively, closing the thirty yards that separated them down to about twenty-nine. 'But what I do not know is why are you not still on the boat?'

His arms were beginning to feel heavy above his head. Don't let them sink. Keep them up. Now choose your words carefully, for there is a rifle aimed at your forehead.

'There was problem on the boat. It is long story. It is about officers on the ship and it will be of no concern to you, but I can explain if you let me come over.'

'Everything here is our concern. Come forward. Slowly. Keep your hands up.'

He proceeded very deliberately, treading gingerly to avoid waking someone, the rifle perhaps, progressing in a smooth steady rhythm at low pace, head bent slightly forward in subservience but eyes up to meet the men's stares so as to retain their respect. Harder to tighten a trigger finger when you're looking into a man's soul.

Someone else in the group pulled out a pistol and trained it on Naveen, but he continued his approach.

At ten yards the man with the rifle yelled out, 'stop there!' So he froze.

The rifle was lowered and pointed to the ground and the man rested his weight on it. But the pistol was still pointed.

Naveen was too intent on formulating his story convincingly to take in their countenances or the dusty look of their clothes. Or the depth of worry in their eyes. He was keenly aware only of the speaker and of the pistol, and everything else was faded in an impressionistic blur.

'Are you Israeli?'

'No.'

'Are you British?'

'No, I am Indian.'

'From India?'

'Yes.'

'Is your boat from India?'

'Yes.'

'Why did you fall off the boat?'

'I jumped.'

'You jumped?'

'I was being chased. The Chief Officer went crackers and I was afraid he would kill me.'

'Went crackers?'

'Went insane.'

Azim pondered this for a minute while Naveen's neck and forearms covered themselves in sweat, his pulse slow but heavy in his throat.

Naveen wondered if he was being watched from the ship with binoculars.

Azim gestured to one of the privates.

'Feel him for weapons,' he said in Arabic.

And to Naveen, 'keep your hands up.'

Naveen was frisked slowly, the man patting him lightly but thoroughly in every place, then reporting, more Arabic, to Azim, who remained silent for a minute.

Then, having made his decision, Azim smiled broadly at Naveen.

'Welcome to Egypt.'

He turned to his colleague and spoke to him in Arabic and the pistol disappeared. He then walked forward and extended a hand, and Naveen grasped it in a wash of relief. Just men like him.

183

'What is your name?'

'Naveen.'

'I am Azim. These are my friends,' and he introduced each one in turn. Somehow he had evolved into their unofficial leader now Lieutenant Hamid was gone. 'Now I will ask you an important question. Did you see something unusual a few minutes ago?'

'*Most* definitely. The bridge...'

'I will ask you again. Think before you answer.' He paused. 'Did you see something unusual here?'

Naveen looked at Azim quizzically, but then understood.

'No, I saw nothing.'

'Why is the bridge in the water?'

'I don't know. Perhaps it was bombed by an airplane.'

Azim smiled and clapped Naveen on the back, and gestured for everyone to pick up their things and get moving.

He turned back to Naveen. 'Please. Come to my home with me. You are most welcome.'

Umbrellas

TODAY he had an umbrella. She'd called him at home last night.

'Roper.'

'Jim? It is Gefen.'

'Gefen. Lovely to hear your voice. How are you?'

'Shall we meet tomorrow?'

'My answer will always be 'yes'. No need to ask. Just give the order, and there I'll be.'

'At the same place.'

'Same time?'

Click.

So he assumed the same time, and she came promptly at one, and had her own umbrella.

They faced each other awkwardly for a minute, rain pouring off their respective convex canopies, water on the toes of Roper's shoes, but none on Gefen.

'Glad you could get away today. I know you're busy. Shall we find someplace dry?'

'No, let's walk again. In England I like to walk.'

'Whatever you wish.'

They processed along the path in the park and he felt no need to end their silence. Sharing the activity of one step after the other and smelling the fresh wet green scent of rural England that only graces London in its parks in the rain, and then only in weak traces.

They passed a man in a raincoat walking a very little dog, its long beige-brown hair glued into irregular and miserable spikes from the wet, but its panting, hopping jubilance not the least bit dampened.

Dead autumn leaves were plastered to the path, and without warning a shot of joy thrilled through Roper and he turned and looked at the nape of her neck and loved her. Her hair was clipped up and there were unregulated bits of downy black frizz persisting out of the clip down the upper inch of her neck in stubborn, defiant beauty. Sheltered under a corbeau parapluie.

She stopped walking and turned to meet his look.

'Tell me about your life, Jim.'

They resumed their step.

'Oh, not much to tell, really.' His life at that moment? In the last weeks? At work? Since infancy? His professional life? His personal life? The request was dramatic in its broadness and had no sharp point of focus at its tip. He was accustomed to definition and precision in his phrases.

'Don't be boring,' she entreated. 'You are not boring, but don't make me fight for...'

'Alright. I was born in a village in Kesteven.'

'You are from a village?' She laughed. 'I can't imagine you outside of the city. Did you play games in fields?'

'A little, I suppose.'

'What was it called?'

'The village? The full name or the swallowable one?'

'The full name.'

He adopted a theatrical posture. 'I hail, my dear, from the distinguished Hamlet of Woolsthorpe-by-Colsterworth.' Direct to your kitchen table. Never mind the grammar school and the unlikely scholarships and the university and the hard work and the stringing up a network of sympathetic lawyers that ran between an Oxford college and the City, the cultivating a pool of people who appreciated my talents and charm and would put in a good word if they heard my name mentioned. Never mind losing out on my one promising pupillage opportunity to some posh bastard from Winchester. That part doesn't matter anyway. If I'd been reclining in a plush chair in the smoking lounge at Gray's Inn instead of getting a headache at a crowded Mayfair party I wouldn't have met you.

'Why did you come to London?'

'Why does anyone come to London? Went to school, left home, looked for a job. The better jobs are in London.'

'For an Israeli diplomat the better jobs are in Paris.'

'Yes, well, I'm sure they are.' He thought for a moment. 'Would you rather be in Paris?'

'Oh, no, I would rather be in Israel. At my junior level I should be in Israel working for the Ministry of Foreign Affairs, but because my brother is here, it was considered that I might be valuable in London. They want to use his connections.'

At your junior level? The entire ministry was only eight years old.

The rain dwindled and they closed their umbrellas and he persuaded her to stop and sit next to him on a bench. He spread his jacket across the wet slats for them to sit on, heedless of the grimy damage that was likely to the cloth. He tilted his umbrella against the front of the bench and she hung hers by its j-handle over the armrest to her side.

The cloud was heavy everywhere except for one small triangle of blue, a lone tunnel of dry purity through the density of low floating damp, drawing the eye away from the dripping urban shab towards a glinting window of stratospheric lume.

'Tell me more about your life.'

'Maybe I'm dying to know even the slightest hint about you.'

'Maybe. But you first.'

Her hands were in her lap and her gaze was forward into the park and he leaned one elbow on the backrest and faced her.

He spoke to her ear, her cheek, her temple.

'Maybe the only important thing about me is that from the moment you looked at me in the party you've lived with me every day. You left an imprint on the surface of my eye and it won't leave and I don't want it to leave.' He startled himself with this.

She deflected it. 'Why are you a lawyer?'

'Oh, I don't know, really. Thought it was a good thing to be, I suppose. Came from a family of tradesmen and surprised myself and everyone else by getting into Oxford, and on scholarship. Thought law was a sensible balance between being someone clever and earning a living by a respectable craft, if you will. But I almost didn't go. My dad's not been around since the war, and my uncle, he lives in the same village, was having a rough enough time of it himself, and I wasn't sure about leaving him to support his own family as well as my mum. But I took a gamble that a few impecunious years would pay off in the end, and they have. I'm comfortable, mum's comfortable, and my uncle doesn't have the extra burden anymore. Of course my mum got money from the government, but it wasn't really enough.'

'So you are a good son.'

187

'Well, I don't know. I suppose I do what I can.'

'You English are so modest, and sometimes I think it is false modesty.' But actually she liked it very much. It showed a very different sort of confidence than she was used to seeing displayed by her compatriots.

'Do you think?' he replied. 'Just because it's automatic doesn't mean it's false, I don't think.' He softened the effect of the criticism by considering it the way he would an academic proposition.

'I think it is your own way; not *yours*, don't think I'm attacking you, but the British in general; of being arrogant. Like you're *so* superior you don't have to make any show of success.'

'Well, I was about to say 'you're probably right', but then I might be committing more of the same offence you so elegantly condemn.'

She remembered she was not talking to an Israeli, and was concerned for an instant she might have overstepped the limits of acceptable criticism in a social situation. Had it been any other Englishman she wouldn't have worried, but it was Jim, and she didn't want to frighten Jim away with her thorniness.

'Jim, I did not mean to attack you or your country. I hope...'

'Don't worry. I'm not bothered an iota. Besides, anything you say is music to my ears. I really think you're wonderful and I really enjoy your company...'

A glance at her watch coincided unfortunately with his profession of besotment and she could not help interrupting with urgency.

'Jim, I'm sorry. I must go back to work. I'm already late.'

'I'm sorry if I...'

'No. It is not you. You don't understand. It is very important for me to be at work now.'

'Can I walk you back?'

'Please do.'

He picked up his umbrella and carried it at his side, and they went back down the path. Just as they passed the gate and joined the street, the rain resumed and splattered down with unusual force. She had left her umbrella at the bench. He opened his and held it over her, and she had to step a few inches closer.

'Shall we go back for your umbrella?'

'There is no time. I will have to get another one. Perhaps you would be as kind as to cover both of us with yours? It is quite large.'

'I think I might just be able to manage that.' *If* I can keep walking in a straight line and not be utterly overwhelmed by your proximity.

His elbow brushed the side of her arm repeatedly and he was barely able to string together a series of simple thoughts. Hold umbrella steady. Walk straight. Walk forward and turn left at the embassy road. Brush against her again, but don't seem too obvious. Say something.

'Nearly there.'

Say something else.

'I imagine you want me to walk you all the way to the door this time.'

'No. Leave me at the street corner please.'

'You'll get drenched.'

'Don't worry about me.'

'Fine. I shan't. And I'll see you when?'

'I'll call you soon.'

She left his shelter and he watched her run in her flat-soled shoes up the pavement, a young oryx out of her habitat, and disappear through the embassy gate.

He remained there a minute at the corner in the rain, then went back to the park bench and retrieved her small, blackish-green umbrella.

*

'Roper, where the *hell* is that bloody ship? Is it or is it *not* in the Suez Canal?'

'Mr Selling, my information is as good as Calcutta Maritime's information.'

'We're going to lose a big client, Roper.'

'I'm sorry. I'm doing my best.'

Upturned Palm

BUMPING ALONG in the back of a lorry, sitting opposite each other on sturdy crates of unknown content, Azim and Naveen provided each other with hasty and disjointed but cheerful verbal sketches of their backgrounds and occupations, their voices raised over the noise of travelling.

Naveen sat leaned forward with his elbows resting on his knees, knuckles touching, and Azim reclined to the left, arm leaning on a metal ledge, his head cradled between thumb and forefinger. He was more than a decade older than Naveen, and listened to the younger man's story of the sea with a patience that soon stirred into mild interest. Maybe he ought to go to sea. It would mean leaving his family for even longer stretches than he did already, which weighed heavily against the idea. He might avoid bullets, but he would have to absent himself from his apartment for months without a single week off to sleep with his wife or pat his children on the head. How he was wearily looking forward to both these activities in the very near future. He could already smell his wife's underarms, already see his children's earnest faces.

Before they set off for Cairo, he had pondered reporting to his barracks but quickly decided against it. His commanders didn't know how long his assignment was to continue, and from the looks of it Lieutenant Hamid, if that was his name, wasn't about to tell them. Nobody would be expecting him back, and he would be a fool to present himself voluntarily. Besides, he wanted to keep an eye on this Indian for a few days to satisfy himself the boy wasn't going to stir up any trouble about the bridge. He didn't care if the world knew that Egypt was responsible for the bridge's destruction, but the last thing he wanted was for anybody to know he was involved. He took death warnings from Egyptian officials very seriously.

So they left the others to find their own ways, and caught a lift to the outskirts of Cairo in a passing lorry, Naveen's clothes still

190

slightly damp, then walked for several hungry and thirsty hours until they reached a busy square. There they boarded a wobbly white bus to Giza, which was so suffocatingly crowded and stinky that even Naveen, who was accustomed to the sweaty hive of urban chaos that was his neighbourhood in Calcutta, was made uncomfortably claustrophobic. Azim paid the fare for both of them.

On the journey from the Canal they had passed dozens of military transports, and approaching Cairo, Azim had immediately noticed an abnormal preponderance of nervous-looking young policemen. No roadblocks nor any special commotion, just a lot of uniformed men milling about, driving by, standing in pairs. He'd not learned that Cairo had been lightly bombed, and they saw no ruined buildings as they entered the city, but he knew enough to guess the police visibility had something to do with the war.

Now, as they drew further from the city centre on the Giza bus, the tight crush of bodies was gradually loosened as stop by stop a passenger or two squeezed himself out of the suffocating cram of people compressed against each other with arms and heads leaning out windows, and Azim started asking around for news of the war. He learned about the bombing by the British and French and the damage to the international airport, but was unable to gain a clear picture of what had happened in the Sinai. One man swore the Israelis had overrun the peninsula, while another reported hearing on the radio that Egypt had captured half of Israel, never mind keeping the Sinai.

Certainly, he was told, foreigners were having to watch their backs, and many Jews in Cairo had been rounded up by the authorities and told in the most persuasive terms that they would be better off leaving the country.

Naveen, meanwhile, was catching glimpses of the wide paved avenue with many honking cars, flanked on both sides by apartment blocks of dirty stone, and a filling station and a Coca Cola billboard and not very many people about on foot.

In Calcutta there would have been pedestrian traffic everywhere, as well as creaking bicycles with ringing bells, and careering rickshaws and animals and motorcycle exhaust and heavy grey sky and bright colourful fabrics. Here people seemed to dress drably and the swell of city movement had a different flavour. If Calcutta felt like a burden of thick smiling rainbow wetness over cutcha dwellings with flecks of mud and dung and spice, Cairo was an astringent black-orange haze with shades of rusted metal and floating cigarette smoke interrupted by scattered vital flashes of greenery.

It was the warm upturned palm of a great hand cradling millions of souls, surrounded by sand. He had not passed through the lusher, statelier districts of Zamalek or Garden City, nor paused yet to behold the magnanimous laziness of the flowing Nile. Much of Cairo proper is blessed with many grand trees, but Giza is not.

Almost empty now, the bus reached the stop for Azim's stretch of Giza.

They alighted, and before their feet even touched the ground off the bus they were swarmed by a cluster of children, all of whom seemed to know Azim. He noted with approval that his own weren't among the group, and enjoined them all sternly to stop causing a ruckus on the streets.

They carried on along a road lined with low-rise buildings of flats, and as they approached the one where Azim lived, he turned to Naveen and said, 'you were on an airplane from India to Europe, and your plane had trouble and there was a forced landing at Cairo International. You are stranded here because your plane was damaged in the bombing while it was undergoing repairs on the tarmac.'

'What about my luggage?'

'It was lost.'

'Why am I staying with you?'

'Because it is my decision. That is enough of an answer for my wife. If someone else asks, you can tell them the lorry I was in stopped at the roadside to give you a ride and we became friends.'

Why *was* he staying with Azim? He pushed the question to the back of his mind, happy for the time being to have found a place to eat and sleep so effortlessly. And happy to have some friendly and interesting company in this strange land.

They climbed worn terrazzo steps up to the top floor of the building, where Azim pulled a key out of his wallet, unlocked the door, and called into the house that he had arrived.

'Azim! *Habib!*' His wife rushed to him from out of some shadows.

He embraced her as Naveen stood shyly in the hall. Then she glimpsed him and stepped back from Azim, embarrassed.

'We have a guest, my dear. Make him comfortable.'

Her English was not as good as Azim's, but he knew she understood.

'*As-salaamu alaykum*,' she met Naveen's eyes only for a fragment of a second before turning hers to the floor.

They were not a religious family, and she wore modern clothes, but she knew well that in front of her husband it was an unquestioned expectation that she would conduct herself with a large degree of the traditional modesty.

'Please, you are my guest. Come in, Naveen. Make yourself at home. Zafirah will prepare coffee. Will you bathe straightaway or do you prefer to eat dinner first?'

'Well, I wonder; I need to dial somebody in India. Can you tell me where is nearest telephone?'

'There is a post office up the road. You can phone from there. Do you have money?'

Naveen was hesitant to reveal he was carrying gold, but also felt he would have to trust this man if he was to take the benefit of his hospitality, so he confessed to having them.

'Gold coins?' Azim tried with difficulty to conceal surprise. 'You cannot take those to the post office. We must go into the city and I will help you sell them to somebody honest. For now I had better give you some Egyptian money.'

Naveen was beginning to feel overwhelmed by all the favour he was being shown. It made him a bit suspicious, but at the same time he had no particular indication that Azim was not simply a sincere and generous man.

'Thank you ever so much! If I am able to reverse the charges, I will return the money straightaway.'

He pattered down the stairs rapidly, eager to make contact with the Company. As he was almost out the main door, Azim called down to him, leaning over the banister at the top of the stairwell.

'Wait! It is after three o'clock. The post office will appear to be closed. You must keep on banging at the window even though the place will look empty, and somebody will come eventually. Tell them I sent you.'

*

'International operator, please.'

'To which country, please?'

'India.'

'One moment.'

Click. Rushing static. Click.

'This is the Indian operator. How can I assist?'

'Yes, I would like to connect to Calcutta Maritime company offices and reverse the charge. My name is Naveen Patel.' It would be late in the evening there, but he knew there would be key people in the office at least until five o'clock Greenwich Mean Time, even on the weekend.

'Bear with me. I will try.'

'Wait. Please tell them I am calling from the *Majesty*. That should help.'

'Bear with me.'

He waited for some time.

'Mr Patel, they have accepted the charge. You can go ahead and talk.'

'Thank you...' 'Hello?'

'Hello? Pankaj Bhattacharya here, with whom am I communicating?'

'Mr Bhattacharya, this is Naveen Patel, cadet from the *Majesty*.'

'Yes, Naveen, we are highly eager for information. I understand you are placing your call from Cairo. What is the status of the *Majesty*?'

'It was in good physical shape when last I saw it this morning, but it is in the Suez...'

'Then it is trapped. It is most fortunate that you are able to convey us this information. We had no communications.'

Naveen heard muffled instructions being issued. 'Sandip! It is in Suez! Contact London immediately... Yes, I know it is Sunday... Saaaan-*dip*! Do as you are told!' Then back to Naveen. 'What is status of officers and crew?'

'Sir, I believe there has been some bobbery. Chief Officer has gone crackers and I feared for my life. I was forced overboard.'

There was a long silence at the other end. Eventually the Company man said, 'that is most remarkable. I find it hard to believe Fernandes could be mad. He is a very stable man. Never mind. We will formulate a plan. I have many questions but first I must confer with directors about the ship. Let us communicate in two days' time. Ring me back please.'

'Very good, sir. I will revert to you on Tuesday morning.'

'We may need to contact you sooner. In case of urgent communication, where can we cable you?'

He wasn't sure, so he approximated the likeliest option. 'Care of Mr Azim Husseini, Giza Post Office, Egypt.'

'Alright. We will be in communication. Goodbye.'

Naveen rang off and stood slightly dazed for a minute. The Company man had so instantly taken full charge of the conversation that he had no chance to relay the bits of recent ship history that would make the situation intelligible to the directors. All the man seemed to care about was the simple fact that the ship was in the Suez. He hoped he wouldn't be faulted for not having divulged more in that initial conversation once the full picture did eventually become clear to the Company.

Well, at least he could return the money to Azim. Accepting hospitality was one thing, but accepting cash had a more unpleasant feel and he would be glad to give it back.

The Royal Borough

'THAT'S NOT something I can accept, Constable. My daughter is at stake here,' he began calmly. 'I'm at home and she is not, and nobody seems to know where she is. I don't know if that means anything to you. I don't know if you have a daughter. I don't know where *you* are, but I need to reach the detective at his home if he's not in the office... No, no, he doesn't, he has a duty to me,' he began to escalate. 'He's a police officer. He's a *police* officer! *You*'re a police officer! So *so* do you! What did you say you were called? Byng? I'll see to it they shut you down, Byng, I swear I will. I need an update! I need. His. *Up*date!!!'

A breathless pause, and then, as an afterthought, he added, 'who do you think you are? Do you know who *I* am?'

Clare shivered at the sound of her father's focused, wrathful impertinence. He might be the devil incarnate, she considered, and that would make her the devil's daughter. She certainly was making her father go through quite a whole rigmore roll for her, she thought, and now he was making the police do the same roll.

It made her wonder whether every activity of every person in every place in the world towards any other person got carried on to yet another by that next person. She was making her father fret, her father was making the police fret, the police would have to make somebody else fret, and so on. It was sort of like the way she assumed everybody felt the same towards each other. If you loved someone, they loved you back the same. If you hated someone, they hated you back the same. Just one of those unexplained patterns in human relationship that she surmised were fundamental operating schemata for the whole world, though had she thought more carefully, she would have identified examples out of her own experience to disprove this.

Overhead, her father placed down the telephone handset and leaned his head in his hands. He dealt in the unexpected every day of his life, and was keen to the snares held out by uncontrollable fortune. He knew that reacting effectively meant not struggling

196

against sudden wrong swings of luck, but knowing how to bounce back flexibly. Control every last variable possible, but know when to concede a battle was unwinnable; know how to move swiftly on to the next thing, and not waste attention or emotion or self on futilities.

Rotors whirl and gears tooth together and conveyor belts speed forward in the enginehouse of a master's business, and his two hands spring and flash and shove them all continually into motion, an invisible flurry of concentrated dexterity, trained in the agility of perpetual withdrawal, never catching a finger in the grind. To dwell on an unwelcome but uncontrollable intrusion into this process is to lose focus on the leading goal. It is to look over one's shoulder just a second too long at a window shattered by some errant projectile, and meanwhile to catch that finger between two gears, killing the finger and bringing the machinery to a halt. All this he knew.

But now his heart was outside the enginehouse of his trade and the goal was different and there was something infinitely more invested at stake. The rubric was now his household, the goal its cohesion and the happiness of its members and its outward appearance of harmony and success. He was not so self-trained in meeting domestic crises, because they were only *partly* a game. You could only prepare yourself to an extent. The loss of a daughter was a real loss, not a pretend loss like the loss of a shipment, and though lessons taken from the game-world of big business in how to be emotionally disinvested could help loosen the adhesiveness of the loss, they could not scoop into him deeply enough to get out all the traces of its shameful, hurtful grit.

Of course the only way was to do one's best and carry on. He decided to call a friend at Scotland Yard and bypass these local buffoons who had inflated senses of their own importance and stickled for procedures they probably did not understand. He dug out the number from a drawer, but just as he reached for the phone it pre-empted him and rang, and he lifted the handset gingerly. He listened into it for a silent while before speaking, which was a habit of his.

'Yes?' he asked eventually.

'Roger Selling here.'

Oh, let me tell you something, Roger. I'm sorry to have to say it, but I'm through with your firm. I was thoroughly put out last week by that trip with your young lawyer up the garden path, and I'm afraid it's just the proverbial last straw.

But he knew better than to say such things.

He lit up a cigar.

'I'm afraid I'm somewhat preoccupied at the moment, Roger. Could you possibly ring back tomorrow?'

'Just wanted to pass on a quick word, old chap. Thought you might want to know your shipment's trapped. Definitive word just in from Calcutta.'

'The shipment.'

His wife chose that moment to open the door and barge into his study. She stood in front of his desk and they stared at each other as he held the handset to his ear with one hand and held his smouldering cigar in the other.

'Yes, I thought it best to inform you straightaway. Of course you're covered under *force majeure*, so there's nothing to worry about now.'

'The shipment?' she said at him in a whispered rage, and he delivered her back a gaze of steel.

'I'll speak to you later, Roger.'

He tilted his head and looked at her as Selling carried on.

'I think...' resumed the tinned voice on the telephone.

'The shipment?' she asked again, yelling this time, supporting herself with both arms on the edge of the desk, leaning towards him and the telephone.

'...we'd probably better meet just so we can clarify your position and be sure we're on the same page, so to speak, old chap, and that...'

He disconnected the line.

Now he was off the phone they stared at each other mutely, he leaning back into his chair and she leaning forward into his desk space, her head momentarily enveloped in a cloud of sharp smoke.

She wore an expression of disgusted astonishment.

'You don't care, do you?' Slowly and deliberately, stated in a tone of sudden enlightenment, 'you don't give a damn.' Then repeated, with more force. 'You don't give a *damn*.'

A strong feeling restrained him from speaking up in his own

defence. The accusation was so outrageous it would have been unseemly for him to dignify it by reply. Instead he looked with pitying superiority at his broken down wife, no inclination to disabuse her of her perceptions. Not worth demeaning himself.

'The only thing which interests you in this great world is your business. Your filthy, all-important business. I knew you didn't care about me, but I thought, perhaps, at least, your daughter might stir some humanity in you. When I married you I thought you could do everything. Can you *imagine*? But of course you can't. There must be a weakness somewhere. And the weakness is laid bare, *dar*-ling. You can't look after your own family. So *you* just carry on with your *ship*ments. I'm going to the police.'

She turned and stormed out, to her husband both ridiculous and desirable in her explosive severity. The door slammed shut behind her, punctuating her exit with a floor-shuddering crash.

A ceiling-shuddering crash.

Such was the exchange that Clare heard, with none of the visual interpretive aids that would have painted an explanatory context. But the resulting conception she formed of her father's villainy was shortly soothed by his calm follow-up. She heard him ring for the butler.

'Dewey, go after my wife please and be sure to catch up with her before she reaches the police. Let her know I'm in touch with Scotland Yard and that she mustn't meddle by making appearances of her own at the Kensington Police Station. And bring her back and see to it she takes some rest. She's in quite a state, poor woman. Take Jane along with you for help.'

*

In a distant sphere of existence, but, as the crow flies, less than two hundred yards from the house on Melbury Road, Roper and Gefen strolled for a third time in the park. They each, without the boldness to say as much, considered it was their park now, the garden of their pairing. Its title was in their joint names, survivorship imponderable, remainder to the birds. He was aflight in legalistic sentimentality.

'So you promised to tell me more about yourself,' he began.

'I did not promise.'

'True. So you did not.'

She smiled back, cruel, quiet.

'But don't you think that's a bit unfair?'

'Yes.'

'Oh. Well, then, I suppose we could talk about...'

'What do you want to know about me?'

Ah.

'Well, I suppose anything that helps fill in a richer picture of your origins. So that I can place you as the object of focus in a palette in my mind and get all the colours right. Where you came from, what you did as a child, who your family are, what your interests are. What you choose to do when you're all alone in your home at five in the afternoon on a bank holiday. Whether you prefer walking barefoot on cool grass or on warm sand.'

'It is better that you do not place me. I can't be fixed like that. Not without mistakes.'

Oh.

'No... I suppose nobody can. Well, then. Tell me about Israel.'

'But I thought you British knew everything about Israel. Everybody I meet here seems to want to tell me things about my own country, as if they know about it better than me.'

Surely, he thought, this was not the way they trained diplomats to speak. But then maybe they didn't train them, as such. Too soon since independence to have developed a thorough system.

'Alright. Defeated. I'll let *you* choose the topic of conversation.'

Maybe she had a man already.

'Let's walk back to the high street.'

Defeated.

'Alright.'

They were wordless until they reached the departure corner. It was sunny and cold that day. He was afraid to ask about next time.

'I have to go back,' she said.

'Yes, of course, you have important work to do. I'm sorry I've kept you.'

She shook her head but said nothing. It wasn't what she'd meant.

Her lips pursing obliquely, she stepped away slowly, then spoke as she left.

'Jim.'

'Yes.'

'I go barefoot on the sand.'

Kingdom of Dust

SOMETIMES one's first evening in a strange land, one's first leisured wander on foreign pavements after the blurred rush of arrival, possesses a uniquely unreal quality, and becomes wrapped in a sort of mystical cloak within the visions of later recollection. All the more is this the case when that evening just happens to contain an encounter with monuments of great, transcendent history, and vistas of breathtaking, elemental force.

Naveen was looked after by Azim's entire household. As Zafirah laboured with apparent effortlessness over elaborate meal preparations, Azim directed his children, who had arrived home while Naveen was out at the post office, to minister to Naveen.

Bring him soft, loose clothing. Bring him a towel.

Did you know this is the finest Egyptian cotton?

Bring him soap. Draw him a bath.

After soaking his skin in hot water and dining with surprising luxury on *koshary* and roast lamb (he was lenient with himself concerning *ahimsa*), wondering incredulously how they had come by such succulent meat, and how Zafirah had prepared it so quickly, he said he would like to take a walk. Azim, out of hospitality and concern, and the suddenly remembered need to be supervising his guest's contact with others, offered to accompany him. But Naveen, mainly because he was already longing for an independent jaunt, but also out of sensitivity to the likelihood that Azim and his family would want a chance to reunite without his presence, persisted in politely declining Azim's company.

On the latter count he need not have concerned himself. He did not know that they were, in terms of their freedom of behaviour, indifferent to his presence. They always conducted themselves within the slightly affected atmosphere of paternalistic and quasi-theatrical formality common in Egyptian households, but were, conversely, just as open in their dramatic expressions of genuine emotion whether or not a stranger was with them. Guests were like close family members. Even a sworn enemy, for as long he was taking hospitage under a man's tent (or plaster ceiling), must be honoured there as his brother.

But Naveen was politely insistent and they let him go. He tread steadily down empty streets dusted with sand and it hit him that he had been awake for over two days. Two days of insanity.

And now peace.

Rather than exhaustion, he felt restfulness and satisfaction and was settled of mind.

Already as he walked among the flats, passing a beggar folded up on the ground in a doorway, he saw with a charge of predictive excitement three angular tips coloured in earth and glowing the setting sun, pointing, neither dully nor sharply, over some rooftops. Ancient vertices of death under rock. Of course. Giza. He'd not even thought of it til now.

The streets led his feet to the edge of civilisation, to the stark delineated end of habitation and the start of the kingdom of dust. You could go three thousand miles overland in a straight line from that point and not encounter a sign of life, except maybe the marsh at Qattara and some lone, wiry shrubs. An ocean of land. Only ships in the sky, out of reach.

A little yellow desert flower somewhere along the way to Nouakchott, where dry again meets wet? It must be a miracle.

Standing solitary in the distance, sentries at an absent gate to the Sahara, the world's most famous trinity of structures. Their companion a sphinx, sensual rock. Did the architects plan these pyramids so that in four and a half thousand years a man might look out and see the ball of sun hovering near; three points, a glowing circle and a cat, and be transformed into an aesthete no matter how impoverished the poetry of his soul?

It was a trek he had to make. He followed a path down the vacant open way for many minutes, and saw camels bending knees at the ground in the distance, leaving, actually. Time to retire with the day.

Not yet for him. He left the path for sand underfoot, and made on until he reached more paths and then the bases of the pyramids. Some people moved nearby, shadows in the closing dusk, but nobody intercepted him. He went for the biggest pyramid and touched the great chunk of worn stone that was one thousandth a part of the whole, or maybe one ten thousandth. His feet were on the ground and the height of the rock reached almost to his shoulders.

He had not come all the way from India just to sit at the foot of this wonder. So he hoisted himself up on top of this ten thousandth stone and heaved his way on to the next and the next and up nook and foothold, and forged a panting ascent to the top.

Meeting his eye as he sat on the upper ledge was a captivating vista, city interlocked into desert, a barren sea of sand grains touched by concrete tentacles. Which was encroaching on which?

Behind it all, the daylight looked on in a glowing half-circle of fire, a slowly shutting eye.

And the thin dry air hummed a deep silent tone of ancient truth around Naveen.

Unsatisfied

ROPER'S subsequent and unavoidable encounters with Penny had been embarrassing. Had Gefen not revisited his life straight after his rendezvous with Penny, he might have cultivated an interest in her and pursued the promise she held out of ready satisfaction and soft comfort. It would have meant making a strenuous effort to keep what was between them secret, or shouldering the burden himself and bearing the unspoken (or, knowing some of the people in his firm, spoken) disapproval of his colleagues. But his general interest in women evaporated in the face of the chance that he could be with Gefen, the only woman.

To make things worse, Penny was entirely and humbly accepting of the way he shamefacedly rushed through the reception area, giving her a stiff nod without slowing his pace, leaving his jacket in his office so as to avoid interaction with her, departing late in the evening, after she had gone home. She still smiled at him and wished him good morning, and was there to greet him when he returned from having disappeared for the long, mysterious lunches he had been taking lately.

It would have been much easier for Roper had she been cross with him, or emotional and accusing, or begging, or anything but her natural kind and friendly self. They had chosen a very professional receptionist, he noted with guilty approval.

Now, having made his way once again past the awkwardness of the reception area, he sat in his office and was unable to concentrate on his work. He had just come from meeting Gefen. There was a ream of material gathering dust in his in-tray, and a stack of little pink notes in the middle of his desk with hand-copied telephone messages in Sarah's script. But he just left them there, making himself and the firm vulnerable to professional liability in contract and tort. Gefen was so inaccessible and abrasively defensive.

Her avoidance of his questions was starting to frustrate him; eat away at him, even. He felt more pressingly than anything else the need to know more about her, the desire to learn everything there was to learn. Rather than seeking to know her in the biblical sense, he was intent on knowing her in every other way. He wanted to possess her by uncovering her veiled origins. He sought to gain self-assurance in their relationship, a little bit of power, by developing a catalogue of fact.

He decided to ring Bradley, the one who had introduced him to Gefen's brother at the party.

'Bradley? Jim Roper.'

'Jim! To what do I owe this dubious honour? And don't say you're after free accounting advice, because I don't even provide that to my own mother.'

'Perish the thought, Bradley. I wouldn't dream of seeking anything remotely approaching advice from you, financial or otherwise.'

'Now, Jim, that's a bit harsh. Just because... Oh, excuse me for just a moment... Oh, hell, I haven't time for banter right now. What are you after, Jim? Wanting to take me for dinner, I hope?'

'Do you remember the party in the flat on Brook Street?'

'Oh, yes, I shan't forget it for a long time. Remember that beautiful blonde woman from Virginia?'

'Er, yes, I think so.'

'Just between you and me, Jim, she had the softest touch and the sweetest taste this side of the Mississippi, so to speak.'

'You scoundrel, Bradley.'

'And such moaning, Jim.'

'Bradley, that'll be quite enough, thank you.'

'I haven't been able to stop thinking about that night. You won't tell anyone, will you? She's the daughter of somebody in particular and I'd hate for him to...'

'My lips are sealed, Bradley. Now let me give you something else to think about.'

'I haven't really got time today, Jim. Huge backlog and the boss is on my back and, oh, just massive amounts of auditing for the third quarter reports.'

'Who was the man we were talking with about murder?'

'Man? Er... um, ah, yes, the boring chap who was rambling on. Samuel... it was Samuel Perl. Now an Israeli, I think. Definitely Jewish anyhow. I believe he does something at UCL. Knows the

Ramptons because John's mother took him in as a refugee. An orphan, otherwise. Interesting story, actually. He got put on some train to the Hook, then a ferry over here, while his sister was smuggled to Palestine as an infant. They rediscovered each other's existence much later. She was there at the party too, I believe. Why do you ask?'

'Well, because...'

'Oh, Jim, do excuse me. I really must go. I'm afraid you'll have to ask me to dinner another time. Coming! Bye, Jim.' He hung up.

'Bye, Bradley,' he spoke into the dial tone.

He sat at his desk staring out the window for the remainder of the afternoon.

Sarah came in at one point and wondered if he was alright, only he had been acting oddly lately.

'I'm fine, Sarah,' he said absently, without looking at her.

She waited for something more, wondering why she went to all the effort if he wasn't even going to look at his messages.

Eventually she left his office, unsatisfied.

*

As an infant?

That would mean she was less than twenty years old.

She seemed so much older. Bradley probably didn't know what he was talking about.

Roper had a lot of trouble sleeping that night.

VI

Closing In

ON THE FIFTH of November, while Roper was lying in bed, his eyes open and his mind exhaustedly resigned to the fact that he would not sleep; when it was a quarter past five in the morning in London and a quarter past seven in Egypt, the Gamil airfield at the Mediterranean shore to the west of Port Said lit up with deadly fast activity. It was being trampled upon by a thousand British boots as one of Her Majesty's Parachute Battalions thudded sturdily onto the tarmac.

The men, hitting the ground running, unclipped their harnesses and rapidly cleared the field, making their way for the cover of nearby buildings. They were fired upon from the moment they landed, and some were forced to engage individual Egyptian soldiers even as they were floating some feet above the ground.

Foot-first into hard action.

Precisely fifteen minutes later, four hundred fellow paratroopers, one of the Régiments Parachutistes Coloniaux, took their positions at Raswa, south of Port Said. This French group insisted on making a spectacular debut, arriving with a daring and mortally dangerous drop from only four hundred feet onto a treacherously narrow landing area, and they pulled it off.

The Egyptian General Staff had predicted that such landings might occur, even though the General Assembly in New York were already preparing to mandate the formation of an international peacekeeping force in the expectation that hostilities would now be ending.

The General Staff were right about the landings, but they were wrong about their location. They brushed aside the Colonel's insistence that Port Said would be a target, and succeeded in keeping him in the dark about the concentration of their defences at Alexandria, which left Port Said wholly vulnerable. The Colonel only discovered the weakness the evening before the Allied landing, but managed to have several powerful Russian cannons delivered early that morning with troop reinforcements and to distribute small arms among the populace in anticipation of street fighting and house-to-house combat.

The Colonel himself set out to meet the people of Port Said the evening before the enemy parachutists arrived. His mood was grim from being at odds with his own generals, and it worsened when he saw the burnt-out tanks along the roadside, destroyed by the European planes, Egyptian soil tarnished by the smoking shame of the whole scene.

He was persuaded to halt partway along because the road onward to Port Said risked being all shot up with a rain of bullets from overhead, and so he slept in Ismailia.

The next morning he awoke to the distressing double blow of two concurrent pieces of breakfast news. The Allies had landed around Port Said and the Israelis had taken Sharm-el-Sheikh. Paratroopers seemed to be swarming everywhere on the surface of his mind, insect-like. A vile infestation.

*

And battles seemed to be flaring everywhere. As the Colonel was speeding away from Ismailia back to Cairo, military targets were being bombed from the air north of the capital.

The Secretary-General of the United Nations was beside himself at the continuation of hostilities and in particular the unwillingness of the Israelis to submit to a United Nations cease-fire scheme.

Parliamentarians in London were readying for a stormy day of shouting and flinging brash words across the floor. Members of the Opposition had caught wind of some heavily intimidating radio propaganda poured towards Egyptian receivers by the British military out of Cyprus, and the Prime Minister would shortly find it very difficult to maintain the credulity of the House of Commons with respect to British neutrality as between Israel and Egypt.

In Eastern Europe, the last bit of Hungarian resistance was being snuffed out by the stolid butchery of Soviet armour in Budapest, and back in London, unaware of it all, Roper was dying under his sheets for Gefen.

*

Eventually he got up out of bed, and as soon as he was standing he knew he could not go to work. Not only was his body not up to being hauled down stairs and through turnstiles and pushed along crowded pedestrian crossings, but he was also weak of spirit and could not stomach facing Penny this morning. His heart was beating too fast and he was a nervous wreck and would be useless in the office in any case.

Rather than being leaden with fatigue, he was feeling disconcertingly light. His joints and muscles ached from lack of sleep, but his head was too clear. The spiders of his brain would not spin cobwebs as they were meant to, so he remained bright eyed and wished in vain to be borne upon by the weight of slumber.

He rang the office and told Sarah he was ill and would not be coming in and that it was no big concern as he had no appointments anyway. Then he disconnected the telephone and lay back in bed and thought about Gefen some more. For the first time he desired her physically, and thought about what was beneath her blouse. He guessed her breasts were curved pertly upwards and her areolas dark and her nipples little firm berries, ripe. He thought right through the seat of her slacks to concealed roundness and wondered if her skin was olive everywhere. Not pink like the English girls in their secret places. Dark and Middle Eastern.

Barefoot in the sand.

He got out of bed again and reconnected the phone and dialled the forbidden number.

'I told you not to call me here.'

'I have to see you.'

'Did you know I have just walked out of a meeting with a UN representative to take this "urgent" call?'

'I'm sorry. I had no business interrupting you.'

'And somehow I knew it would be you.'

'But still you left the meeting.'

No answer.

'Meet with me.'

'You must *never* ring me here again... I will meet you tomorrow, but you will not like what I am going to tell you.'

'Impossible.'

'Bye, Jim.'

He disconnected the wire again, sank into his mattress, and

was asleep in seconds. He slept deeply all day, waking now and then for a moment, but only to roll over and bury his head under the cover and sleep some more.

At dusk he got up, the taste of daytime sleep coating his throat, his head heavy, his balance almost imperceptibly askew, and he put on some clothes and went to work to sift through the backlog of messages and produce some memoranda on firm management so he would have something to leave on Selling's desk to keep the old sailor happy.

*

The great sea convoy from Malta had arrived off the shore of Port Said ahead of schedule, and the Task Force Commanders were debating the possibility of shelling the port at dusk to pave the way for the paras to storm the streets rather than waiting until the next morning.

The French, meanwhile, were heavily engaged, closing in on the town from their southern position. For a little while, as they knocked out one vital Egyptian installation after another, they thought they would be able to capture Port Said without the help of shelling from the British fleet, but the local resistance slowed them down too much.

On the way up to the port they opted for an unmeasured approach. While the British commanders were wringing their hands and delaying and imposing self-limitations on the calibre of guns to be used in civilian areas, the French parachutists were ploughing on to Port Said at a good clip, using machine guns indiscriminately to clear their path of every living thing. The small contingent of British sappers who accompanied the French saw no reason to complain. Better behind the crazy Gallic gunners than in front of them.

*

As advance units were cutting the phone lines around Port Said in preparation for the onslaught, the British naval chiefs decided to wait until morning, when it could be ascertained better if and precisely where Allied soldiers had entered the town overnight.

Communications were patchy and a night-time bombardment with poor visual scope could blow out the friendly along with the enemy.

*

The French general insisted on watching everything unfold out the window of a lone airplane circling overhead.

Things were getting hairy.

Night Life

IN AZIM'S flat, the sound of bombs in the distance.

'Naveen, my friend, let us discuss politics.'

Naveen was not too sure about politics, and had never given world affairs much thought. He knew that in India his parents were ardent Congress supporters and expected him to vote for the same. As he saw nothing strikingly wrong with the party, and generally minded little about election outcomes, he was content to ignore the confusing goings on in halls of power, to vote as his parents wished, and to keep away from the noisy politics of the street. India was a place where it was possible for a person of virtually any stripe, so long as he earned more than a basic subsistence income, to be very politically active if he had the interest and the patience, and Naveen left his country's politics to those who possessed such qualities.

As for international affairs, he was confident to the extent of recognising that the world appeared to be entering a post-colonial phase, symbolised not least by India's emergence as a regional great power, that the United States were advocates of this new world order, at least as far as it concerned India, and that Stalinist communism was the alternative to the American ideal of open democracy and capitalistic enterprise.

He was, as was every Indian, deeply conscious of the colonial imprint of Britain upon his country, and, like most of his compatriots, was able to sustain mixed feelings towards Britain without feeling self-contradictory. Britain was a great nation with many admirable features. Sound government, honour and top hats and fine tailoring, sublime literature, the greatest seats of Western learning, industrial expertise. Britain had also dominated the subcontinent for centuries, possessed it, sometimes strictly and forcefully. India was a forlorn bride in a forced marriage, who had come to serve her husband out of resignation and necessity and just a little bit of admiration *ex post facto*. Because it is better to love than to hate. Because it is *something* to be the most favourite of the many brides of the world's most powerful man.

The British could not have hoped for a more tolerant and complementary woman and indeed they did not. They were pragmatic bastards. Stiff and imperious but somehow easygoing when it came to policy. And eventually predictable enough for enterprising Indians to manipulate this devil-they-knew to profitable advantage whilst appearing to humour the white men at the same time.

Now they were gone. They had left behind, among much else, from the wonderful to the horrendous, their language. And now there was also Pakistan, full of wild religious militants in Naveen's Indian imagination.

This was what he knew about the world.

He did not realise that to satisfy the requirements of conversation with Azim, his knowledge was far more than enough. All he really needed was the ability to craft sweeping judgments about the course of the global power arrangement, to point his finger in dramatic indictment at the rogues of the world, to display firm convictions, and to avoid causing insult. Supporting empirical data was not necessarily an asset in Cairo parlour talk.

*

Beyond Suez, other big political and military things were going on in the world too. All across America, the sovereign people of the Union would soon be out at the polls reelecting the incumbent presidential candidate. In France, negotiations were being wrapped up in the final stage of the creation of the European Economic Community. In Moscow, the Soviet General Secretary and his Marshal had made up their minds about crushing the Hungarian government and, having given the order for the tanks to roll on Budapest, felt a great weight lifted off their chests. They had done the right thing. Now they were liberated to turn their minds to other matters, the foremost of which was to get themselves properly involved in this Suez business.

It was time to have a bit of fun with the West. Dabbing the corners of their mouths to wipe away some drops of Hungarian blood, they stood up at the dinner table of world politics and announced to Britain, France and Israel that it was the height of unfairness to attack a weaker state that had only recently gained national independence and which lacked adequate ability to defend itself. The General Secretary had to restrain the urge to take off his shoe and whack it upon the table to make his point (it would not have been polite), and the Marshal vociferously deplored the attack on Egypt as 'inhuman', and called upon the British Labour Party and trade unions to intervene to halt the barbarity. The Marshal then communicated with the United States, suggesting that America and Russia take immediate joint military action to eject the old colonialists from the Middle East.

The President was disgusted by this overture, and even while America was voting, he busied himself with assuring his loyal Secretaries that no matter what foolish exploits the British and French had got themselves up to, and come hell or high water, if the Reds attacked any NATO Allies, America would go to war to protect its old friends, so help us God.

But, Mr President, Congress is not in session.

Well, hell, boys, that don't matter.

So he sent some U2 planes to reconnoitre the Middle East and see if there were any Soviet installations in Syria. If there were, they ought to be smashed to bits.

Still, it would be better to stop the Brits and the French before things escalated, so at the same time the CIA got busy pumping disinformation through the intelligence networks, feeding in some 'credible rumours' that the Soviets were rattling their sabres something serious, and that big trouble was brewing up ahead. They spread fictitious word of Soviet Air Force overflights menacing the Turkish skies. The feared *Voenno-Vozdushnye Sily*. If the juvenile Europeans were made to recognise just how much and what sort of fire they were really playing with, maybe they would come to their senses and back off from Egypt.

*

In London, the rule of law persisted as always. The police went about their business and conferred on the wisdom of widening the search for Clare. Focus on Kensington with more intensity, or involve other police branches and spread the net wide? It was a matter of resource allocation and of strategic preference. They settled on the options and decided to present them to Clare's father and learn his inclination.

Clare herself thought she was ready to come out from hiding, but each time she prepared to leave the room, something told her to stay. Returning to the open was a frightening prospect. Whether or not her parents were angry, and she did not really care anymore, there would be a very great deal of explaining for her to do. When she started this whole escapade she had been motivated by imagining the effect it would have on others. She had been fed up with the world and her disappearance was meant to teach everybody a good lesson. They were to learn that she was not to be taken for granted, and that her feelings were as important as anyone else's. That she counted.

But now all her anger and frustration had evaporated into the thick, dusty air of seclusion, and she was calm and at peace with humanity. She begrudged no one anything and would be happy settling back into the ordinary routines of her life. The problem was, now it would be impossible for her to slip out quietly and resume the course of her previous existence. She could not go back to the *status quo ante*. Not possible to reemerge and drop once more into the swing of life as if returning from vacation.

No, the reemergence itself promised to be a whole new source of trauma, and now she had made her spirit easy, she was hesitant to step out again into the plain free air of normality, worried that her emotional gain would have to be traded in in return for retaking her place in the outside world.

She heard the detectives file into the room upstairs and begin discussing with her father how they should proceed.

After nearly an hour's debate, he made a decision.

'Alright,' he said. 'My daughter's the most important thing. I'll put up the reward money and take out newspaper advertising.'

There was palpable relief in the room, and a minute's silence. The policemen's expressions communicated everything. They had been afraid they would have to override the man's wishes, and widen and publicise the search without his blessing. It was in the public interest and ultimately not his decision to take, but having him alongside and with the benefit of his money, the work to come would be far less ugly.

Nobody noticed a slight stirring beneath their feet, some

scuffling noises. They were too caught up in being relieved.

'Now get busy with your search so I don't have to spend the reward money!'

They rose slowly to leave, and Clare's father did not get up to see them out. They were a bit unsure whether they had actually been dismissed, and there was some awkward hesitation and hovering before anyone went for the door.

*

A British Brigadier who was the most senior Allied commander on Egyptian soil was helicoptered behind French lines during the shooting. Accompanied by the French paratroop commander, he made his way to the local waterworks building, which was in French hands, to meet with the Egyptian General in charge of the Port Said defences. The Egyptian and his staff entered the building under a white flag, and everyone stared at each other. It was very tense. Throughout the entire meeting, nobody sat down, nobody shook hands, and nobody smiled.

'We will agree a cease-fire if you stop killing civilians in Port Said, and reconnect the water supply.'

Some of the French who were present thought that were they in charge of the meeting, they would be able to work out a satisfactory arrangement. But the Brigadier felt bound to insist on full and unconditional surrender in the traditional form.

'Unconditional surrender? If that is your request, then we must contact Cairo for their instructions. I do not have the authority to hand over Port Said.'

They agreed a temporary cease-fire during which the matter was to be relayed to the Revolutionary Council Building in Cairo. The British secretly believed it would become a permanent cease-fire, assuming wrongly that they had severed every wire link out of Port Said, that the Egyptians were thus unable to contact Cairo with the message, knew as much, and that 'temporary' was really a face-saving description.

In fact, the overconfident wire-cutters had unknowingly passed over one submarine cable, and the Egyptian General was able to use it to apprise Cairo via trunk line of the surrender request. The Colonel was none too pleased at the message, and after the war he sent the General off to an early retirement.

For his part, the General always insisted that he never meant to surrender, and that the temporary cease-fire and message to Cairo were simply ways to buy time in which the Egyptian army could distribute weapons among the residents of Port Said so they could present the enemy with a more stubborn and spirited resistance the minute the truce expired.

The evidence suggests he was telling the truth. Between five and ten thirty in the evening, local time, endless crates of brand new, grease-covered Czech rifles and machine guns were deposited in large piles in the streets of Port Said for everyone living in the town to take from freely. Vans carried loudspeaker messages through the streets.

'World War Three has begun! The Russians are on their way to defend us! London and Paris have been devastated by nuclear bombs! Oh, brave people of Egypt! People of Port Said! Take up these guns and kill the invaders! Kill them with all your might and courage! The war is being won!'

At half past ten, well after darkness had descended on the port and the streets lay bare, empty crates strewn about and gun barrels pointed out of windows, the Egyptian General communicated the rejection of the surrender terms.

The crack of bullets ricocheting on the pavements was immediately heard, the shatter of glass on cement, the soft hurried pounding of feet down silent alleys, the furtive hand signals of group sergeants directing their men through the fearsome task of urban assault. Port Said crackled and shouted awake and became engulfed in lead-spitting, head-splitting combat.

Night life.

Missing Complements

HE LED HER by the hand to a large old tree and turned her gently by the shoulders so her back was to it. They kissed there, under the rustling branches, and some golden brown leaves fluttered to the ground about them. It was calm and natural unlike other first kisses. He knew as they walked hand in hand that it was to be done, and he knew as he reached the tree that it was to be done there, and he knew that she knew the same. There was no explaining it. There was just the living of it.

No charge of energy that made you faintheaded. Just the comfortable love of lip, to lip, on lip. Like they had done it before.

She had been unusually tender with him this time. She had spoken no brash words and said nothing provoking, and had been feminine of body, as always, but also of manner, submissively so. Almost.

It felt by her closeness as they walked that he should take her hand, and he did and she clasped her fingers round and through his and it was like she wanted to intertwine with him but without force or need. Her touch felt assured and yet soft and it gave as much as it took.

He had expected sternness but there was none.

She said little at all, but she seemed to him more human at this encounter than at any other, and not just because he was feeling her skin on his. Because her mode was changed. Or his. Or it was both of them together merged as two parts of a one.

Was it a wistful look in her eyes he saw that afternoon? Like she had already lost something between them? Certainly he would think so later.

Now all he knew was that he was in utter balance in himself and with her and on the world. No big feelings in him, only the smooth pulse of coasting along the surface of life like some wood down a river, on course for the sea. Like his world could be upheaved around him and he would scarce feel any shock of it. Constant he would be. A splash in the river by a boulder but the wood keeps on drifting. A part of nature. Just a normal thing.

We'll meet next Saturday.

Yes.

*

Order once again having dissolved on the streets of Port Said, the Allies making systematic progress from block to block, clearing out every last room of every last house and apartment of potential fighters, but facing tough resistance at each step (just hard luck, they told themselves), the British commanders received word that the Prime Minister had conceded under great pressure from the United Nations that all British bombing would cease.

The British Permanent Representative at New York had been telephoned by the Secretary-General, who had heard from his man in Cairo that things were being bombed over there.

There had been a bit of misunderstanding. The report was of indiscriminate bombing of populated areas in the Egyptian capital when really there had been hits only upon the rail line, an airport (the military one this time), and the main barracks. But the mood was hostile enough in the United Nations, with respect to the British and French presence at the Egyptian coast and in Egyptian skies, that knowledge of the more restrained scope of the bombing would not likely have changed any minds in any case.

The Representative notified London of the seriousness of the exception being taken to the British exploits in Egypt, and to prevent some drastic resolution being carried out in the General Assembly which would, by its morally persuasive force, end up freezing the British advance entirely, the Prime Minister let it be known among the Queen's military men that bombardment of Port Said must be avoided if at all possible.

The word was transmitted by emergency signal from Cyprus headquarters to the Land Force Commander, who then relayed the order to the officers concerned.

A major amphibious landing had been planned for first light, and there was strenuous protest from the officers against the notion of rolling up on the beaches, which were live with Egyptian armoured defences, without the cover of naval bombardment.

Never mind, was the reply, and if it could have been sent with a wink it would have been.

Government said 'no bombardment'. They said nothing about 'gunfire support'.

The fine English art of verbal pedantry finds its useful place well outside the confines of law, politics and the academy.

*

One o'clock in the morning. The marines would meet the paratroopers on the ground in the town in a few short hours. Some of the men tried to sleep. Others found their eyes would not close, instead staying peeled open at the dark emptiness of the night sky, the boundless tilting sheet of black; ears taking up the quick, impatient lapping of nervous water against the boat hulls.

*

Not tired, because he had slept once again for most of the day and gone into his deserted firm late in the evening, Roper left work in the wee hours and wandered the empty ways of the City. The square mile, the financial heart of London, is barren at night, and it sent up lonely echoes from the contact of his hard leather soles on the pavement. Not even any drunks were around to make him depressed. Just the soft blanketing of night.

He thought he might walk all the way home through the cool, dark breeziness of the capital.

Along a wide street and around a deserted circus.

A couple of taxis sputtering idle at the kerb. The drivers black ghosts, not really there with him. The silent unnoticed face of London, out of the poor estates where they too slept the days, happy to be earning an honest living in a rich land, but sure lonelier than Roper. Often shunned even within cabbie society, which was almost exclusively white and home-grown.

Their wives in distant foreign places, along with their children, of course; all earnings sent to the faraway families, probably through the hands of corrupt handlers. No money left over. Not for drink, not for sex. They had only the melancholy companionship of each other's expressionless stares.

Roper passed them by and walked and walked, and reminisced

about the day before.

He had been transformed since they first met.

Had the change begun as soon as her existence sparked through his synapses from her tangible stare at the party? Had that been a seed planted in his heart, waiting to be fertilised by a second encounter? In hindsight it seemed to be so, though had he never stumbled into her that day at the embassy after the impatient client had so fortuitously left him alone, he may never have had reason to think this was the case. The seed from the party might have dissolved away into the recesses of his veins, filtered out of his blood, and he would have thought those brief visions of her just a passing madness. No germination of a romance.

Was it that her company highlighted, brought out from hiding, a part of him already there, but which he had not known existed? Was she his missing complement, come to unbind the element of his life vigour from its stable compound, raise it from its unconsciousness, expel it from its complacent state of subnormalcy? Or did she actually add something to him, remoulding him after including a fresh ingredient, infusing him with a new brisk breath of paradise to suit her glowing essence, so that she would never find herself in the company, as otherwise she would, of an ordinary man?

He *was* now another person, letting himself be occupied by such thoughts with any seriousness.

Was she?

He kept up his pace through the city and wondered.

Resurrection

'MY DAUGHTER'S the most important thing.'

She would have to come out, she knew, at some point, and it might as well be now. She heard her father and the police talking about her, and considered it would be a good opportunity to hand over the coins and bring full circle the whole episode of her drift away from the friendly society of people. Besides, her father had just said she was the most important thing, and she reckoned that if capitalised upon soon enough, those words could be used to her profit.

Already thinking like her father.

She left behind her hiding supplies, ran up the steps, opened the panel, slid down off the ledge, and stepped her two feet onto the floor of the open hall.

Just then, a police officer walked out of her father's study. He glanced at her for a second and she smiled at him to be polite, and he smiled back, and carried on. A second uniformed man filed out behind him, and did not turn in Clare's direction to notice her. Then, just as a third man was stepping out into the hall, the first policeman stopped dead in his tracks, and the second policeman collided with him, and the third with the second. It was very comical and Clare laughed. They swivelled in unison to stare at her, and they all looked like friendly astonished straw men with axles through their heels, frozen still with their eyes stitched open wide.

'Now *what* is this about?' asked the first slowly but noisily.

Clare took a little step back. They looked silly and harmless, but the man sounded very serious.

'Are we being had?' asked the second.

'What's your name?' asked the third.

Clare's father poked his head out the door of his study to see what all the fuss was about, and Clare watched his face take on an open-mouthed, dumbstruck expression, which looked, as she would recount in later years, as though he had just witnessed the resurrection of Christ.

'God in heaven,' he said finally.

Then, after a few moments, hating not to be in control of a situation, he ordered everyone back into his study.

'Seat yourselves, gentlemen. Clare, first question. You look a right mess. Are you alright?'

'Yes.'

'Then you sit down as well, on that chair. Now let's get to the bottom of this.'

'Perhaps you'd like a few moments alone?'

'No. You've been put to some trouble over this, and I don't want anything concealed from you. This way you'll see we've been acting in good faith. Though in return, of course, you'll be discreet, and not let anything you learn here escape the ranks of the police.'

The policemen nodded.

'You've been gone nearly three days, Clare. Your mother has suffered a nervous breakdown and is now unable to leave her bed. I have sacrificed a great deal of business to attend to the vexing matter of your disappearance...'

A knock at the door interrupted his lecture.

'Come in.'

It was Nan, and she was visibly struck at seeing her young charge sat before her. She blinked, and it was no apparition.

'Oh, Clare! Where on earth have you been?'

Clare could not restrain herself from getting up off the chair. She ran over to Nan and leapt off the ground and wrapped her arms around her wizened neck, and though everyone saw the flash of emotion in Nan's eyes, she composed herself quickly.

'Now, Clare. You'll snap my neck in two. Go back to your seat and start conducting yourself in a manner appropriate to a young lady.'

Clare retreated to her chair.

'And as soon as you're finished in here you'll need a thorough scrubbing. Goodness me.'

Nan had come to inform Clare's father that she had been harassed by some newspapermen on the street, who had heard rumours of Clare's disappearance. She said she had denied everything and declined to comment further, and Clare's father assured her she had done the best possible thing.

'Oh, I'm glad. Thank you,' she said, and left.

'Now, Clare, you'll kindly tell us everything.'

'Please, can I first fetch something from my room? I promise to return straightaway.'

'I think we'll all come with you.'

So they proceeded purposefully down the corridor and up the stairs and into Clare's room; one little girl, three awkward policemen, and a millionaire in a starched white shirt and gold cufflinks.

They stood watching her, and she reached into a drawer and pulled out the coins, and turned to face the four men, looking up at them.

'Which one of you is the more important policeman?'

The officers looked at each other and chuckled.

'Wells is the more senior detective here.'

She held out the coins to him.

'These belong to the bus. Please, sir, can you see that they get returned?'

He leaned over and looked at the contents of her palm, and seeing their low value, he accepted the coins and put them in his pocket.

'Of course,' he said solemnly. He did not consider it wise just then to ask which bus, or what she meant.

'Now, Clare,' said her father, 'I think we've been very patient, considering. So let's hear it already. Where were you these last days, and what, for God's sake, were you up to?'

She didn't know where to begin the story, so instead she walked out of her room and led them all to the secret place, and took them down into it, and told them all not to be scared and that she was going to find the torch and things would be lit up in just a moment.

She picked it up, flicked it on, and shone it about the room.

'Blimey,' said one of the policemen.

'I'll be damned,' said Clare's father. 'I assure you gentlemen I never knew about the existence of this place.'

'You were down here the whole time, Clare?'

She nodded.

'Blimey,' repeated the policeman.

'Why?'

'You and mother needed to be taught a lesson.' She paused.

'And I needed some time to myself.'

She saw the corner of her father's mouth curl in slight suggestion of an amused smile.

'Go and see your mother, Clare, and tell her you're sorry.'

'Yes, father.'

'Right now.' He was stern again.

She ran up the steps and went to her mother's bedroom, leaving the men hunched over in the low room, looking round and round in amazement, not knowing quite what to say.

*

'I suppose we'd better tell them what we've learned from the CIA.'

It was dawn and the Port Said landing was to take place in thirty minutes.

'Even though the Prime Minister is not in the least concerned?'

'Look. He thinks so long as we're in step with the Americans that the Russians wouldn't dare. But we don't know the Russians. We never have. With all respect to the Prime Minister, he's under tremendous strain, and it's been showing. If you hadn't noticed, he's surviving on stimulants. And I'm not so sure we're as closely in step with the Americans as he thinks.'

'We're military men and he is not, and you know as well as I that concealing strategic knowledge of this magnitude is a grave disservice to *Musketeer* and to the armed forces. Have some faith in our Commanders.'

'Letting the Commanders know will only be providing them with another source of undue strain and confusion.'

'This is serious enough that we have a responsibility to inform them, and they certainly have a right to know.'

The other sat and thought for a minute, his forehead in his hands. 'Yes,' he said finally. 'I know you're right.'

So one of the Chiefs of Staff in London dictated a message to be sent by highest priority cable to the Allied Commander-in-Chief at the operation location.

FLASH 060536Z. URGENT – BEAR IN MIND.
RUSSIA INDICATING READINESS TO USE FORCE

IN MIDEAST AND HINTING NUCLEAR THREAT.
USA WARNING RUSSIA ANY FORCE WILL ENCOUNTER
USA OPPOSITION.

And the fate of the world seemed then, for just a fleeting while, to rest on British shoulders. The administration had, in a perverse kind of way, got what they subconsciously wanted: a reaffirmation a decade after they stared down the obliteration of free Europe and won the confrontation; fifteen years after their brave men were all that stood between the sceptered isle and the storm troopers; and now, in 1956, after all it had weathered, that the British man-of-war was still sailing strong. That Britannia possessed the global might and broad freedom of geopolitical manoeuvre which belonged to her by imperial birthright. That she could still step into the fray and hold her own, and that her men and money and machines could yet, by firm and resolute action, tip the balance of the world. Now the nuclear world.

*

Naveen was young and muscular and handsome and exotically brown, with a brilliant white smile and the unseasoned confidence of youth that Zafirah had not seen so near to her in a long time. He was exuberant in the energy he unknowingly projected from his frame, while at once being almost shyly retiring in his conscious posture, and deferential within her husband's realm of authority.

As she ministered to him at her husband's command, unobtrusive and nearly unnoticed, like a good servant, she felt half mother, seeing to his corporeal needs, tender, and half maiden, wanting, guilty, for him to see to her. Also tender.

Daylight was business and childcare and servience, and desire coiled itself away at the base of her spine, patient for the dark.

Her husband's long absences built up the spring inside of her and she would have taken ten men, not just one, or two.

Deep in the night, flushed from a dream and not all herself, she entered the living room in a light cotton robe, nothing covering her flesh beneath, and made sure the sash was undone. If she moved too suddenly her body would be revealed, and she would casually and not too quickly pull it back around her, belatedly closing the window of skin. She would imagine he had been awake and had seen it.

She went to stand next to the couch and hovered there. He had been given the children's room but roundly refused it when he learned they would have to sleep on the floor in the sitting room and kitchen. Instead, over the strenuous objections of her husband, Naveen had taken the couch.

She put her hand on his foot and rested it there, then slid it upwards, curving her fingers around his hard smooth calf above the ankle. He inhaled sharply and she stopped moving her hand, but did not remove it from him. He settled back into his dream, and she waited some time. Then she moved it again, further up his bare leg, and now he opened his eyes and looked directly at her.

Her heart pounded in its cage as he stayed there, motionless, expressionless, suppressed under the weightless heavy ton of her lightly leaning arm. He did not resist her touch. He did not know what to do. She saw him growing quickly large under his loose shorts, and saw him squint and purse his mouth in indecision. Her breaths became sudden and she was being pulled by an invisible cord back to her husband's bed and being drawn like a magnet onto Naveen's body, and she would yield to neither force until one was exerted more strongly.

Naveen withdrew his leg from her touch and with much power of will turned over so he lay on his front, and put his face down into his folded arms. Turned his back on her offer which was more a request, foiling her brave expedition. And she retreated to her husband, soft as she left him.

Judgement Calls

IF THE Prime Minister in England did not take the warning of Russian rockets very seriously, the entire French Cabinet, camped out at their leader's palatial residence in the seventh arrondissement, were scared to death.

The previous November, the Soviets had test-detonated the RDS-37, their first two-stage radiation implosion weapon, at Semipalatinsk in Kazakhstan. It had a yield of 1.6 megatons.

In Britain they had reason to feel confident. If the Soviets decided to wipe the British Isles off the face of the planet, British subjects could rest easy in the knowledge that Her Majesty's fission bombs would be put to good use in decimating large swathes of Russia in second-strike retaliation. Destruction was mutually assured, so everyone could sleep soundly at night.

But France had no nuclear capability, and the Cabinet men were desperately worried that they would lack the means to kill off the Soviet people if they were themselves attacked by fissile devices from out of the great enigmatic goliath to the east.

The anxious French leader summoned the American Ambassador to the hotel at two in the morning, and demanded to know what the Americans would do if Paris found itself the target of a Soviet attack. Everyone was very jittery, and the fatigued Ambassador found the whole thing pretty unpleasant. Inappropriately, the French leader was also using the occasion to try and wrest some statement of commitment from the Ambassador that the Americans would ensure free elections in Egypt once the fighting was over.

The Ambassador didn't take happily to rooms full of uppity politicians at such ungodly hours, especially if they were very animated and French and overly talkative. But he kept up his perpetually pleasant demeanour.

'Oh, a Russian attack would engage the NATO treaty. No doubt about that. The United States will be at your side.'

'Can you get confirmation of this now?'

'I'm afraid you'll have to take my solemn assurance at the

moment. Everyone's all wrapped up in the election just now.'

'I see.' The French leader was clearly unsatisfied, but recognised that he would not get anything more firm at that hour. 'But,' and this was a pet concern he simply would not give up, 'there *must* be free elections in Egypt.'

'The President is aware of your position on Egyptian elections, Mr Prime Minister. For now, I suggest we all take things one step at a time.'

*

In a large fire-proof, bullet-proof, sound-proof, and radiation-proof chamber with monitored ventilation shafts and radio signal interrupters, deep inside the American Embassy in Moscow, the US Military Attachés were toiling through the night. They were sweating, poring over the unread reports that had been stacking up on their desks, analysing the previous evening's posturing by the Kremlin men, nervously bouncing their legs up and down in a way that only heightened everyone's tension, their hands trembling from the excess of coffee, their minds jumping disconnectedly from thought to exciting thought. To scary thought.

Caffeine pills had also been passed around.

They had been told to make their best 'judgment call' before the night was out. The question they had to answer with authority, and with their careers possibly on the line, was whether the Ruskies were bluffing, and if not, what exactly they might be expected to do.

By dawn they had prepared a summary, reporting that Russia had really sent the West an ultimatum in all but name, and that the Soviets, now they had weighed in, could not afford not to follow through with some decisive action if Britain, France and Israel did not back down very soon. Their 'great power credibility' was at stake.

The Attachés conjured up a few specific scenarios they thought might unfold, involving such frightening Soviet acts of brinkmanship as operating submarines against the Allies out of the Adriatic, flooding Syria with MiGs, ready to take to the skies against the colonialist invaders, and providing armies of skilled Russian 'volunteers' to engage the Allies directly on the ground.

Escalation, a giant beast crouching at the sidelines and waiting to be unleashed, menaced Western leaders that night, gnashing together its sharp metal teeth and exuding the thick morbid stench of physical destruction.

*

In that corridor in Clare's house which had recently been the stage for so much drama, there were now five paintings resting upright on the floor, leaned against the wall in a row.

A thin, bony man with little round spectacles and a fitted brown suit was kneeling next to one of them, inspecting, and running his finger now and again along the frame, feeling. Every so often he would pull out a handkerchief and wipe his fingers into it, replace it in his pocket, and then, using the freshly wiped finger, push his spectacles up the bridge of his nose.

One of the first things Clare's father did, once the commonly felt shock of his daughter's return slipped away from the domain of the sensory and into the realm of history, was summon one of London's leading art experts.

The servants carted up the paintings from the closet in the secret room under the man's direction, stirring up a century of dust, and one of them began sneezing uncontrollably.

The art expert, who was an incurable hypochondriac, and also not a very pleasant man, told the servant angrily to stop sneezing in the same room as others, at which the servant stumbled away up the steps and down the hall.

After all the paintings had been brought out, they could still hear the poor man sniffling in a room behind a closed door, once in a while punctuating the silence with a great trumpeting sneeze.

Nobody spoke as the expert, on his knees, over and over again, leaned close to a canvas and then swayed back, then got onto all fours to inspect some point near the bottom, then got up onto his knees again and reached behind the painting and tapped at the backing with one hand, holding up the other hand to request utter silence.

Clare's father became impatient with his theatrics and left. He went to see his wife and sit next to her without speaking a word, and gave her a prolonged look that said 'you see, you had nothing

234

to worry about, and yes, I know you were under strain and I've already forgotten anything nasty that might have passed between us', restoring her faith in his dedication to her and just possibly in his character generally, and she resigned herself delicately to accept once again the shelter of his wealthy, paternalistic wing.

Her hands were in her lap and he rested his on hers for an instant; his warm, hers cool; and she let him, passively reaffirming their matrimonial bond. And he stood up, satisfied, and left, returning to the art.

By the time he arrived back at the corridor, the expert was no longer examining the paintings, but pacing now, slowly back and forth, his hand on his chin.

'What's the verdict, then?'

The man stopped, turned deliberately to face Clare's father, paused, clasped his fingers together in front of him, and said in the most disinterested tone he could muster, 'I think you might have something here.'

'Oh?'

'Early pre-Raphaelite. Sterling condition, which is quite surprising. I'm hesitant to say anything more at the moment.'

'Valuable?'

The man paused, considering his response. It looked as though he had something to say but was not sure it was prudent to say it.

'I should have thought,' he said eventually, mildly, 'that they constitute a national treasure.'

VII

Toggles of the Mind

NOW THE final day of battle in the Suez war, heralded at first light by the journey, cutting sharply across the momentary centrepoint of the world, of a lone artillery shell, hurtling swiftly against a dark red dawn, bursting violently into some shanty huts by the beaches of Port Said and setting them aflame... and followed in immediate rapid blasting succession by a torrent of further ordnance arriving on the sandy shores, from the sea and from overhead, a vertical and horizontal convergence of explosive insanity at coastal Egypt.

Valiants swooped low and loosed their payloads over the port, demolishing neighbourhoods, hiding them under columns of ash and smoke, and suddenly, with an earthshaking tremor, hitting a nearby oil installation, sending up a dead hot burning ball of awe that was visible in its thermal splendour from the decks of the armada, reflecting like a little mad sun on the excited surface of the early morning sea.

Amidst this firestorm, the Royal Marine Commandos commencing their approach to the Egyptian shore in landing vehicles; small transport boats that get converted into beach crawlers upon contact with land. Steady on, protected by the 'gunfire support' from above and behind, and soon to be joined by a squadron of Centurion tanks, which were being floated ashore on special landing craft.

Then, twenty-five minutes after the non-stop barrage began, it was cut off simultaneously from all sources at a word from the Task Force Commanders.

For the forty-five endless seconds that followed, there was nothing at all to be heard at Port Said.

The only sound, the mechanical splashing of the approaching landing craft, was drowned out, hidden from the hearing of any Egyptian unlucky enough to be present, the noise smothered by the enforced soundlessness after a bombardment when the ears refuse to register anything that does not match in decibels the great tumult of the previous minutes.

So just the silent scene of no more bombing and the steady approach of the invaders' helmets in ugly dark metal boats and many long muzzles protruding out from them in all forward directions.

Forty-five seconds of lull.

Until the sweeping return of the Hunter aircraft.

They swung buzzing out of the quiet sky and in perfect formation they bellied low, noses angled to the sand, and strafed the beach thoroughly from east to west. In coincidence with the air assault, the shanty huts began exploding in little banging puffs as stores of ammunition, abandoned by fleeing residents, gave way to the lapping flames ignited by the bombardment, the 'gunfire support', just past.

When the planes lifted away the landing stage was set, cleared of immediate opposition, the arrival of the troops by water now an easy thing. The boats tracked their way onto the sand, and the men leapt out, bent over but with their heads up for trouble, and made their way across the beach under light fire, which was emanating from some concrete buildings in the distance.

Only when they found themselves entering the town streets were they faced for the first time with the split-second decisions and flashing scenes which would trouble them for the rest of their lives. Civilians with guns running in all directions, terrified, undisciplined, fleeing, but some staying, hunched, concealed behind a pillar, crouched beneath a window sill, letting off bursts of defiance in the soldiers' direction.

If you see a ragged-looking man, maybe in his sixties, with a beard and sandals and no uniform and a fatherly face and a machine gun clasped tight to his body, not shooting and not aiming at you but running across your field of vision in fear as firefights blaze around you both, do you fell him with a quick easy shot while you have the chance? Or do you let him go, maybe later to kill your mates, or kill you, or maybe only to find his wife and children and protect their lives?

Come on, lads, be decisive. No time to make a wrong choice.

Such was the bitter taste of action for the young British marines on that early morning of their first engagement.

*

240

And the paratroopers who were closing in to meet the marines had to take similarly wrenching decisions, although they were for the most part somewhat older and more battle hardened, particularly the French ones.

By the time the marines landed and entered into combat, the Parachutistes Coloniaux had been fighting all the previous day and most of the night, and had racked up quite a lot of killing among the jungle of sand, gravel, concrete, and now rotting flesh, the sea splashing pleasantly in the distance and the moist saline breeze soothing the mortally wounded, easing their last waking minutes. Comforting the slaughtered.

Once you have shot eight uniformed Egyptians in close quarters in the last few hours, watching the pained look of surprise common to all their eyes as the fatal bullets entered, seeing lifeblood spurt thickly from severed arteries, and trying, the hardest part of all, not to hear the agonised screams; once you have accomplished this, turn your gun on a civilian who is bearing arms and you might find the action no longer poses so great a shock to your psyche. You have reverted to a primordial state of moral calculation, where an enemy national with a gun becomes simply an enemy national with a gun, never mind what he's wearing and whether he's pointing his weapon at you.

Then, from that diminished stage of consciousness, after twenty hours of brutal hellish street work, of killing anyone with a weapon who does not wear your colours or those of your friends, you find you're just in plain elimination mode, complex identity discrimination switched off because it does not seem to be a necessary condition of your own survival. It becomes you or them, dead or alive. Two simple toggles of the mind.

So when you encounter at dawn, as the French soldiers did, a group of terrified but peaceful and unarmed elderly fishermen, huddling by their boats, their livings, by the water, their hands raised in the air and begging to be spared, no threat in the face of your machine guns; when you encounter them in their humble supplicating state you might just, as the French did, shout at one another in a murderous frenzy to mow them down, and shoot them all to death by the water where they stand. Bodies splashing undignified into the sea, and the waters taking on the earthen red of spreading blood.

Prisoners are inconvenient in such chaotic circumstances. Everyone's dying anyway. It must have been their turn too.

Bad luck.

Come now. Is it our fault we have to kill all these Egyptians?

*

Along with the men, their souls, and the bombs, fell the pound. Britain was isolated diplomatically to an uncommon degree, France the only unreserved friend at the moment, and City bankers quickly fled the sterling market, the rest of the world promptly following suit, divesting itself of the dirty imperialist currency.

The Chancellor of the Exchequer could only stand and watch, horrified, as the sterling area appeared to be collapsing. For once, the Americans could not be approached for the propping up which they normally gave the Treasury with unquestioning magnanimity.

The Prime Minister was notified of the looming disaster, but for the time being there was nothing he could do without upsetting the careful balance of the constitution of the United Kingdom. He was obliged to sit, possessing full knowledge of the immediacy of the economic crisis, in a state of immense frustration. The Queen's Speech, with all its slow ritual, was being performed in the House of Lords, and to get up and leave would have been unthinkable. He knew exactly what had to be done, but he would have to wait patiently in order to do it, millions of pounds sinking steadily away in the meantime. Tens of thousands of pounds sliding down a drainpipe with every word uttered carefully by the young, graceful monarch.

The soon-to-be Common Market chiefs, the French and German political leaders, would have to be leaned upon for emergency support of the sterling reserves. That was the urgent plan running back and forth along the limbs of his body, tightening his joints and plucking at his nerves, and yet he managed to sit through the dragging proceedings with the external appearance of remaining unflapped. He had good stiff control of his image. Imperturbability.

Ways Out

AS LONG as he was recalling the touch of Azim's wife on his skin, Naveen was a bit uncomfortable rubbing bare forearms with Azim as they sat next to each other on the jerky bus into the city. So he told himself it had been a dream, and swore he would think of it no more, and for the most part he succeeded, because he had not yet saturated his spirit in sexuality, and was not tormented in the nights by the lure of the feminine, or the masculine. His energy still channelled itself outward to adventure, deflecting the onslaught of temptation without him even knowing it.

Being borne upon by a wanting woman was exciting and educational, and cause for self-congratulation, but it did not, as it might have done to an older man, penetrate the skin of his mind and give rise to tumultuous, agitating, even violent, inner obsessions. Instead it just became another memory as he moved on to the next bright episode of discovery. Firmly blocking out the recollection of her touch was not so hard for him that morning as they headed into the city, that day of the Port Said landing.

Azim was accompanying him into Cairo to find a good black-market moneychanger who dealt in gold. If things got worse and the capital was attacked by ground forces, such errands might become much more difficult. Better have cash on hand in advance.

So he changed three coins and kept the rest, walking out of the dingy back room of a perfume shop in El-Dukki with several large wads of American dollars. He had declined the moneychanger's kind offer to hold the cash in safekeeping for him. He would rather risk losing the dollars out of his own hand than return one day to the shop and find the man gone, or the shop gone, or the man and the shop still there but the memory of the trade evaporated.

'I am holding your money? Don't be ridiculous. What idiot would leave so much cash in the hands of a stranger? You traded gold here? For American dollars? I doubt it. But wait, wait, do not look so upset. Let me try and recall. I am thinking. Please have some patience. Maybe...

'Hmm. No. It is no use. I see so many people every day. I am sorry, my friend, but I think you must be mistaken. Your face is not familiar to me. I wish you good fortune. Now please, I have important business to attend to. Goodbye.'

Naveen would have none of that, so he purchased a small satchel and carried the money inside it, and bought some clothing, and concealed the money in the bundle of fabrics, then he bought a bottle of water, and placed it on top of everything in the bag to help account for the volume of the contents. But all of this only increased his paranoia. Eventually, just like he dispensed with the shaded mental image of Zafirah leaning over him, he simply forced himself to shove this worry firmly out of his mind.

Then, because it was Tuesday morning, they went to a post office so Naveen could contact the Company.

'Mr Bhattacharya?'

'Naveen? We have been in contact with the Egyptian government and made arrangements with them, and also we have finally established contact with the vessel. We have informed the Captain of the situation and ordered all hands to disembark and accept accommodation in Ismailia, which will be provided by the Canal authority. Now, I have spoken with the Captain, and, from what I understand, you have behaved very courageously. We need not discuss the goings on that were taking place on the ship any more than that. Our insurance brokers do not need to know anything about it. Do you understand?'

'Yes.'

'Now, as for you, there are three options. If you would like to return to India, that is your choice, but we would encourage you to remain in service, and we will not consider there to be any disruption in your contract. So the second option is to join the men at Ismailia. But I understand it may be dangerous to reach there, and, moreover, in the light of recent events, we think you might be better off with a different complement.

'The Captain told me about giving you some of the gold, and under the circumstances I am prepared to support his decision. I understand he also used Master's prerogative to release your passport to you. This may prove to be a blessing, and I applaud the Captain for his foresight.

'Vessels are being diverted around the Cape. We expect that one will be making a call off Mogadiscio. If you think you can reach Mogadiscio in three weeks' time, I would very much encourage you to join the *Liberty* at that port. We have an understanding with some Italian agents, and if we make arrangements, they will receive you there. But it is not the simplest journey to take, and I'm afraid we at the offices are not the ones to advise you. You must ascertain this for yourself. It will not be held against you if you choose not to embark on the trek to Somalia. But please let us know by Thursday.'

Naveen's head was reeling from this barrage of surprising information, and he could not think on the spot how to reply, so he gratefully accepted the postponement.

'Very well,' he said, 'I will dial you by Thursday.'

'Alright. Think about it. Goodbye for now. Oh, and mind yourself, Naveen. I hear there is some bombing around Cairo.'

'Thank you. I shall. Goodbye.'

'Oh, and Naveen?'

'Yes.'

'Well done, my boy. You're something of a celebrity at the Company. Enjoy it while it lasts.'

Naveen laughed. He liked the sound of that.

All the way back to Giza he found it difficult to make conversation with Azim, his mind preoccupied with the exciting prospect of fresh adventure. Things were looking better than he had conceived possible, and the new possibilities for travel stimulated his imagination. And it would be on Company money and fully authorised, to boot.

✳

After having his bone set and his arm encasted and lying for nearly a week on a creaky bed in an otherwise quiet military hospital, recovering from the traumatic shock of his hours at Mitla, attended by gentle hands in the open, breezy ward with windows ajar and flapping white curtains, overseen by pleasing young faces, Walid was handed his bag of effects and discharged. Free to go home.

Home?

Home was a tiny one-room flat overlooking the water in Port

245

Said. And it was the sixth of November. He had heard nothing of the war while in the hospital bed, but when he walked out of the building into the street (and discovered for the first time that he was in Ismailia), he wandered over to a café and sat and drank a little cup of thick coffee, and told the other two men sitting in the early afternoon laze all about the insanity of Mitla and about his brushes with death, spinning an enriched tale (though it need not have been so in order to achieve the desired effect), keeping his listeners at the edge of their seats, sowing awe in the dark room under the revolving fan blades.

'So now where will you go?'

'Thanks to God, back to my home in Port Said.'

The men looked at each other.

'Port Said?'

'Yes. Why not? What is wrong?'

'I had a niece in Port Said. She escaped last night with her husband on a motorcycle, and we had a desperate message from her that they are coming to stay with us here.'

'Escaped. Why? Are they fighting there?' His words were sharp and abrupt. He fought back a surge of primitive fear at the thought of Israelis fighting in the streets of his town.

'Yes. There is terrible fighting. Destruction. You must not go.'

He must not go home.

For once, he thought himself lucky not to have a family. No one to rescue.

The only place he could stay would be with his hospitable friend, Azim. The latter had taken him in once before, in more impoverished times, and Walid had no doubt he and his wife would take him in again. The thought struck him suddenly that Azim could be dead, and he hoped to God he was still alive. That he had not been butchered by the Israelis wherever he had been assigned.

His mind now elsewhere, he bid the men a hasty goodbye and set off for Giza.

*

He was hugely relieved when Zafirah told him that Azim was in town with a guest, and please, would he like to come in and make

246

himself comfortable? Azim would be so happy to see him when he returned.

Yes, yes, thank you, dear woman. And do not mind if I help myself to some sweets and cigarettes.

Of course, it is your home here. But ahh, look at that arm! What shall I do to help?

Oh, it is nothing, dear woman. You are too kind. I will be fine. It is a minor injury.

From the Israelis?

Yes.

Bah! The filthy devils.

Never mind. It was nothing. Please, do not let me disrupt your chores.

Oh, thank you, Walid. You are a kind and a very brave man.

He smiled to himself, and reclined comfortably in Azim's dozing chair.

Leaving Egypt

AS WALID rested there in the flat, the war ended. The British administration held back the tide of international and domestic pressure as long as it could, so the armies might gain as much ground as possible before the inevitable cease-fire. But the delicate breakwater of diplomatic and political manoeuvre finally gave way, on the sixth of November.

A week earlier, the Canadian Minister for External Affairs had got busy working the diplomatic circuit in New York. He commiserated with the American Secretary of State, expressing grave disappointment at the Anglo-French 'ultimatum', which had risen without advance notice out of the blue. He was accustomed to being confided in by his British and French counterparts. He was used to it all being very gentlemanly, old school and civilised. The activities in the Middle East rubbed him coarsely in the wrong direction.

Three days into the crisis, after the Americans proposed a cease-fire resolution in the General Assembly, the Canadian statesman stood up at four in the morning and called for some calm amidst the argumentative grip that had been squeezing the chamber. The cease-fire resolution, though adopted, was not binding in international law. Let's take some time for informal chats. Let me talk to my contacts, to some Commonwealth men, and maybe throw together something of an emergency military presence, a peacekeeping force for the Suez. Strictly under United Nations mandate, of course. Nobody wants a repeat of the Korea debacle.

Of course.

The American Secretary of State loved it. He interrupted the Canadian to give the idea his firm and enthusiastic endorsement, and let it be known that America would throw itself behind such a proposal if introduced formally at the next session.

Newspapers in Britain, public opinion, the Universities, the Opposition in Parliament, they all seized upon the cease-fire resolution and the Canadian plan, and the ideas, gaining popular momentum, became a nightmare to the British government. Crowds gathered along Whitehall, and their chants (moralising, treasonous?) could be heard right through the brick walls of the Prime Minister's residence, vibrating the floors.

∗

The day the El-Firdan bridge blew, the Old Man who led Israel, knowing that the army would shortly possess Sharm-el-Sheikh, permitted his man at the United Nations, the Israeli statesman who had made that impassioned justificatory speech a few nights before, to accept the cease-fire proposal. They had nothing else to gain by remaining in the fight.

A few days later, after the most severe and substantive chastisement their country has probably ever received from the United States, the Israelis withdrew from the Sinai and handed it back to Egypt via United Nations soldiers.

Even before that, Israel simply having stopped its advance, acceding to the pressure to lay down arms, there truly appeared to be no legitimate excuse for the Europeans to be in Egypt. The Canadian peacekeeping resolution was passed without obstacle, and an Indian-sponsored resolution for the fighting to end entirely within twelve hours was carried with only five votes of opposition.

The French administration, were it not for their intimate partnership with the British, would have cared about none of this. They were content to ignore world opinion, knowing full well their affair would soon be forgotten, buried in an archive, wrapped in a coil of microfilm, some footnote; knowing that even if it did not so quickly escape the popular consciousness, their diplomatic position would in the long run be little changed regardless.

Yes, we had gone into Egyptian territory. Yes, it had probably been a bit of a silly idea. But it's over know. So let's just forget about it.

But the British Ministers, who would not sleep at night knowing the world thought badly of them, accepted that their time in Egypt was limited, and so the French, who were insistent on the Egypt action remaining a joint venture throughout, understood that their time in Egypt would be limited too.

The parachute drops and the Port Said landing had been undertaken on the now shaky pretext, because Israel had just accepted the cease-fire recommendation, that Israeli troops had not yet withdrawn from Sinai and that Israel had voted against the Canadian plan. But things soon got worse for the Prime Minister and it looked as though the government could fall. So he stood up in the House of Commons and announced at long last, for it had been an interminably hellish few days, that British forces would observe a cease-fire from midnight.

The House broke into loud cheering, and everyone felt much relieved.

*

Walid stayed sitting, blissfully at rest with his life and his freedom, appreciating the experience of doing nothing, admiring the natural pattern of the lines in the wood on the table, of the supple energy in the movement of Azim's children's limbs when they pranced in, home from school; of the music of voices dancing to each other in the room's air about him.

When Azim and Naveen came home, in the split second before Walid rose in effusive greeting to embrace and kiss Azim, Naveen watched the infinite contentedness of Walid's expression and thought he understood why it was there, though he knew nothing at all about the man or his history. He was sure Walid had been playing games with Azim's wife and that his look had been one of smug satisfaction, and Naveen worried greatly that if he remained much longer he would again find himself in the awkward position of having to reject the overenthusiastic woman.

She knew she would never again approach Naveen, and probably not another man but her husband for a long while. But Naveen had no idea of her thinking. He knew that whatever she did, it would be awkward for him to remain. Quiet and small as she was, a soft, gentle part of the woodwork, her presence in the crowded flat would be loud as thunder to Naveen.

Discovering, moreover, that Walid had arrived to stay, he knew beyond doubt that he would part for Mogadiscio sooner rather than later. Preferably not even spend another night in the flat. It would be too much of a burden on the family.

Never one to impede or delay his own firm decisions to act, he informed Azim with solemnity that he would have to leave; it was the Company's request; that his gratitude could not be told in words, that on his pledge of honour he would never mention to anyone what he saw at El-Firdan, that Azim was the kindest and most decent man he ever had the fortune of meeting, and that he would not be satisfied if Azim would not accept a small gift.

Just a shiny commemorative medallion, he said with a sly wink, slipping a gold coin into Azim's shirt pocket.

And slipping quickly out before there could be too much protest. Out on his own again, hand sliding speedily along the railing and feet bumping lightly down the stairs, out the door, along the road...

And away!

Away

AWAY ALSO went his vibrant energy, departed from the flat, leaving a depletion in its wake. Just the old and familiar. Azim, Zafirah, Walid, and the children.

'But mother, why is Walid's arm made of plaster?'

Zafirah had been in a foul mood all day.

'Because,' she replied, 'a rocket from a brigand Zionist imperialist invader army broke his arm in half. And the poor innocent have to suffer because the rich people in the world are greedy executioners.'

'Oh.'

The boy twirled his curled black hair between his fingers and turned his attention to the arm. Not interested in his mother's abstractions.

She hadn't meant to speak up so loudly. It silenced everyone in the room, so all that could be heard was the background noise out the window, the sorry sound of beggar children playing with empty bottles out in the street dirt. The sound of glass shattering and children crying and shouting and swearing. Breaking bottles on pavement and kicking the shards of glass the only amusement in the long hopeless alleys.

*

Looking along the aisles between the desks in the classroom. Children breaking pencil lead. The rows and columns drab in their squareness, dreary straight lines, an endless collection of hard right angles. Perpendicularity.

In school again.

She had been home ill for a few days. A white lie. It's just *so* much simpler, Clare. And more appropriate in these exceptional circumstances. And not only because father, mother and Nan had all three of them said so, but because she saw herself the value in not sharing the reason for her absence with her schoolmates. They simply would not have understood. Not remotely. They...

'*Stop* breaking the pencil lead!'

Miss Berkhoff flew into a holy fit and sent five students, selected apparently at random, into the corner, which she swore to them was only a holding cell until such time as she felt they had provided sufficient example of what befalls those who destroy precious resources entrusted to them by a benevolent institution such as a school. Then it will be off to the headmistress, and we shall let *her* decide the rest.

Ominous.

But wholly unworrying to Clare, who had lately transcended the bounds of such ordinary threats, not at all afraid of the teacher's mundane words.

Oblivious.

Who cared about being sent to the headmistress for a quick talking to? She had been in *hiding* for a near *eternity*. For heaven's sake.

When school was out for the day she gathered her things and walked out the door out the schoolyard to the gate to Nan, heedless of her passage, her thoughts far elsewhere, and could not believe her mind when it informed her that the familiar person standing there waiting for her was not Nan.

It was father.

Who swept her up in his arms, a great knight, and kissed her on the cheek and replaced her on the ground and said how would you like to come with me for an afternoon?

No need for a reply. The answer was obvious. Obvious to her. It would be like a precious dream.

She just looked up at him and nodded vividly, her eyes asparkle.

'Good.'

He had driven himself, and now he was driving himself and his daughter, a man in poised and elegant control. The greatest man in the whole wide world.

So this is what comes when you take matters into your own hands and show a bit of independence. You get to be with father, like an equal. To go with him to...

'We're going to Mincing Lane, Clare. It's auction time, and I need someone to stand by my side and make me look important.

Are you up to the task?'

She nodded again, and it was enough of a reply, because he saw it out of the corner of his eye.

'Good. Now I'd better give you a bit of background.'

'Yes.'

'Yes. Well, let's begin with the tea itself. The leaves begin their journey to my company out of the high hills of Darjeeling. Or sometimes from Siliguri. They're harvested and selected according to grade. There's the good whole leaf stuff at the top of the ladder, then you have the brokens, then the fannings, for the middle classes, Clare, then there's the dusts, for your honest working man. There's something for everyone. And I; we, Clare; we provide something for everyone. And I'm not crooked like half the merchants in this country. If the package says Darjeeling, it contains Darjeeling. I challenge anybody to prove otherwise.'

They curved gracefully around a bend, and Clare turned her face out the side window and watched a new part of the world passing by. Unfamiliar buildings. Strange and wonderful streets.

'Then the tea gets here and is auctioned off by merchants, to merchants. It used to be that I did the selling at auction. Now mainly I do the buying. And because I'm an old hand at importing I bypass the auctions as well from time to time, buying my own tea cargoes so that they belong to me from the moment they're loaded onto a ship in Calcutta; that's a city in India, Clare; to the time they leave my packaging plant in lorries.

'In any case, we're now going to an auction. In the end, it's been a real blessing that I was distracted away from the markets these past few days. Everybody's been buying up stock like mad, like there will be no more tea grown as of this Saturday. Ever. By order of the Queen. If I hadn't been preoccupied I would have done the same, just another fool. But the war is ending and the price reached a plateau yesterday, and no doubt that means it will begin to fall.

'Make sense so far?'

'It makes perfect sense.'

He turned to look at her, and the car seemed to drive itself for a minute, loyal to its master and not losing its way as the gazes of generations met there above its soft seats, two looks clasping together in firm acknowledgment of the shared destiny of lineage, the common experience of bloodline and spiritline.

He turned his eyes back to the road and continued.

'Half my reason for going to this auction is to pretend to look desperate. Make my enemies think I'm losing it. I don't really mean to buy anything. Just force up their bids so that when the price does begin to fall *they*'ll be the fools.'

'I see,' she said, which seemed the appropriate response.

'You see? It *is* competitive. Those blockheads at the Monopolies Commission think we're all in league, all us big seven brokers. But we're at each other's *throats*!'

Yes. At each other's throats. Pirates. Her father the lone good man in a ruthless sea, dodging the waves and the cannonballs and the glinting pirate daggers.

And the best man would prevail. And she would be at his side.

With her father.

Whisked wonderfully away on the wide sloping waters, rocking gently on the sea with his infallible protection. Her very best wish.

The Third State

ROPER'S much anticipated wish. It was to lunch with Gefen like they were a pair of ordinary people falling in love, doing the usual things such people did as they courted, though there would only be one person to fall into love here, because he knew he had already inhabited that place for some days now.

It was to do the lunches and dinners and movies, and because he was a comfortable lawyer and could afford it, the theatre and a fancy boat ride on the Thames, and then a trip for just the two of them to a seaside hotel in Torquay where they would do their strolling in a bit more style on an English beach, even though it was autumn or maybe winter already, depending on whom you asked, and the breeze would be cold; even though there would be a bracing damp chill, they would walk, because she would be kept nicely warm under a thick woollen cardigan, and if that were not enough, perhaps because they would be showered upon by a scattering of raindrops from over the sea, she would have his jacket to cover her, and they would be heedless of getting sand on them everywhere, and would bring it back with them between their toes because it had got into their shoes, and into their bed, and grinding roughly between their skins as it spread from their feet to the sheets to their legs intertwined and all over their persons; their persons, apart from the whole wide world, just them in a garish cozy hotel with a florid coloury carpet and pale pink walls in their suite and an ornamented ceiling long ago coated over with white paint and an elaborate ironwork grille at one edge for him to look into as she dominated him in their shared springy bed that you sank into deeply as you do only in the beds in those hotels, seeing through the design of the iron grate covering the vent into a long dark place of invisible passage, which converges with other such long dark places and leads only God knows where, but to a damned good place, that was for sure, because with her for the rest of his life and forafter there only were damned good places.

Though today it was still part of the waiting period and so back to the habitual illicit phone conversation. Because he'd heard about the cease-fire and she had a promise to keep to him, and he would see to it she kept it if it was the last thing he did, because she owed it to him, because he had pulled himself through all this anguish of waiting for her. For a few days.

Now on the phone.

'You remember you made me a promise?'

'I don't know. What did I say?'

His love teetered dangerously towards hate and then righted itself, just barely.

'That you'd come to lunch once the war ended. And I think it's ended.'

'I'm not so sure.'

'But the cease-fire.'

'A cease-fire is not as clean and neat as it sounds on the radio news.'

Blast her and all her self-important knowledge of the way things work in the world.

'Yes, well, how about lunch?'

'I think that would be very nice.'

Do you?

'So on Saturday then? I know you're busy in the meantime.'

'How would you know?'

'You indicated as much the other day.'

'Oh, did I?'

'Yes.'

'Yes.'

'At one on Saturday, then?'

'Yes.'

*

'Gosh, you're looking really beautiful today, Penny.'

'Why thank you, Jim.'

She didn't know whether it was a compliment or if she should be insulted and feel even more degraded, but because she was a very sweet girl she pretended it was a compliment, imagined it was meant for her and was not just some cruel by-product of his frustrated wants, and so she smiled a nice genuine smile at his back as he passed. Maybe he would even turn around and see, like he used to do before.

*

Then his Saturday came.

They were to meet at a different location than usual, more neutral a place, as it happened, than the park by her embassy. A quiet little spot he knew in Wapping, tucked away by the bank of the Thames, under-visited but a gem of a place, exotic by local standards, where Mediterranean gulls cried and swooped and bickered on a rest stop along their modest November journey from the south coast to East Anglia, and a matronly Italian kept a restaurant with a patio and served mouth-watering Umbrian fare in a not too pretentious, almost provincial, atmosphere on the inside. A peaceful bit of London on the outside.

He thought it perfect for the two of them. For a romance by the pier. He looked around. So perfect.

He asked for a table indoors, but positioned himself outside, on a seat at a spot on the empty patio, declining a glass of wine while he waited.

At twenty past one he rose and stretched and took a slow pace across the road to the footpath opposite, and turned and leaned his back against the railing, the water not far behind him and the restaurant across, and a view along the road in both directions.

He ambled casually, back and forth just a few steps each way, then venturing further from his base, always keeping the patio within view, then eventually letting that go for brief stretches as he turned his back and covered longer distances, until at a quarter to two he returned to sit.

Perhaps the gentleman is a bit peckish? The matron had noticed his reappearance and come out with a basket of bread. She spoke with a heavy accent out of the Umbrian hills.

'No, thank you.'

She nodded in a wise old way and retreated without a word to leave him to his waiting.

Had she not been able to find the place? Unlikely. Had something urgent come up? Possibly. But she had never let urgent business stop her from keeping a date with him before. Cut it short, yes; prevent her from setting a meeting in the first place, yes; but her record of turning up, not that it was a long record, was reasonably good. She had only been late that first time.

A part of him now seemed to know she would never show up for him; not now, nor ever again. But another part of him, the stronger part, wrote that off as unfounded nonsense. And yet a third part of him, a calm and disinterested part, permeated the rest of his mood, and he felt unbothered by her failure to appear, like it was nothing. It was a careful way of fooling himself. A protective mechanism against his worst fear.

The fear that it was over, that the frame of his existence had been shattered.

And in that third state of mind which shielded him, it might have been no more than the mild and passing worry that he had lost an ordinary pair of gloves on the underground. Inconsequential. Something you forget about. Write off. Just gloves.

Just a woman.

Just a woman?

And that was when it flooded over him, breaking the defences, his childish logic failed, and he felt sick and faint and humiliated and angry and the pavement bent up at him, and the poles leaned in upon him, and the distant sound of heels on the walkway kicked into his head and pounded his skull in. He looked up at the sky for escape and it was laughing at him.

He stood up, dizzy, and felt drunk though he was not, and noticed the soft touch on his arm of the matron who had appeared out of nowhere, at which his manners took over, unfailing, and he began an automatic apology that was so instinctive and practiced it sounded genuine, as though he really was troubled at the notion that he had taken up space in the restaurant for all that time and in the end not placed an order and that there was nothing else weighing on his mind than his guilt over that.

She gripped his arm now and tightened her hand around it, surprisingly strong for a woman of her appearance, and silenced him.

'It's a nothing, my boy. You will have a better one a in the future. A better luck.'

She patted his cheek and sent him off, her strong eyes smiling for his comfort, and he wandered away bewildered.

*

Monday when he called the embassy they told him she had been reassigned.

And no, they were not at liberty to disclose her new whereabouts. And would you like to speak with her successor? Or perhaps the Trade Representative, who was her superior? No? Alright. Then pardon me, sir, but may I ask where you got this telephone number?

He hung up the handset and leaned at his desk and saw with a pang that her blackish-green umbrella was still leaning against one of his filing cabinets. A pang of hurt.

He thought he noticed a funny smell in the air, and he imagined it was making him ill, and he got up and left.

Just as he reached the way out to the reception area he heard Selling calling after him, but pretending not to hear he pushed on, passing Penny and looking at her blankly without a thought, leaving the building for the open street.

If Fate Sees Fit

CLARE'S WORLD seemed to be contracting around her. For yesterday she had been in a bold new expanse of life, rich with importance, heiress in training to her father's tea empire, and today she sat at breakfast to learn he had already departed for work, and that what awaited her that day, and the next and the next, was school, and no more auctioneering.

She sat dejected at the table, the sparkle gone from her eyes, the verve left from her movements, her joy evaporated. For the moment. Because Nan soon noticed, and she looked up at Clare from across the table with porridge spoon in hand, her eyes drooping tiredly and seriousness etched into her face as ever, years of it, and she knew exactly what she saw in Clare's demeanour.

'Clare?' Her tone slow and severe.

'Yes, Nan.'

'I want to tell you something important and I want you to listen carefully, and take it to heart.'

'Alright.'

'You remember what you did yesterday with your father?'

'Yes.'

'Well, it is likely never to repeat itself.'

No reply.

'What you did yesterday was extraordinary, and life is ordinary, and one of the things that helps get you through all the ordinariness is keeping vivid memories of the extraordinary parts. So you can cherish them for as long as you live.'

'But *what*'s the use of that, if...'

'One day, if fate sees fit, you shall be as old as I am. And a memory of an afternoon like the one you spent with your father yesterday will be one of the most valuable things you own, and you must keep it with you always. Nurture it, refresh it, and guard it safe, because one day you will want to live it again in your mind. You will want to turn it over and over and look at it, and walk through it, and repeat its words to yourself, Clare.

'So you must see your experience for what it was: a cause for joy and celebration in years to come. It was a time of unique closeness with your father, and that is why it is special. Instead of moping about it having ended, just be thankful you had it at all. Because moping is for spoiled brats.'

'Yes, Nan.'

'Now finish your breakfast so I can pack you off to school and have my rest. And *I* shall fetch you this afternoon, so don't go entertaining any false hopes.'

'Yes, Nan.'

*

When she was at school, she decided that what her father had done must be classed as a good turn. It was the first time, she reckoned, that she had ever been on the receiving end of a good turn, and she knew of course that one good turn deserves another. She resolved to do lots of good turns so that others might feel as happy as she had been the day before.

At lunchtime she stood up on her log and surveyed the schoolyard, her eyes skipping over clusters of girls, laughing, babbling, jumping, running, until she saw what she was looking for. The quiet one who sat all on her own, engrossed in a book in the far corner by the brick wall of the schoolhouse. Whose name was Prudence and who had wondered if she might join Clare's group, only she was new here and had no friends. None at all.

Clare manoeuvred her way through the animated, shifting, unpredictable crowd until she reached the wall, and then nonchalantly sidled up next to the girl with long dark braids, and broke her attention away from the opened pages.

'Hello, Prudence.'

Prudence looked up at her, a bit surprised.

'Hello, Clare.'

'What's that you're reading?'

'Oh, it's just a story.'

Clare sat down on the ground next to Prudence, and settled herself into a comfortable position.

'I like story books,' she said.

'Me too. Reading is my favourite pastime.'

'Don't you ever want to have adventures like the people in the books?'

Prudence laughed.

'Of course. Otherwise I wouldn't like reading them so much.'

'Well, would you like to hear where I was yesterday?'

'Yes.'

Clare thought for a moment.

'Well, it's a long story. It will be better if I start at the beginning.'

'Go on, then.'

So she did.

And Prudence listened with delight, and the next day told Clare a few stories of her own.

By the end of the week they were old friends.

✻

But in Roper's office it really did smell bad.

He had returned from stomping down the streets despondently, hurling his hate at the institutions of Finsbury, abusing the old patient edifices, projecting ill at the walls and the iron fences, spilling out hurt onto the pavements.

He had found his way back to his desk without remembering having made any decision to return there. It had just drawn him, senseless, like a magnet.

Now the door was closed to keep out anyone, everyone. And the window was shut to seal out the creeping chill.

Why was he at work in a state like this? Because he was a lawyer and had a responsibility, which he had been neglecting grievously in recent days, to the partners, and of course to his clients. And even now all he could do was stare at his desk.

But that smell! It was so stuffy in the office. Too cold outside to open the window. The firm's rules. Don't waste heating in the winter months. And there was no way he would be persuaded to open the door only to have Selling barge in and give him an earful of patronising, paternalistic, self-important rubbish. Not that a shut door ever stopped Selling. But at least it was a deterrent.

But the smell. It was becoming unbearable and he was going to open the window, sod the rules, and then he looked up and rain began pattering on the panes, and the windows were stupidly designed such that opening them let in the wet and he cursed them and cursed the rain and London and Selling and above all that bloody smell.

He got up anyway to look out the window and down at the street. And as he stood up the smell became even stronger. It was distinctly sour, and he thought it seemed almost alcoholic. He was trapped in a chamber with no air circulation and the odour of rot. Where the hell could it be coming from?

Then he was greatly startled, for there was something moving in the corner of his office by the window next to a filing cabinet.

He calmed himself and tried to pull himself together and told himself he was thinking like an adolescent and what was wrong with him? He could always control his angers and frustrations and why now all of a sudden was he not able to disperse them? Breathe deeply. Dilute the bad in a wave of mental calm. Cultivate a field of the mind and till its soil; turn it down on itself and cover the disappointment under a clod of earth so that it is buried, your troubles buried, sunk away. Deep breath. Now put your mind on something else and go investigate that movement by the window.

This he did, and when he approached the space where the movement was, the source of the smell became clear to him. The movement was a happy jumping dodging leaping swarm of fruit flies, and their feed was a crate's worth of decomposing pears. He had forgotten about them entirely. It was now all gone to waste. Wasted money, wasted food (though not if you could ask the fruit flies); a wasted ten days. And he had come out of it all worse off, although later he would think himself better off for having met her.

Now he tried to switch himself into automatic, and get some useful things done despite his mind and feelings being all over the place.

He leaned over the crate of pears, not thinking to avoid a deep inhalation as he did. His lungs filled with alcoholic vapours, his head became foggy and he had to grasp the cabinet for support, and he generally felt quite ill.

He staggered away from the corner and made for the door, and opened it, and stumbled out into the corridor, and tripped on, what was that?

His knees on the floor, and then his whole body, in a rapid folding heap.

He picked himself up quickly before anyone would see.

And saw what it was. A roll of carpet. Yellow carpet. Sarah. Bless her. She must have done it herself. The people here were so kind to him, and he felt such an ass.

He carried on to the reception area and tried to appear normal, and he passed Penny and felt a rush of emotional warmth for her.

'Forgive me, Penny,' he uttered, and carried on out the front entrance.

It was raining and he knew he had to head for cover. For the pub. But by the time he got there he was wet as the rain itself, his hair a soaking mop and his suit a wet, dripping rag. He thumped himself down on a barstool and had one whiskey, then another, and another, and then a few more, and the world tilted, then spun, but he righted himself, because he was sober. Yes, he was sober. Only had one or two. And asked the barman why women are cold and heartless and given to such, to such, to such… It's not as if we done nothin to them ever, did we? And why do you serve such awful tasting whiskey? Give me somethin smoother. And you think that's enough? Why, you bastard! Look at me. You're just a Nazi. I'm perfectly in control. No! I don't want any more. I know my limits, I do. Here, and you know I'm good to my word. You know me. I been here before. You don't trust me, but you can have my whole wallet, you can. And he left it there on the bar.

Stumbled out onto the road and somehow made his way back to the firm. Cause he had work to do. Cause they had to stay two steps ahead. Old bluster said so.

He took the stairs slowly, one step at a time, cause that's the sensible thing to do when you've had a drink or two. And he pulled open the door and the world swayed dangerously around him. Why wouldn't everything stay put? Hard for a man to keep up his footing when the swaying starts. They must stop the swaying in this age of technol… in this age of technology.

There was Penny again. Such a lovely girl. She was all he ever wanted. And he went for the reception desk and lurched and teetered and somehow reached it even with all the blasted shifting of the floor and the walls around him. Like he was on a boat.

He thudded his elbows down on the counter and leaned over

and reached and touched her, and she withdrew her hand. A lump grew in his throat, and he thought they had all turned against him. But Penny? Even Penny? Maybe because of what they'd done. But he would show her commitment. He loved her. Show her what he was really like. And the lump became more of a blockage, and he could barely force out words, and it hurt his head.

But he said it, for her.

'Marry me, Penny.'

She sighed and he thought he saw her arms trembling, and she stood up. Yes, that was his girl. His Penny. She came round the desk and took him by the arm.

No, not took him. Put his arm around her shoulder and held onto it with both of hers. It was to keep him from falling, he thought she said, but he didn't believe her. It was because she was his Penny. And he found himself on a chair in the cloakroom and the poles with hangers and coats and hats all about, and kneeling in front of him there was Penny. She had been bent over and tying his shoelace.

And now he looked at her, and there were such tears in her eyes. Streaming down her face now. A torrent. So beautiful.

VIII

Trajectory

NAVEEN'S journey from Cairo to Mogadiscio is a special tale all its own. It took him across the Horn of Africa, through sand and mud and heat and cold and every manner of natural extreme. By rail along the Nile to Aswan, passing the monuments of Luxor and then disembarking by the ancient settlements of Elephantine. Across the border into newly independent Sudan, where he marvelled at the water scene and the great wide sandscape from a promontory over Wadi Halfa, guns being pointed all through that area, but never at him. And no shots ringing out.

Then more rugged, in the back of a lorry, getting stuck in ruts on muddy trails til Omdurman, avoiding militias along the way, wandering the wide streets and losing himself in the markets of Khartoum, past spice stall and café and pushing through herds of goats. Then off along the Blue Nile and on through Abyssinia, a rich verdant place of old civilisation; a loose fringe at the edge of Christendom, over mountain and through gorge and bartering his way out of trouble, and wilder still as he roughed it through the really untamed parts. Rushing rivers, deadly wildlife, bandits and fighters and swarming insects. And plenty of fever. Parts of it all just a blur.

But arriving finally, ragged but intact, reaching his new destination. The gentle shore of his Indian Ocean, where the thin fresh breeze blew soft and free off the eastern waters as he stood at the edge of the city of Mogadiscio, a stately mix of mosque and colonial architecture. Elegant cars and European suits and also robed men from the caravans out of the desert across the open.

Veiled women.

The silvery green of the leaves on the trees against the silvery blue of the sea, tinselling in the wind.

There had been harrowing misadventures along the way, a treasure trove of stories to be stored away for later, to ripen and gain value with age, bettering with each passing season to come, to be told and savoured and relished.

'Years ago, when I was just a cadet, I was on board a Calcutta Maritime Company ship. We ran into a spot of, well, difficulty. And that is to put it mildly! Our daring, my friends, and yes, I will be the first to admit it, our penchant for serious trouble, it knew no bounds... So let me begin at the beginning, leaving the docks at Calcutta, and end at the, for now, at the middle...' And so he would spin his story.

'When I boarded another ship for England, on course once again, sailing it past the white cliffs of Dover and into the Thames via the longer way; maybe the better way; surely the more peaceful way; it was one heck of a time we all had. One memorable journey...'

Now time to meet the new.

He leaned over the railing on the deck of the *Liberty*. They were clipping along nicely, about to change their bearing and swing north up the west of Africa.

A strong breeze picked up and landed a spray of ocean on his face while gulls circled their natural patterns in the distance, the sun high, high up in the sky. It must have been sometime about midday, and someplace about midway. To Hay's Wharf at London. Rocking along with a new set of men, there was land visible to Naveen in the near distance; a long, lone finger of rock jutting into the sea, pointing them gently on their way. They were slinging slowly along a great arced trajectory, all carefully navigated, the helmsman steering them expertly on, and the vessel sliding, ever graceful, round the Cape of Good Hope.

E I Vernon lives and works in Toronto, Canada, where he was born in 1979. He studied history at the University of Toronto and jurisprudence at the University of Oxford. *The Ears of a Dog* is his first novel.